The Sunshine Solution

The Sunshine Solution

A DIGGER DOYLE MYSTERY

Rosalie Rayburn

Copyright © 2023 by Rosalie Rayburn

All rights reserved. Except in the case of brief quotations embedded in critical articles and reviews, no part of this publication may be reproduced, stored in a retrieval system, transmitted in any format or by any means—digital, electronic, mechanical, photocopying, recording or otherwise—or conveyed via the internet or a website without written permission of the author. Rights inquiries should be directed to: RosalietheAuthor@gmail.com.

This is a work of fiction. Unless otherwise indicated, all the names, characters, businesses, places, events and incidents in this book are either the product of the author's imagination or used in a fictitious manner. Any resemblance to actual persons, living or dead, or actual events, is purely coincidental.

Cover photos: Woman, istock.com, credit: Nachosuch; Albuquerque at the base of the Sandia Mountains, istock.com, credit: Noël-Marie Fletcher. Title page illustration: Jan Luyken, etching (detail): "Joshua orders the sun and the moon to stand still...", 1708, Wikimedia Commons.

Publisher's Cataloging-in-Publication Data

Names: Rayburn, Rosalie, author.
Title: The sunshine solution : a Digger Doyle Mystery 2023 / Rosalie Rayburn.
Description: Albuquerque, NM: Rayburn Publications, 2023.
Identifiers: Library of Congress Control Number: 2023920481 |
    ISBN: 979-8-9892110-1-2 (paperback) | 979-8-9892110-0-5 (ebook)
Subjects: LCSH Hispanic Americans—Fiction. | Lesbians—Fiction. | Solar energy—Fiction. | New Mexico—Fiction. | Political fiction. | Mystery fiction. | BISAC FICTION / Mystery & Detective / Women Sleuths | FICTION / Political | FICTION / Romance / LGBTQ+ / Lesbian
Classification: LCC PS3618 .A93 S86 2023 | DDC 813.6—dc23

To my beloved son Patrick

CHAPTER 1

The fuzzy black-and-white picture showed a young teen, face wasted and body rail thin, pulling away from an older man. The man was tall, well-dressed, Hispanic. He looked as though he was trying to drag her down the street. The flier headline screamed, "Saturday night on Central Avenue: Orlando Garcia likes them young. Is this the man we want running our state?"

Orlando Garcia stared at the flier his aide had handed to him. She said she found it on her lawn that morning. His stomach churned. There had already been the rumors, the attack ads. He'd fought those off, but piece by piece they'd cut at his credibility. He knew now that the moment people saw this picture his political future would be over.

It didn't matter that the photo was not what it seemed, that he was not harming the girl but trying to stop her from another drug overdose. None of that would make any difference now. He wished he could make it disappear, undo its existence on this earth, roll back the clock. But one shredded flier made no difference. There were probably hundreds of fliers out there by now, and thousands of eyes would see them—HAD already seen them. That was how the political game worked. Your opponents would seek out a tiny vulnerability, something meant as a good deed in a dark world, and they would forge it into a deadly weapon. He could try to fight back, but he would always see the doubt in people's eyes. He'd seen that happen before to other candidates. You never got over a smear like that. It was over, everything he'd worked for.

He squeezed his eyes shut and felt dizzy, as if he stood at the edge of a cliff, hearing the voice inside his head praying to a god he no longer believed in to deliver him.

There would of course be no deliverance. When Orlando opened his eyes, the pieces of the poster still littered the floor; what had happened, had happened. He could see no way out. He'd failed them: his family, his supporters. He sat down at his desk, found a notepad sent to him in thanks for his contributions to helping the homeless, and wrote a note to his wife, pleading for her understanding. He wrote a note to his son and daughter, begging them to look after their mother. Then he went out to the garage, got in his car, backed out without looking, drove out of the city, and onto to the freeway, speeding south through a night sharp with stars, heading toward the canyon. Yes, that would be the place.

CHAPTER 2

Twenty Years Later

Snow had begun to fall shortly after two that afternoon—light, feathery flakes that floated teasingly through the sharp, thin, high-altitude air. Chris Lovington entered the Roundhouse, the seat of New Mexico's part-time legislature, which looked uncannily like a Spanish bullring, and was often the scene of verbal bloodletting. He stopped in the lobby and showed his ID card to the security guard, who checked the appointment book and frowned, "Hmm, the Governor doesn't usually see people up there."

"I know," Lovington nodded, "but he specifically asked me to meet him there." The guard shrugged. "Well, I guess he's the boss around here."

Lovington looked at his watch and opted to take the stairs rather than ride the elevator up to the fourth floor. He was apprehensive about the meeting, curious why the governor had asked for him, and puzzled as to why the meeting would be held in a room usually reserved for high-level discussions or critical announcements. When he reached the top floor, he expected to run into an aide who would announce him, but there was no one around. He knocked on the dark wooden door and waited; breath shaky, heart fluttering. A moment later a voice summoned him, and he entered.

Governor Joe Sheridan stood on the far side of a vast table. There were no lights on in the room and his face was ghostly pale in the low afternoon light. He was well over six feet tall, with iron-grey hair smoothed back over his scalp, deep-set eyes, and a long straight nose. Snide online Tweets sometimes called him "professorial" and today he looked the part, dressed in a gray tweed jacket over an oatmeal-colored V-neck sweater.

He pulled out a chair and motioned for Lovington to take a seat next to him. They sat silently, Lovington keeping his eyes on the polished surface of the table. Sheridan cleared his throat. "Thank you for coming at such short notice, Chris. I hope I didn't inconvenience you. I know things can sometimes be hectic on a Friday afternoon." His voice was deep and formal like that of an old-time newscaster.

Lovington shrugged. "No problem. My assistant Andy Whitaker can handle anything, and if he can't, he can always call me."

Sheridan nodded slowly. The skin around his deep-set eyes was dark and his lips were stretched tight, as if he were suppressing inner pain. Lovington knew Sheridan was in his late fifties. Today he looked much older.

"I'll get to the point quickly," he said, "I asked you here today because I'm going to be making an important announcement on Monday." He paused and looked directly at Lovington. "I've decided not to run for a second term."

Lovington's jaw dropped. Sheridan was popular and his poll numbers were good, the election was months away, and campaigning had barely started. Anyone in his right mind might say "Why this?"

"I know it's a surprise, Chris." Sheridan paused briefly as if gathering energy. "But I've had some news recently that's made this decision inevitable." He sighed. The murmur of air leaking from his lungs was like a slowly deflating bicycle tire. Lovington said nothing, waiting for the sound of Sheridan's lungs to re-inflate enough to fuel his next words.

"About three weeks ago my wife noticed some unusual pain. She'd been experiencing pain for a while. She always thought it was indigestion or something minor. But this time the pain was so severe she could barely stand. She went in for tests and a tumor was found on the liver...."

"Oh, it's not...?"

"It is cancer, and I don't think I need to spell it out for you. There are of course options for treatment, but she probably doesn't have long."

"Joe, I'm, so sorry, I ...."

Sheridan held up a hand to ward off any further commiseration from Lovington. "I know, Chris, and thank you for your thoughts. Martha and I have been married thirty-three years. That sounds like a long time, but when you know your time is limited, there is never enough time. That's why I decided not to run. I want to be there for her as much as I can. I think you understand that from your own experience."

Lovington understood the reference only too well. He had lost his wife three years before to a brain aneurysm. They'd been married almost twenty-two years. Sheridan was peering at him now, and he sensed that another shoe was about to drop. He braced.

"That's one of the reasons I asked you here today," Sheridan went on, "I want you to know that I have been watching you as we've worked together during my term. I've been impressed by your integrity and your conscientiousness."

"Joe, I ..." Lovington interrupted.

Sheridan held up his hand again. "I know. I know you had some questionable issues in your past. There was some ugly stuff, but the Chris Lovington I've gotten to know is not that guy. As State Land Commissioner you have a lot of responsibility. You're overseeing millions of acres, making sure the leases on those lands benefit our schools and colleges. I see how seriously you take your duties. I know you're under a lot of pressure from the oil and gas guys; especially because the state can make so much money from exploiting those resources. But since I've been governor, my major concerns have been water and climate. The hotter it gets and the more wildfires we have, and the poorer our state will become. I'm thinking about the long-term, and I think you get that."

Lovington nodded. He wasn't sure where the conversation was headed but he felt deep sympathy for Sheridan. The man had always impressed him.

"Anyway, the other reason I invited you here today is that I wanted to ask you to run for governor in my place. I think we share some of the same goals, especially when it comes to the environment. I've heard the way you talk about renewable energy. We need more of that, and that's why I believe you are the right person to carry on my legacy."

Lovington sank back into his chair. Relief flowed over him. Sheridan knew about his past, but he was willing to trust him. Still, he could never have imagined this. "I, uh, I don't know," he stuttered. "This is, uh, unexpected. What about Sylvia?"

Sylvia Sanchez, the Lieutenant Governor, who frequently appeared in evening news broadcasts, seemed the most obvious choice.

Sheridan shrugged. "Yes. I suppose everyone would think that, but I don't have the same confidence in her. My sense is she would take New Mexico in a very different direction and that would not be good for the land. So…well, I'll give you the weekend to think about it. Martha and I have managed to keep things quiet up to now, but it's going to get out. I'm planning to make a statement to the media this coming Monday afternoon. If you agree, I will use the opportunity to announce that I will be endorsing you for governor. So, I'd like your answer before then. Okay?"

Lovington knew the conversation was over. Sheridan had made up his mind. Now it was up to him. He stood up, thanked the governor, and left the room quickly, heart pounding.

Once outside the building, he stood for a moment staring at the street with its white dusting of snow. He looked at his watch and noticed it was just after four o'clock. It was Friday. The old guilt stirred within him, the dull ache of it had grown worse since Christine died. Shame. Deeds that could not be undone. He walked out to the street and turned left on Old Santa Fe Trail, heading for the Plaza. Because of the snow and the traffic, it took him longer than expected. It was nearly four-thirty by the time he reached the cathedral.

Entering the building, he saw that it was almost empty, with only a handful of tourists. They wouldn't notice him. Standing for a moment just inside the door, he let the familiar stillness settle over him like a comforting wrap. His feet took him towards the dark wooden structure where he could make his confession. Lovington was not Catholic, but he had discovered that this ritual soothed him more than any therapist's words. He saw no light glowing above the door, which meant it was available. He entered and knelt in front of the fretwork screen, shielded from the world, where his words would be heard in secrecy and safety. "Bless me Father, for I have sinned."

CHAPTER 3

Five Months Later

Thin air is cold at high altitudes, and nights without clouds are the coldest, leaving the dry earth exposed to the vastness of a dark sky pierced with innumerable stars. Chaco Canyon is such a place. There, the walls of an ancient civilization stand empty and silent in a desert baked by the relentless sun. The ancient Puebloan peoples aligned the walls precisely so the first rays of the rising sun at the summer solstice would stab through the darkness in a dagger of light.

The air was frigid, but the campsites were not aligned to celestial rules. Former reporter Elizabeth Doyle, whom everyone called Digger, and her fiancée Maria Ortiz were asleep in the campground at Chaco Canyon Historical Park. Light seeped gently into their tent, signaling the approach of dawn. Digger stirred, burrowing her face into the curve between Maria's shoulder and her chin. Maria snuggled her body closer, and they stayed that way for a little while, sharing their warmth as the day began to unfold. They had made the one-hundred-mile trip from Albuquerque the evening before. It should have taken them about three hours, but even in Maria's aging RAV4, the last thirteen miles over the washboard dirt road felt like forever. They arrived at the campground just before sunset, in time to set up their tent and heat the pizza slices they'd brought.

The trip was a pre-wedding "gift" from Digger's new boss, Julia Montoya, Secretary of the Department of Cultural Affairs. Digger's brow furrowed when Montoya made the offer. The department supported cultural activities and organizations and museums throughout the state, but Chaco Canyon was not its responsibility. Moreover, June was not the best time for a visit to Chaco Canyon. The place was known for glacial temperatures at night and blazing heat during the day. Still, the idea of getting away from family and friends, and the endless pressure of Maria's political campaign was appealing.

"I'll check with my fiancée but I'm sure she'd love to go. That's very kind of you," Digger said.

"That's settled then," Montoya nodded, looking at her agenda. "Could you go on Monday?" She asked it casually as if it were an afterthought. But there was nothing casual in her expression—or her wardrobe. Julia Montoya was a small woman, maybe five foot three, with impeccably cut mahogany brown hair, piercing dark eyes, perfect nails, and expensive outfits. Something about Montoya's expression—that's settled then—made her immediately cautious.

"So, is this an actual work trip?" She'd asked it cautiously.

"Not officially, no," Montoya said briskly. "But there is something I'd like you to do while you're there. There's an event scheduled for Tuesday afternoon. The State Land Commissioner is expected to announce a new solar power project. I'd like you to attend as an observer and report to me afterward. I would like to keep an eye on these developments. We can discuss them later."

There was a pause in their discussion. Digger stared at her boss, trying to read her face. Why, she wondered, would he be willing to travel all the way to Chaco Canyon to announce this project? Tourists and historians loved the place, but the State Land Commissioner?

Aloud she said, "Why isn't the Commissioner making the announcement in Santa Fe?"

Montoya's slim eyebrows knitted. "I suppose he is trying to appeal to the environmental groups that oppose oil and gas exploration in that area. So, you will go?"

Digger decided not to ask any further questions. Despite her suspicions, Montoya might be right. Someone was always protesting about drilling near Chaco, so choosing the location for an announcement about solar energy made sense.

"Okay," she said, "We could arrive early and explore the canyon before the presentation."

"Very good," Montoya said, looking at her agenda. "I'll arrange everything."

The news conference was scheduled for some time in the afternoon, so after a quick breakfast they drove the short distance to the Visitors Center, where Digger introduced herself and checked on the time of the event. Then they set off on the Una Vida trail. At that hour of the morning, the air was still cool and fresh, the sun still low in the morning sky—no sounds except the crunch of their hiking boots on the sandy trail, and now and then a distant bird call. The canyon rose in a sheer wall on their right, its surface etched with geometric shapes and stick-figure images, the *petroglyphs*.

They went back to where they'd parked the car and drove on, continuing to the start of another network of trails. They hiked without talking, appreciating the morning air and the quiet, until they saw the curved walls of Chetro Ketl, and beyond that, the iconic Pueblo Bonito. Digger stopped, taking in the vastness of the place, the age-old ruins, the massive rocks. Above them, the sky arced deep blue above the sandstone cliffs; below, the land stretched out in greenish grey, dotted with the creosote bushes and cacti that could grow in such dry conditions.

As she stood gazing at the ruins, she felt her heart pound. This was why she had come back to New Mexico. Yes, she could have chosen to go to Houston when the newspaper where she worked closed. Her old colleague Tim had gone to work for the *Chronicle*. She missed being a reporter, but there was nothing like the beauty of Chaco to be found in Texas. This place had allowed a unique community to flourish for hundreds of years until it withered and left only these ruins.

Maria reached out and took her hand. "Come on, let's go inside."

The women spent half an hour exploring the complex before continuing the trail toward Pueblo Bonito. They walked softly on the sandy path as if they otherwise might disturb the long-departed inhabitants. When they reached the ruins, Digger pressed her forehead against one of the old stone walls, feeling the rough surface worn by time. What were the beliefs that drove the builders to haul stone and timber miles across the desert by hand? How had they lived, sustained life, and worshiped?

It was late morning when Maria and Digger emerged from the shelter of the walls, and they immediately felt the crushing heat. The sun was nearing its zenith. It had taken longer than they thought to explore the ruins of the ancient community. Digger stared at her near-empty water bottle. If they headed back to the campground now, they'd have time to have lunch and change before the presentation. She had no desire to go but it would be too hot to continue hiking and she'd told Montoya she would do it. The whole idea of holding a press conference way out here was nuts.

They were almost to the trailhead when they heard a voice that sounded more animal than human. A figure appeared from behind one of the ruined walls. A man with wind-tossed hair and a scraggly beard, wearing nothing but a pair of faded cut-off jeans, was walking toward them. Despite the harsh sun, his eyes were fiercely focused on the two women.

"Should we run?" Maria whispered.

The man waved a hand at the ruined walls. "Vanity of vanities! This was a great civilization, but they did not heed the warnings. Beware the fires of hell! The engines of death are everywhere!"

Digger put an arm around Maria and steered her away. As soon as they reached the trail, they broke into a run and raced back to the car. Arriving at the Visitors Center drenched with sweat, they stumbled inside and found a park ranger. It took Digger a few moments before she could gather enough breath to speak.

"There's a guy out there! He's wandering around shouting crazy stuff."

The park ranger smiled and nodded. "I see you've met Cedric. Yup, he's our most regular visitor. He freaks people out, but he won't hurt you."

Maria frowned, unconvinced. "He's kinda creepy. Why do you let him wander around?"

The ranger laughed. "I don't make the rules. This place is supposed to be open to all. I'll go find him and drive him back to his shack. You guys need water?"

"We're good. We're on our way back to the campsite. We have to get ready for the presentation this afternoon."

"Oh. The big wigs from Santa Fe. Gotcha."

The ranger waved as they left the building and headed back to the campsite to change and eat lunch. By the time they'd returned to the Visitors Center, the meeting room had already been set up for the event. Shades had been drawn over the windows, creating a semi-dark atmosphere. A large screen covered most of one wall. A dozen or so people seated directly in front of it—all of them outfitted like park employees. The screen glowed with a huge picture of Pueblo Bonito, while sinister music filled the room. The picture morphed into an aerial view of a nearly empty lake, with the water level just a series of puddles in a sea of mud flats. A man's deep voice intoned,

"Do we want to be like the ancient civilization of Chaco Canyon and disappear? That could happen. Our summers are getting hotter, wildfires are destroying our forests, and we are running out of water. Our state is in crisis. It is time to wake up to the realities of our climate emergency and take serious action."

The picture abruptly changed to a massive solar array: rows of iridescent blue panels shimmering in a desert landscape. A man appeared from behind the screen and stood to one side of it. "Good afternoon, everyone. I am Chris Lovington, the State Land Commissioner." He smiled as his eyes swept the room. "I suppose you're wondering why I asked everyone to come all the way here to Chaco Canyon instead of holding a press conference in my office in Santa Fe. It's because I wanted you all to take in the majestic beauty of this place and to ask yourselves why it was abandoned. And while you're still thinking about that now, I want to show you what we can all do to avoid a fate like that."

He pointed at the image of the solar array. "For decades," he continued, "New Mexico has been dependent on revenues from the oil and gas industry. Our electricity comes from burning coal. But we have another resource—one that can put us ahead. We can be a leader in solar energy."

As Lovington spoke those words, the screen went blank and the blinds slowly rose, until the room was filled with softly filtered light. Lovington beamed at the audience, his toothbrush mustache twitching with energy, eyes prominent behind round wire-rimmed glasses that glinted when the sun caught them. Digger had read about this guy a few months back when Governor Sheridan had announced he wouldn't seek reelection but would endorse Lovington to run in his place.

Lovington radiated an upbeat spirit as he spoke to the small audience. But Digger realized he was intending his speech for a larger audience. She noticed a man with video equipment at the back of the room. As Lovington's speech wore on, she guessed he was going to use the presentation as part of his campaign.

"I have a vision for our future," Lovington concluded. "A future where the sun, not fossil fuels, will power our state. New Mexico is rich in an all-important resource: sunshine!"

He paused to give his audience time to react. When the clapping stopped, he went into his spiel. "So, I'm proposing a project that's going to mean jobs—and I mean a lot of jobs—for our state. It's a project that's going to make us proud." He paused, looking around the room to confirm the small waves of further applause.

Digger suppressed a groan. She figured now that he'd hooked them, he'd go back to his same old stump speech routine. She'd bet money on it. But no, his next words surprised her.

"Best of all, this project is going to be good for the environment. In these times when we are seeing the effects of climate change every summer in the form of huge wildfires and drought, I believe this is the right thing to do. So, I'm going to introduce you to the folks representing Solar GRX that are going to bring this great development to New Mexico." Lovington turned to the couple now standing beside him. "Tony, Janet, take it away."

Tony Kramer was tall, fortyish, gray-suited with hair so perfectly groomed it had to be a toupee. But maybe not. Maybe men really could look like they did in those magazines you found in dentists' waiting rooms. Still, she'd put her money on a toupee.

Kramer stood, looking around the room as if to make sure he had everyone's attention. The smooth, salesman-like way he smiled at them reminded Digger of a preacher at a Pentecostal church she once attended with a former girlfriend.

"I guess you could say I'm somewhat of a visionary," Kramer

began. "I believe the future lies in developing new resources and I've made a career out of it. So, like Chris said, our company Solar GRX is really interested in New Mexico's potential for solar energy. We have the experience of working with solar energy projects in Arizona and that's why we approached the State Land Office."

He waved an arm toward Lovington who nodded back. "Chris and I, we've been talking for a few months now and we recently reached a deal that will let us develop what we believe will be a major generating site with an array of solar photovoltaic panels that will be capable of producing enough power for thousands of New Mexico homes. My business partner Janet Macy and I are really looking forward to extending our expertise and bringing jobs to this state. Isn't that right, Janet?"

Janet had big Texas hair, bright nails and a voice that was mostly Southern Belle, with a steely corporate-flack undertone. "You're absolutely right," she said, taking Kramer's cue. "Power from the sun makes a lot of sense here in this state. Chris Lovington is a real visionary, and we look forward to working with him for the benefit of New Mexico."

Digger wanted to puke. This was such an obvious campaign plug. Why weren't there any reporters or TV people here? Was this a dress rehearsal for a bigger event? Like trying out a show before taking it to Broadway? She was ready to leave when Lovington broke in to announce that the state would be kicking in around $15 million in economic development incentives and tax breaks. *Fifteen million!* That caught Digger's attention and her reporter's instinct kicked in. Who were these people? Had the state folks really checked them out? She stole a glance around to gauge reaction to the announcement. That's when she saw him, half hidden behind a pillar near the back of the packed room. That wavy white hair of his was unmistakable: Danny Murphy.

Everything Digger knew about Murphy made her wary. She was sure he'd been the man behind Johnny Raposa's scheme to defraud taxpayers over a failed subdivision project. Raposa was now locked up and doing time. Meanwhile, Murphy's public image remained unsullied, and he was running for the state legislature—against Maria!

Now, the million-dollar question was, "Why would a Las Vistas developer come all the way to Chaco Canyon to hear an announcement about a solar project? How did he even know about it?"

CHAPTER 4

Digger was standing by the window, watching as the sky above the mountain crest grew paler, changing almost imperceptibly, second by second. Today they were getting married, and the way the mountain glowed as a sliver of fire peeked over the ridge felt as though the sun was sending them a blessing. She felt Maria's arms slide around her waist and her lips brush the back of her neck. Her voice was barely above a whisper.

"I love seeing the sun come up."

"I love it even more when I can watch it with you," Digger said.

They were silent for a while, watching the bright crescent grow, turning the sky above it golden. Digger felt joy flood through her chest. Just days before, Maria had won the primary election for a seat on the state legislature. Maria never gave up. That was what made her different from all the other women she'd dated. Back in the days when she went to the women's bar every Friday night, her friend Lexi had accused her of being a "player." Digger had denied it. She'd given her usual excuse, "I don't like people trying to get inside my head and I don't want someone moving in with me on the second date."

Maria had a knack for inspiring trust without ever asking for it. She had faith in herself, and she had Abuela. Maria's grandmother was the one who took her in when her parents rejected her for being a lesbian, the one who saw the same need in Digger and embraced her within the family. Abuela—the tiny woman with a voice, smooth and worn like the handle of an old wooden tool and the enduring spirit of an olive tree.

Abuela's strength had given them the courage to take the leap. Would getting married change anything? They could go on just the way they were, but something about the idea of getting married appealed to them both. She knew nothing in life was certain, but this felt about as close to certainty as it got. She had never been so sure about anyone before, so ready to make room in her life for someone else. It was time.

She eased around and nuzzled her head on Maria's shoulder, breathing in the scent of her bed-warmed skin in the predawn air. It was so still she sensed the beating of her lover's heart.

Later, long after light had invaded the room, Digger rose again and brewed a cup of Piñon coffee. Maria was already up, freshly showered and brushing her hair.

Digger stopped, mugs in hand, marveling as she watched Maria swing her shiny dark mane to one side and swiftly wind it into a bun at the back of her head. Even though she'd seen Maria do it dozens of times, it always looked to her like a magic trick.

"What time is our appointment?" Digger asked.

"Ten-thirty at the County Clerk's office and then we go to Abuela's for the ceremony. You'd better hurry."

Digger's rented tux hung on the back of the closet door. She let friends talk her into wearing it for the ceremony. Now it seemed absurdly pretentious. She'd wanted to go in a Western outfit. Abuela always called her Cowgirl because of the boots she wore. But Lexi, her mentor in all things proper in what she called the Lesbosphere, said it had to be a tux.

She felt clumsy buttoning the white dress shirt and fumbling with the clasp of the bow tie. Maria was already dressed in an indigo blue blouse and skirt, the fabric shot through with silver threads that caught the light. She came to Digger's aid, swiftly fastening the clasp and patting down the collar.

"You're nervous?"

She was nervous, but not about Maria or the ceremony. It was her grandparents she worried about. They'd flown in from Houston the night before but declined Digger's offer to meet them at the airport.

"I'm wondering how Grandma Betty will react to coming here."

"You said they'd never been back after the accident?"

"Only a couple of times. For my parents' funeral, of course, and graduation from UNM."

"I couldn't understand why they didn't want us to meet them last night. We could have picked them up and taken them to the hotel. Are you sure they'll be able to find Abuela's home? Maybe Lexi should go get them?"

Digger knew exactly why her grandmother didn't want them at the airport. She would be afraid of breaking down in front of a stranger. In Grandma Betty's eyes, showing emotions was showing weakness.

"They'll be fine," she said. "That's what map apps are for. Don't worry. It's not because of us." She smoothed a hand over Maria's hair. "It's just the way she is. I know she's happy for us, Grandpa too. It's just hard for them. My dad was the eldest of their kids. They didn't want me to come back to New Mexico, it felt like losing him all over again."

Maria cut her off. "Don't go there. I know you didn't have the same kind of close relationship with her as I have with Abuela, but you've told me she always stood by you. That's what counts in the long run. What I've heard about her, I like."

Lexi, her wife, Susan, and Abuela were waiting for them outside the County Clerk's office. Digger had asked Lexi to be one of the two witnesses and Maria wanted her grandmother. Abuela was as dressed up as she ever allowed herself to be—wrinkled linen pants and the blue jacket that she boasted was her best Thrift Store find. Tears ran down her lined cheeks.

"Mija!" Abuela murmured, clasping Maria tightly. She reached out an arm and drew Digger into the embrace. "My girls! Such love. I knew it from the first time Cowgirl came to the house."

The office door opened, and a secretary motioned them inside. After many hectic days of agonizing over the election, the civil ceremony was brief and anticlimactic. Digger had been afraid she would forget essential paperwork or laugh at the wrong moment, but the ceremony was over in minutes. In the eyes of the law, they were now married! Just outside the door, they stopped, embraced, and laughed. "Hey, come on, guys!" Lexi barked in her best bar owner voice. "Let's go get you married for real."

An immense wreath of white crepe paper flowers hung on Abuela's gate to welcome friends and family home. Abuela led the way, ushering them into her tiny front yard, where a small crowd of friends had gathered. Maria's father and two sisters rushed to greet the couple with hugs and tears. Maria had not invited her mother, as they hadn't spoken in months. Jackie, the celebrant, was a Native American friend who taught at Maria's school. She and the others took refuge under the tent erected to provide shelter from the usual harsh sun. Digger and Maria stood by the gate waiting for Digger's grandparents to arrive. Digger felt sweat seeping down her back and wished she could shed the tux jacket.

"Hey!" The familiar voice that came from behind made them turn round. "Let's get a picture of the happy couple."

Rex, her old colleague from the newspaper, who had been standing ready by the gate, was waving his camera at them.

"Rex!" She had stayed in touch with the photographer in the months since The Courier, the paper where they'd both worked, had closed.

At the sound of a car horn, everyone turned to see who else had arrived amidst the shutting of car doors. Digger recognized her grandmother's voice. Forty-three years in the US and she still hadn't lost her Irish accent. The gate opened and suddenly there she was, all five foot two of her—all that silver white hair and those piercing blue eyes.

"Nana! Grandpa!" Digger rushed and wrapped them in her arms. "Come, come! I want you to meet the other two most important people in my life."

Abuela held out her gnarled brown hands, taking hold of Grandma Betty's soft pale palms. "Bienvenido. You are welcome to my home on such a happy day for these girls."

Grandma Betty's face lit up and Digger was surprised to see tears glistening in her eyes. "I'm happy for them, and happy we could finally meet. Elizabeth—and I think I must be the only one who still calls her that—has said such good things about you."

Then she turned to Maria. "Ah, you're a lovely girl. Here, I've brought something for you both. Jack, can you hand it over to me?"

Grandpa Jack fished a small, decorated cardboard box from his jacket pocket. Grandma Betty took it, placed it in the palm of one hand, and removed the lid. She held it out to them.

"It's your parents' rings, she explained. They won't fit you, mind, but I thought this was the right time to give them to you two."

Digger shut her eyes. Her grandmother had safeguarded the rings all these years since her parents died, and she had chosen this moment to part with them. Digger swallowed. Her throat ached so badly she couldn't speak, but she felt Maria's supportive arm encircle her. She opened her eyes to see Maria kissing her grandmother's cheek.

After a brief family ceremony, they all headed to Frankie's—the bar that Lexi ran. A small crowd of regulars lined up at the entrance, cheering as Digger and Maria walked in. The DJ had put on Cher's hit "Believe" and the place rocked as everyone began belting out "Life after Love."

Digger glanced back toward the door where her grandparents were standing beside Abuela, the three of them looking awkward but happy. The air vibrated with the beat of the music, and the dance floor was suddenly crammed. The smell of french-fries and beer filled the air. Lexi guided the older people to a quiet table near the wall, returned to the bar, and came back with bottles of beer for them. A few songs later, the music died down and the DJ shouted, "Time for our favorite girls to show us how to dance!"

Maria led Digger to the middle of the small dance floor. Digger gave a sheepish grin to the women looking on. She could never keep up with Maria, who moved as if she had learned to dance soon as she could walk. To Digger's relief, the DJ put on a slow song, so they could wrap their arms around each other and tune everything else out.

Not everyone was enjoying the party. Maria's old girlfriend Izzy Chavez stood alone at the end of the bar, frowning. She couldn't help but think—there was her Maria, dancing with "that other woman."

Izzy hated the way they were wrapped into each other, totally in the moment. Pangs of jealousy stabbed her in the chest. Whenever she saw Maria, her body reacted with the same aching hot desire. That should be me, she thought, the words racing through her head. We used to dance like that, she told herself.

She remembered the feel of Maria's body against her and thought of the time they'd kissed forever in a cabin in Taos with the hot shower of water pouring down over them. Why did Maria leave her for someone else when the two of them once had so much going for them? She wanted to roll back the clock, run to Maria, rip her out of the arms of "that woman," and shout "you should be with me!" to everyone in the room.

Digger felt Maria's steps falter. "What is it?" She opened her eyes. Maria pointed with her head toward the entrance. Digger swiveled so she could follow Maria's gaze. A tall butch-looking woman was standing by the entrance staring at them. The woman's dark hair was shaved short on one side with long bangs flopping over one eye. She stood with her arms folded across her chest.

"It's her: it's Izzy," Maria explained.

"Your ex?" Maria nodded. "I had a weird feeling she might show up."

Izzy glanced briefly around the bar, then walked straight toward them.

"I hope you're happy," she said, glaring at Maria.

Digger let go of Maria and turned to challenge Izzy. "She's fine with me. So, you can leave us alone now." The music had grown louder and faster as people crowded onto the dance floor. Izzy glared at the newly married couple a few seconds longer, then leaned in close: You should stay away from her," she hissed at Digger, "Take it from me, you think you can trust her, but she'll turn on you."

Izzy spun around and elbowed her way through the crowd toward the open exit door.

CHAPTER 5

The day after the wedding, it was back to work as usual for Digger. On the drive back to Santa Fe, she kept wrestling in her mind with questions about the State Land Commissioner's announcement. It had been frustrating as hell to sit through the press conference and be precluded from saying anything. When did Lovington decide to jump on the renewable energy bandwagon? Had he and Sheridan made the same dirty deal? Was that why the governor picked him instead of Sylvia? Everyone thought the Lieutenant Governor would have been the logical choice to run in his place.

And what about this company, Solar GRX? What did that even mean? The couple of quick online searches she'd done had revealed almost nothing. Why would Lovington offer millions in state incentives to such a little-known company? The closer she got to Santa Fe, the more she wondered what Montoya really wanted to know. She sent her a short email summarizing what she had heard and mentioning that there'd been no news media present; however, she revealed nothing about her concerns. That would be saved for an in-person conversation. Maybe.

By the time she'd parked, Digger could feel the heat was already ballooning up from the asphalt. The city's homogeneous tan-colored buildings would absorb the sunshine all day, so by afternoon the narrow streets of Santa Fe would be boiling like a cauldron. Even with sunglasses, the light hurt her eyes as she walked the short distance to her office in the Bataan Memorial Building. The place drew visitors to this political part of town. It was named in honor of the tens of thousands of Filipino and American prisoners—many from New Mexico and some of them who'd been forced to march across the Bataan peninsula of the Philippines during World War II.

Montoya's office door was open, and she was on the phone when Digger entered. Her earrings, silver hoops the size of Christmas ornaments, gleamed in the light from a desk lamp. Without pausing, Montoya gestured for Digger to take a seat in one of the small armchairs by the window.

Eight months ago, when she had received a phone call from Montoya's assistant inviting her to meet the Cultural Affairs Department Secretary, Digger knew little about the institution. She'd been afraid that the Secretary was upset by an article she'd written that talked about the environmental threats that the nearby road project was bringing to a nearby housing development and historic chapel. But no, Julia Montoya had been so impressed by the piece that she'd invited Digger to Santa Fe to offer her a job. The offer turned out to be a lifeline. The Las Vistas Courier, the newspaper where she'd worked since college, was circling the drain.

Since starting the new job, Digger had noticed that the Secretary liked to handle conversations in an informal setting. Once she'd ended her call, Montoya came over and installed herself in the other armchair. Digger caught the scent of the fragrance she wore, subtle but distinctive. The kind of scent that would have set her hormones vibrating in the days before Maria. Funny how a settled heart changed perceptions.

Montoya fixed her eyes on Digger, raising one expertly

plucked eyebrow. It was a look Digger found slightly unsettling. The secretary's eyes were the color of black olives, with lashes so long they looked almost fake.

"I read your email, but I wanted to get your personal impressions." Montoya's voice was low, with a hint of the Northern New Mexico lilt. Digger recounted the event again, glancing occasionally at the notes she had taken. She kept her response brief and factual. "Anything else?" Still that unsettling look. Digger hesitated. Should she mention her misgivings? Being a reporter made you skeptical of everything. Sometimes people really did what they said they would do. But something about Tony Kramer's upbeat pitch just sounded off.

"Well," Digger said, leaning in. "Apparently the state would be putting up to fifteen million into this project, which just seemed ...."

"Seemed what?" The sharpness in Montoya's tone surprised her.

"It seemed like a lot for a company no one has heard of before." There, she'd said it.

Montoya sat still for a moment, looking aloof or perhaps thoughtful as she twisted a bracelet on her left wrist. She looked back up at Digger, her lips compressed, then shook her head as if irritated.

"I don't think you need to concern yourself. That is Chris Lovington's problem." Digger knew not to protest. If Montoya didn't want to talk about it, then her hunch was right. There was something fishy about it and Digger was sure as hell going to make it her business.

Montoya stood and went back to her desk. She rummaged through a couple of drawers then returned to Digger. spread a map on the table in front of them, studied it for a moment.

"From what you said, it sounds as though this is the location where they plan to put the solar facility." Montoya pointed at a spot northwest of Albuquerque.

Digger nodded. "Yeah. They didn't show us a map, but from the description they gave, that looks about right. Do you want me to do some follow up?"

"We must keep an eye on this, but I prefer to do everything quietly," Montoya said. She swiftly folded the map and took it back to her desk. Digger had learned enough about her new boss by now to know that no further explanation would be forthcoming. She stood and made as if to leave but Montoya gestured for her to pause.

"By the way, congratulations on your marriage. Did you enjoy your time off?"

Digger shrugged. "Thanks. We so appreciated having time with family around the wedding. We've been so busy with Maria's political campaign."

Montoya nodded. "Oh, yes. Of course. Maria Ortiz. She's just won a primary, hasn't she? Her district covers part of Las Vistas and the area around San Fermin pueblo, doesn't it?"

Their eyes met. Digger paused. What was Montoya getting at? She didn't want her boss prying into her life. She shrugged. "Yeah, I think you're right."

Montoya, pursed her lips, looking down at her desk and then back up at Digger. "Thank you for today," she said crisply. "I certainly would like you to follow this." She paused. "But, as I said, quietly."

Dusk was closing in when Digger pulled into the apartment parking lot. She didn't want to leave this apartment. The complex nestled close to the foothills of the mountains, and this evening a three-quarter moon was just visible above the crest. The higher elevations still had the pink glow of sunset, but even as she watched, purple-blue shadows seeped upwards, consuming the light. This place had been her home since graduating from UNM, and this she would miss, but Maria's political campaign meant they had to make the sacrifice to live in the district that she wanted to represent. Maria needed causes the way most people needed fresh air, and her eyes were always on the horizon. By next weekend, she and Maria would be moving in with Abuela. She loved Abuela, but the thought of being squeezed into the tiny home of Maria's grandmother in Los Jardines made Digger anxious. She'd only agreed to it because she knew how much it meant to Maria. At least she could bring her cat. She was willing to do a lot of things for love, but abandoning Lady Antonia was certainly not one of them.

Inside the little apartment, she caught the smell of frying onions and garlic. Four months ago, when Maria had moved in with her, she had laughed at Digger's George Foreman grill and had promptly bought a cast iron skillet. At first, they had taken turns cooking, but Digger had to admit that she was a rank amateur cook compared to Maria's expertise in the kitchen. Since then, she'd been happy to be the setup and cleanup crew. She couldn't argue with the results, except to feel guilty when she looked at the scales. No amount of running could stave off the effect of Maria's enchiladas.

From the kitchen came the sound of Ricky Martin belting out "Livin' La Vida Loca." Digger followed the sound and watched Maria working at the stove, moving her shoulders to the beat. Her dark hair was swept up in a twist at the back of her head. She was wearing a deep-red flowing top cinched with a woven belt, over black jeans.

Digger moved quickly to stand close behind her, wrapping an arm around Maria's waist. She planted a kiss on the side of her cheek. "Preciosa!" Maria whirled around, grabbed Digger by the waist, and led her in a dance around the table. Digger stumbled. Sometimes being with Maria was like riding a galloping horse headed straight for a big jump.

"I'm always on the wrong foot, but I do so love coming home to you," she confessed.

Maria laughed and poked a finger at her chest. "You expect me to say, 'how was your day dear?'"

Digger laughed, went to the fridge, took out a can of lager, and popped it open. She'd been thinking about her conversation with Montoya all the way home from Santa Fe. She sat back, shook her head, and took a slow sip of beer.

"I know that look," said Maria, "So okay, tell me what's going on with you."

Digger sighed and rubbed her forehead, trying to clear her thoughts.

"Julia wanted to see me today to talk about the event at Chaco Canyon. I'm still not really sure why she wanted me to be there. It didn't seem to have anything to do with the Cultural Department. She just said she wanted to keep an eye on it. I think she's got issues with Chris Lovington, the commissioner."

Maria tossed the pile of zucchini she had just sliced into the skillet.

She glanced around at Digger again, eyebrows raised. "Haven't we got enough on our plate right now? Why are you so bothered about that?"

Digger set down her beer and began to pace around the kitchen. "There was just a lot that didn't add up. Lovington talking about the fifteen million, for instance. When I was at the paper, I reported on companies that arrived with promises of better-paying jobs and economic development, but nothing ever happened. That couple, Kramer and Macy... something about those two just seemed off."

"Did you tell Julia?"

"No. I think she's got her own agenda about this, but I'm going to keep poking around and see what I can find out. But I will have to be careful because she'll be keeping an eye on me."

Maria turned away from the stove and confronted her. "I know you, and you were a good reporter. If you think there's something "off" about these people, you're probably right. Just trust your gut."

Digger took another sip of her beer and frowned. "There's another thing. Julia was really interested in the location. She brought out a map, and when we were looking at it, she casually mentioned that the solar array will be just inside the district you're running for. It was just weird the way she said it."

"Hmm. You should maybe talk to Abuela. I think she knew some of Julia's family a long time ago. Sometimes family issues go way back."

Maria spread the plates out and started to dish out the food.

"Hate to rush you, Mi Amor, but speaking of the campaign, we'd better eat quickly because Dillon is coming over for a strategy session."

Digger groaned inwardly. She had been so looking forward to an evening away from campaign talk. Almost as soon as they'd finished the calabacitas dish, the doorbell rang.

"It's Dillon, better open a window," Digger whispered.

Dillon stood smiling in the doorway with rumpled clothes and disheveled hair, exuding his personal brand of body odor.

"Hi! I hope I'm not too early." He smiled and walked in, heading for the living room.

Digger busied herself with the dishes, leaving Maria to help Dillon set up his laptop beside her computer.

When she rejoined them, Dillon was showing Maria examples of the fliers he'd made when running a campaign for Jack

Kimble, the former mayor of Las Vistas. Kimble had lost his bid for a second term as mayor, but he'd recommended Dillon when Maria asked for advice.

Listening to their talk, Digger experienced the same tug of excitement she used to feel when she had covered elections for the paper. God, how she missed being a reporter! Apart from Rex, she'd only kept in touch with a few friends from the newsroom after The Courier had closed its doors. At first, she just saw a few Tweets and some Facebook and Instagram posts, but mostly the rest of them had just melted away. New Mexico could be a hard place to find a job.

Now Dillon was talking about fundraising events. "You're lucky that the incumbent is retiring," he told Maria, "Doubly lucky that nobody knew much about your opponent in the primary. You've got a lot of recognition from the work you do in the school, and the road protest last year—so those sorts of things helped get you over the first hurdle. But the general election is going to be a whole different story, believe me—and you've got just four months to go."

Maria's dark eyes flashed. "When have I ever settled for easy?"

Dillon ignored the question. "You're going to be up against Danny Murphy in the general. He's got support from people with deep pockets." Dillon pushed his glasses up the bridge of his nose and stared at Maria like a teacher explaining a math problem for the umpteenth time. From where Digger was sitting, she could see fingerprint smudges on the lenses. She wondered how he could even see through them. Dillon was difficult to be around. Maria found it hard to be patient with him too.

"Danny Murphy!" Maria said angrily. "That guy's been here, like what? Five minutes? How does he think he's qualified to represent anybody but those entitled people in Las Vistas that moved here from Michigan or New York or wherever?"

Dillon shrugged, as if the answer was obvious. "Murphy runs

the golf course and he's close with a lot of developers. Look at this."

He rummaged in his backpack and pulled out a flier which he spread out on the table. The paper was creased, but the artwork was slick, showing Murphy's face beaming alongside images of homes in the high-end subdivision of Las Vistas with the mountains in the background. The text read, "Las Vistas and its neighbors, our home, your future."

Digger listened, her irritation growing. She'd spent a lot of time poking into Murphy's unsavory background. "Dillon, there's a lot that Maria could hit back with. Murphy was partners with that developer, Johnny Raposa, and that could hurt him. Remember all the fallout from Los Sueños and the other subdivision that went belly-up. Those guys were as shady as they come, and Murphy was part of it."

Digger had written a whole series about how Raposa had twisted arms at city hall to get permission for an access road to his Los Sueños subdivision. Maria had been fighting against the road because it would damage a historic Spanish chapel. Maria's cause won. Digger wondered if Murphy was now looking for revenge. As Maria said, he'd only been in the state a couple of years. His business background was in Arizona. If she wanted to help Maria's campaign, it was time to check up on him again and maybe find out why he'd been at Chaco Canyon that day.

CHAPTER 6

Digger spotted the familiar shock of bleach-tipped black hair as she walked toward their meeting spot at Cafe Pasqual. "Hey, Manny!" she called out. Manny Begay had been a cop reporter at The Courier and she'd heard he'd landed a job in Santa Fe with *The Daily Post.* "Yo Digger! Heard you got married. Congrats!" He slapped a fist on her shoulder. "Heard you landed a big job too. How's life on the dark side?"

"Hey, don't give me that. I work for the state, I'm not doing PR." She noticed he had one arm in a sling. "What happened to you?"

"Bike accident." She held the door open for him as they walked in. They ordered a couple of lattes. The tiny restaurant was half full that morning with a mix of what looked like tourists and the kind of shaggy older couples that were probably worth a couple million each. Digger was glad for the mingled background sounds of voices, clinking plates, and the hissing of an espresso machine. The noise would drown out their conversation. She gestured at a table near a window.

"Really good to see you," Manny said, "I didn't realize how much I missed the old crowd. You keep in touch with anyone from The Courier?"

"Just Rex, the photographer. He and I used to work on a lot of stories together."

"Heard he was doing real estate stuff now." Manny rolled his eyes.

Digger nodded. "Yeah. He hates it. I saw him a couple weeks back. He looked like hell. I think he's drinking a lot." Manny let out a slow breath. "It was tough when the paper closed. We all knew it was coming, but that didn't make it any easier. Anyway...." He looked up. "Jeez! You and Maria Ortiz, the protest leader. You sure kept that quiet." He gave a snort.

"Felt like I had to under the circumstances—but it was hard. It felt like being in the closet because I didn't want it to come out while I was writing about her protest campaign. The paper closing was kind of a blessing in disguise, but I miss it. Anyway, that's not why I contacted you."

He eyed her over his coffee mug. "So, what's going on?"

"I saw your story last week about a wind farm. You following that stuff now?"

Manny gave a lop-sided smile. "Yeah, it's pretty tame, but at least it's a job."

When she knew him at The Courier, Manny stood out as one of the relentless ones—the reporters who sunk teeth into a story like a dog with a piece of raw meat. She imagined stories about wind and solar energy were pretty much vegan fare after SWAT scenes and homicides, but she wanted to see what his take on the solar project would be.

Manny took a hefty bite out of the cinnamon bun he'd ordered and washed it down with a gulp of coffee. "Let's hear it then."

She recounted the presentation she'd listened to at Chaco. At the end, she said, "The weird thing, there were no reporters there. I saw you guys just had a lame story from a press release, but somebody needs to start asking questions. That's why I called you. I've got something I want to see." She'd bought a large-scale map of the area mentioned during Lovington's little dog-and-pony show and she'd noticed a couple of details that weren't mentioned at the Chaco event.

Those details, and seeing Manny's story, convinced her he was the right guy to contact. She took the map out of the small backpack she carried and spread it on the table. "Here's the spot they talked about," she said, pointing to a place northwest of the town of Bernalillo. "It's on state land and it's pretty close to the main power line that comes down from the Four Corners area towards Albuquerque." Manny leaned over and stared at the map. He traced a finger over it, as if taking a mental picture of something.

"Hmm. You're right. This is where that high-capacity transmission line goes. But if that is where they plan to put the solar array, they'll have to cross a corner of San Fermin Pueblo land to get to it." He paused. And they'll have to get the tribe to agree to an easement of some kind."

That was exactly what she'd hoped he would notice. Although Manny was Navajo, not from one of the pueblo tribes, she guessed he would have a better understanding of the implications than anyone else she knew. She let the seconds tick by. Manny would talk when he was ready. After nearly a minute, he raised his face and looked at her. She waited. Then he gave a barely perceptible smile. "You working with anyone else on this?"

Digger shook her head. "Obviously not. None of this came out in that story your paper ran. There was nothing in the article about financial incentives. I heard it all, but I couldn't ask any questions because I wasn't really supposed to be there. I don't know what it is, but my boss—Julia Montoya—wants me to keep an eye on this unofficially. I wanted to know if we could work something out, kind of on the down-low, if you get my drift." Manny's smile widened.

"Just you and me, babe."

There was a lot more she could tell him, but she decided to keep the rest to herself for the time being. She liked Manny. He had proved trustworthy in the past. But she wanted to do more work on her own first.

CHAPTER 7

Tony Kramer took his time washing his hands. He liked the smell of the little round cake of soap stamped with the hotel insignia. Then, staring at himself in the mirror, he tried on the expressions he planned to use in the meeting. He still had it, the smile that radiated sincerity and made people want to believe everything he said.

He smoothed his hair, which was showing a tad more gray this morning than he liked, straightened the new tie he'd bought for the trip, and took a couple of deep breaths. He was ready. Janet was probably still perfecting her makeup. She always cut a good figure with that generous halo of coiffured hair and form-fitting dresses.

Had it only been a few months ago that she'd shown up with her husband at his Sunday morning fellowship service? He'd spotted her there among all the other faces and couldn't' take his eyes off her. Afterward, they met and talked during the coffee social, and the attraction was instant for each of them. For him, the four years he'd been dating Elaine on-and-off suddenly meant nothing. Janet was all he could think about. They'd tried to be discreet, but her husband had found out and had gone to the church elders.

They gave him a choice: forswear Janet or leave. He chose to leave. So did Janet, and her husband made sure she lost her job as a realtor. Jeff, a supporter of his church, had offered them a chance with this solar project. Tony saw it as a Godsend, but he thought they should still be careful. They'd taken separate rooms for the trip.

He'd arranged to meet Janet in the hotel lobby. He found her there already, browsing through the souvenirs on display for the tourists—the usual turquoise jewelry, a pile of rugs, an array of pottery, and Native American art. Despite the throngs of tourists that crowded the narrow sidewalks, Kramer was enjoying Santa Fe. The soft outlines of the adobe buildings in their myriad shades of brown, the winding streets of the small city center, the Cathedral of St. Francis with its oddly unfinished looking towers. Yes, he could see himself here, away from the brash sprawl of Phoenix. It all depended on the solar project. He and Janet had managed to negotiate a pretty sweet deal with Lovington, even though they hadn't got any real financing in place. The folks in Phoenix were supposed to be working on that. The next step here was to hire themselves a good PR person. Janet had good instincts and she was confident the woman they were scheduled to meet today would be ideal. Kramer had wandered into the souvenir shop off the lobby and that's where he found Janet.

"Why, hi there, handsome! I was just fixin' to come looking for you," she drawled.

He grinned back. "I thought I'd give you some time. I knew you were just itching to do a little shopping." "Don't you worry. I've got my eye on a couple of those darling bracelets and I'll be back. Anyway, we'd better go. I told her we'd meet her by the entrance. We can sit and discuss things over coffee."

Izzy Chavez cursed as she circled the parking lot, glancing at the time display on her dashboard. There'd been more commuter traffic than she'd expected, and she'd gotten stuck behind a couple of trucks on La Bajada hill on the drive up from Albuquerque. If she didn't find a spot in the next couple of minutes, she'd be late. Not good for a first meeting with a new client. From what the Texan woman had said, this job could open doors for a lot more lobbying work.

She saw a mother with two young children stop beside an SUV and chafed with irritation as she waited for the spot. Come on! Come on kiddos! You can finish that ice cream in the car! Mom will probably take it to the car wash tomorrow anyway. Finally, they all settled into the vehicle and moments later it backed out. Izzy snagged the spot, pushed dark bangs out of one eye and wiped sweat from her forehead. She closed her eyes and mentally put on her combat face. Right. Time to go nail this!

It had been four or maybe five years since she'd been in the La Fonda. She had taken Maria there for dinner on her birthday. She'd even bought a bottle of champagne. Huh! Maria never appreciated any of it. She was only happy when she was out marching for the cause of the week. Now she was running to be a state representative. That was probably how she met that skinny Anglo girl. And now they were married. Married! Wonder what Maria's parents thought of that? She hadn't seen Maria's mother at the reception. Then again, Consuela Ortiz would have been a disaster. She never could make it through a family gathering sober. But Abuela, Maria's grandmother, had been there at Frankie's. Izzy had seen the anger in those mean old eyes as she walked out of the bar.

Izzy stood now in the La Fonda entrance, looking around at the dark wood, the chandeliers, the people milling around the lobby. No, the place hadn't changed much.

A couple strolled by trailing two young teen-aged girls. The man was wearing a loose shirt printed with bright green parrots, his wife had a shimmery necklace that sparkled in the light. She was frowning at the girls who looked bored. One of them rolled her eyes and exclaimed "Mom!" in a whiny voice. "Watch out!" the mother snapped, as the other girl bumped into a man in a gray suit who emerged from the souvenir shop doorway behind her. He gave her an ingratiating smile. Beside him, a tall blond woman in a neatly tailored turquoise-blue dress caught Izzy's eye. The woman beamed a neon-white smile at her. "Oh hi," she called. "You must be Isabel." The Texas accent was unmistakable.

Izzy walked over to meet them. "Yeah, that's me. Call me Izzy," she said. She held out a hand, but the woman ignored it and gave her another 500-watt smile.

"I'm Janet, and this is Tony Kramer."

"Isabel—er—Izzy," Kramer said, leaning in to take Izzy's hand. "Chris Lovington said a lot of good things about you. I gathered you've worked together in the past."

When they shook hands, his palm felt soft and slightly moist. Izzy fought the urge to recoil. Instead, she nodded and held out the portfolio bag she'd brought. "Sure. I've brought some examples of my work. If we sit down somewhere I can show you."

Janet took her arm. "I think it's still cool enough that we can sit outside," said. "I just love the way New Mexico is so dry, not like where I'm from at all. Dallas is just miserable in the summer." She led the way to a terrace set with several tables. A server came and they ordered coffee.

Kramer leaned over the table toward Izzy, smiling. His blue eyes crinkled at the edges.

"Izzy, when you talked with Janet on the phone, I think she gave you the thirty-thousand-foot overview of what we're doing. And, as I said, Chris Lovington was very complimentary about your work. But now we're meeting in person, Izzy, we'd like to hear more about it from you."

Kramer's steady smile, his kindly but fixed gaze, and the way he kept repeating her name, reminded her of the Honda salesman where she'd bought her car. "Sure," she said, opening her portfolio.

She gave them a brief background and the elevator pitch she'd used plenty of times. Graduated from the University of New Mexico with a bachelor's in political science, internship at a newspaper in Las Cruces, then a job with an expanding public relations firm before starting her own PR company. She'd done work for Lovington when he was with an agricultural products company. She'd also had a stint with a non-profit that advocated for renewable energy programs.

Janet's quarter-sized gold hoop earrings waggled as she nodded appreciatively. "This is so great, Izzy" she drawled.

She turned to Kramer and laid a hand on his arm. "Tony, explain to Izzy what we need for this project."

Kramer took a sheaf of papers and a map from a laptop case and spread it on the table. He went over the details, indicating the proposed site and mentioning the financial incentives. "So, you see," Kramer said, giving her that look again, "The solar array will be able to power thousands of homes and that means reducing carbon emissions from fossil fuels. Plus, it will create jobs in an area where there aren't many economic opportunities. All in all, this is a real win-win for New Mexico."

Izzy was intrigued. "I get it. So, what do you see as my role?" she said.

Kramer and Janet exchanged glances.

"Going forward, Janet and I are going to be back and forth to Phoenix as we work with our backers to secure the rest of the financing. We need a person on the ground here. That's the role we envisioned for you. How does that sound?"

Izzy wanted to know more, a lot more, but money was money, and she needed this job—plus, "renewable energy" always sounded good. Another arrow in her quiver, so why not?

They spent the next half hour ironing out details for a contract and Izzy left feeling pleased with herself.

Tony Kramer and Janet Macy accompanied her to the hotel entrance, and they shook hands. They watched Izzy as she walked down the narrow street toward the Plaza.

"She's perfect," Janet said. Tony nodded. Janet looked at him, raising an eyebrow. "Do we have some catching-up time?"

He grinned. "I thought you'd never ask."

CHAPTER 8

In the six months since The Courier had closed, Digger had gradually overcome her resentment at the commute to Santa Fe. Getting up early was a pain, but the drive had its benefits. It gave her nearly an hour of thinking time and she never tired of the landscape. Every morning the sky—the same deep blue of Maria's paintings—stretched forever in all directions. To the east, the mountains loomed a dark slate color in the morning light. They passed in a series as she traveled north: the Sandia, Ortiz, and Sangre de Cristo ranges. There was her favorite tree, a half-dead cottonwood. In the fall one side blazed gold while the empty branches on the other side stretched skyward like empty claws. Today, the low hills north of Algodones lay rumpled and brown, with just the faintest hint of green from the recent rain.

Moving in with Abuela meant she had a shorter drive, missing the chokepoint at Bernalillo. Living with the old woman had its challenges; noise carried in the tiny house which meant she and Maria had to make love quietly. If they snuck off to the bedroom on a weekend afternoon Abuela's only reaction was a sly smile.

Last night was the first time she and Abuela had even talked about their new situation. They'd finished the last of the green chile stew Maria had made earlier in the week. Maria had cooked, so she took off to her studio while Digger and Abuela cleaned up. That was the deal they had worked out. Digger offered to wash.

She did the plates first then scrubbed the stew pot and set it down for Abuela to dry. The old woman handed the stew pot back to her and gave a dry chuckle.

Digger frowned at the pot. "What's the matter? It's clean, isn't it?"

Abuela's face, brown and grooved as a walnut, was wrinkled with mischief. "You think my old eyes wouldn't see it, but I can still feel that crusty stuff with my fingers?" Abuela's fingers were twisted, the back of her hand a delta of veins. Digger wondered what her own mother's hands would have looked like. She was thirty-six at the time of the accident, so she would be in her mid-fifties now. Odd how thoughts of her parents resurfaced in the most mundane moments.

As if Abuela could read her mind, "I know you grew up with your grandparents," she said, "but did you ever think you would be living with this old woman?"

Digger started to make a joke in reply but caught the seriousness in Abuela's expression. She thought of the day they had met. Maria had invited her to lunch to discuss the protest, and afterwards brought her to the tiny adobe house in Los Jardines. The first time she saw the house, it looked as if its earthen walls had grown straight out of the soil, as if the dwelling were a thing of nature, not man made. Abuela had been sitting on an old bench in front of a window. The indigo paint on the wooden window frame was faded and peeling. It was a hot afternoon, like today, and she had been napping. Digger remembered the look in Abuela's eyes when Maria introduced her. She said it was as if she was recognizing the daughter of a family member, not a stranger.

Digger dried her hands on her jeans and put her arms around the old woman. "You always told me I had a home here. Without you, I wouldn't have Maria. You made it possible."

They stood silently for a moment, Digger leaning down

awkwardly, noticing a tiny twig in Abuela's hair. A large juniper bush grew in the corner where Abuela tended a vegetable garden—where she grew the green chile peppers they had eaten a little while before.

"Do you ever worry about Maria?" Abuela asked, the breath of her voice warm on Digger's shoulder. Digger didn't relax her hold. Abuela was like a small tough tree, maybe a salt cedar. Still, she had her frailties.

"I do," Digger said. "The protest last year against that road was one thing. But the election campaign—I don't know. I've followed elections and things get really ugly. As lesbians, we're already a target and some people will use that against her. But Maria believes in what she's doing. I think the only person she's afraid of is her own mother—and maybe her ex."

Abuela looked up at Digger, her eyes narrowed. "Yes, I saw that one at the reception. That Izzy is bad business."

―――

Shortly after Digger got to the office, Julia Montoya messaged asking for a meeting. Digger had been preparing a presentation about a new program planned for the Natural History Museum that she was supposed to give at the community college in Albuquerque. The presentations were scheduled for the following week, and she was only halfway through the work. Never mind, she was used to pressure. Deadlines were a wonderful way to focus the mind. She picked up a notepad and headed to the meeting.

Julia Montoya was pouring hot water into a small iron teapot on a table in the corner of her office. A wreath of silver bracelets clinked on her wrist.

"I like a cup of Earl Grey in the morning. Would you like some? I have an extra cup."

Digger rarely drank tea and wasn't particularly fond of Earl Grey. "Thanks," she said, "I'm more of a coffee drinker."

Montoya gestured at a jar beside the teapot. "It's just instant but you're welcome to it. The tea will take a few minutes. Have a seat." She motioned toward the armchairs.

Digger sipped her coffee and waited, thinking impatiently about the unfinished presentation on her desk and wondering what Montoya was going to spring on her today.

When she deemed the tea ready, the Secretary brought it along with a sheaf of papers and set them on the low table between the armchairs.

"I've been thinking about that solar project," she said. "We didn't talk about it before, but I'm sure you realized that the site is right next to the San Fermin Pueblo."

Digger nodded but kept her expression neutral while thoughts raced through her head. Where was she going with this? It was impossible to second-guess Montoya.

"You may not know this—you've only been here a few months—but there are a couple of locations of significant cultural interest on San Fermin land." Montoya raised an eyebrow, letting her point sink in. Digger decided to let her play another card before making any response. She nodded but said nothing.

Montoya took her time, drank some tea, played with the silver bracelets, and set down her cup. When Digger still said nothing, she went on. "The presence of those locations, so close to something that may have a major impact on the land, gives my department ample reason to become involved. I approached the State Land Commissioner and suggested we could help negotiate with the tribe, should the need arise."

Digger thought she knew what was coming next.

"I think you would be ideal for this upcoming project, so I suggested it to the Land Commissioner, and he agreed. I know you are working on the project for the community college, but I want you to set that aside for a couple of days next week so you can arrange a visit to San Fermin."

Digger wondered what their conversation had been like. She noted that Montoya didn't refer to Lovington by name. That seemed odd, and she made a mental note to ask Abuela what she knew about Montoya's past. The Secretary was looking at her now as if she expected a commitment to the San Fermin visit.

"Okayyy," she said, slowly. "If that's what you want. I didn't know anything about those cultural sites."

Montoya looked thoughtful for a moment then went over to a filing cabinet beside her desk. After a couple of minutes of searching she pulled something out, returned to her seat and handed Digger a slim brochure. The brochure was printed on glossy paper but the photo on the front was in black-and-white. It showed a Native American man pointing at a rock face. The picture was slightly blurry, but Digger could make out that the geometric images on the rock were petroglyphs. They looked a lot like some she'd seen on cliffs at the edge of Albuquerque. Inside the brochure there was another photo showing what appeared to be the entrance to a small cave. She looked up at Montoya. "I've never heard of these before."

"No, they're not well known. The San Fermin prefer it that way," Montoya said, "but this department has a duty to make sure they are protected." She took another sip of tea, then leaned closer to Digger. "How much do you know about the San Fermin?"

All Digger knew about San Fermin Pueblo was that it encompassed a small area a few miles northwest of the city of Las Vistas. But in the five years she had reported on city and county affairs, she'd never visited the pueblo. It was a parallel universe closed off from the world she inhabited. The tribe only allowed visitors in on feast days. Did they use isolation as a form of protection, she wondered. And why not? Tribes everywhere had suffered betrayal after betrayal. If that was their experience, it could be hard to find a path toward trust. She could understand that. She had her own issues with trust.

"San Fermin," Montoya continued, "is one of the smallest tribes and the people are very private. They don't have a casino or hotel like other tribes in the area such as the Santa Ana and the Sandia. They don't have much water either. Even though the Rio Puerco crosses part of their land, it's mostly dry. So, they depend on selling their pottery and basketwork. You're probably familiar with it."

Digger nodded. She had seen the distinctive black-and-red patterned baskets in several of the tourist stores in Santa Fe.

"This solar project could be a real boon for San Fermin," Montoya said, "or it could be another attempt to cheat them—and I don't want that to happen. You understand?"

Digger wondered if Montoya had her own reasons to mistrust the deal. It was hard to read her expression.

"The Commissioner said he'd get back to me. I think the company representatives have gone back to Arizona, but they have someone here that's handling things for them. Her name is Isabel Chavez."

Izzy. Digger's stomach knotted.

CHAPTER 9

Abuela was in the tiny kitchen making verbal love to Lady Antonia when Digger arrived home. The cat was playing hard to get, eyeing the tuna in front of her with suspicion. Abuela was trying out yet another brand in her effort to please Lady Antonia's palate. Digger had never found Lady Antonia picky about brands. She was just as happy with the cheapest can from Walmart as a premium Albacore, so long as it wasn't immersed in oil. But if Abuela and the cat found a way of bonding through gourmet brands of fish, it made Digger happy.

Abuela looked up from her love session with Lady Antonia and nodded toward the studio. Maria had transformed the small wooden shed at the back of the house into a workspace where she could paint when her teaching schedule allowed. Every inch of the shed was crammed with art supplies: canvases, stacks of drawings, paints, jars full of brushes, a rack of tools. When Digger looked into Abuela's studio, she found Maria absorbed in a half-finished landscape of the burn-orange rock faces and slate-blue ridges near Abiquiu.

"Hi love," Digger said, nuzzling the back of Maria's neck.

Maria set down her brush, wiped her hands on her overalls and wrapped her arms around Digger. "I have good news," Maria said, "Alma, the mother of two of my students, told me she wants to host a fundraiser at her house. She could do it next weekend. I think it would be a good way to reach out to San Fermin Pueblo. Her husband is a member of the tribe."

Digger nodded. She wasn't sure how high voter turnout was in the pueblo, but every bit of support was critical. Danny Murphy had a lot of clout at the golf course he managed, and he was bound to get hefty campaign contributions from developers.

She plumped down on a stool by the door. "Well, my news is a little different," she said, and related the conversation with Montoya. "I have to do the site visit next week with someone from the SLO. And, by the way, Kramer and his lady pal have gone back to Arizona, but guess who they've hired to represent them."

Maria threw up her hands in the universal I-have-absolutely-no-idea gesture.

"Your old friend Izzy."

Maria's eyebrows shot up. "You're kidding. I don't believe it! Will she be there?"

"Not sure. But if she is, it'll be an interesting day. Got any tips for me?"

Maria squatted beside the stool. "Look, I know you're the calm one and I probably don't need to say this. But: don't let her get to you. She's a jealous woman and she's a manipulator."

Digger thought of Izzy's hard face and piercing black eyes when she glared at them on the dance floor. She had a crazy thought. "What do you think Izzy would have done if I'd challenged her there at Frankie's. You know, asked her to step outside. Imagine a couple of dykes in rented tuxes slugging it out in the parking lot."

Maria squeezed an arm around her. "No, sweetie, I can't see you doing that. But Abuela, absolutely! And can't you just see the two of them going at it—an angry Chihuahua fighting a Doberman!"

When they'd both stopped laughing, Digger said, "Hey, it's nearly seven, we'd better get ready. Rex will be expecting us. He texted me a little while ago. He's already at the bar."

Rex had offered to do publicity photos for Maria's campaign. He'd called Digger about it a few days after the wedding and suggested they meet at the Pioneer Saloon, the downtown bar where journalists used to congregate back when people read newspapers instead of iPhones. Digger knew that Rex and some of the older Courier reporters still hung out at the Pioneer sharing memories. The only time she'd been to the bar was after the memorial service for Halloran, the investigative reporter who'd been her mentor at the paper.

They found Rex sitting at a corner table beneath a sepia-toned print of cowboys galloping across a desert landscape. The flush on his cheeks hinted that he'd been there a while. He greeted them with a loose smile.

Bo Sampson, the bar owner, hailed them as they approached Rex's table. "Hey, what're you girls drinking?" If he'd been a woman, the belly Bo sported would have warned of an imminent birth, but the thick curly beard that wrapped itself around his face like a Christmas wreath said Santa Claus, not the Virgin Mary.

Digger ordered a couple of Coronas. "Oh, and we'll each have a taco. Rex? You want one?"

Rex merely shrugged and waved his half-empty bottle. Bo nodded. "Another IPA coming up. Okay, Rex? Been seeing you a lot here lately, almost like the old days when you and Halloran and the rest of the gang would stop by. Man, that was a sad business, him going like that. And then The Courier closing. I never believed any of it could happen."

Bo gave Digger a half smile. "You ladies look after him, okay?" he said, patting Rex on the shoulder. Digger and Maria exchanged glances and Digger ventured a question.

"So, how's the real estate world treating you these days, Rex?

After twenty-five years as a newspaper photographer racing to SWAT scenes and freeway pile-ups Digger couldn't see Rex taking "parade-of-homes" glossy shots.

"It's shit," he said. "I'm either trying to make some cheesy little dump look like a million dollars or taking pictures for rich assholes who insist you walk around in your socks, so your shoes don't scuff the tiles." He took a slug of his beer. "But what the hell, it pays the bills."

Rex had always been a cynic, but at least he'd had a sense of humor about it. Digger hated hearing the defeated tone of his voice. She wondered how many beers he'd had. His face had the same crushed look as Halloran's after they'd all heard that The Courier was being sold.

Rex rallied a bit as they ate their tacos, drank, and discussed photos for the fliers, posters, and yard signs that Maria commissioned from him.

"If you're running against Murphy," he said, a shred of lettuce dangling from the corner of his mouth, "you've got to be what he isn't. He's the business guy, right? So, you go for the family look, all soft and wholesome. Be the one every mom and dad wants to vote for."

Maria rolled her eyes. "Hey, Rex—I'm a Latina lesbian. You think those white-bread parents from Las Vistas are ever going to...."

Rex waved a hand impatiently. "Don't even go there. You stood up to those people at city hall over that road protest and you got a lot of support. People are going broke cleaning up the flood mess from that disaster and they're starting to get good and fed up with the developers—use it!"

"Okay. Okay. I get it. Just make me look more Xena than Martha Stewart, all right?"

Rex raised his bottle and gave her his "get real" look. "I'm a pro, remember?"

When Maria left them to go to the bathroom, he turned to Digger.

"You been following what Murphy is up to?"

"I have a feeling you're going to tell me."

Rex looked serious. "I hear stuff from the real estate guys I work with."

"Oh, So, what gives?"

"I hear Murphy's been looking at some land way out on the west side of Las Vistas."

Digger was all attention. "The area that borders San Fermin land?"

Rex nodded. "I dunno what it means, but it just seems weird. It's not like there's anything out there. Just thought I'd mention it."

"Thanks. I'll keep it in mind—and if you hear anything else like that, let me know."

Digger stared out the window as Maria drove them home. She kept puzzling over Rex's comments about Murphy. Why would he be looking at land near the pueblo? Could there be any connection with the solar project? She was still deep in thought when Maria broke the silence.

"I have an idea. What if I were to come along with you on the visit to San Fermin? I could hand out my flyers and talk with those people in my district. We've talked about how I need to reach out to the community as part of my campaign."

Digger thought for a moment. Montoya had made a point of saying the solar site would be in Maria's district. Why would she do that? Did she think it would be something Maria could campaign on? Digger's first thought was that she'd like to bring Maria along, but there was the Izzy factor. Things could get ugly real fast.

"Much as I'd love you to be there to scope out the lay of the land" she said, laying a hand on Maria's arm, "I think it would be better if you went after this official trip." She didn't say it aloud, but she was thinking that a follow-up visit might give them both a chance to hear what the people at San Fermin really thought about the project.

CHAPTER 10

Andy Whitaker called her from the State Land Office at 8:30 the next morning to set up the San Fermin visit. He told her he'd be by to pick her up at the office at 10 o'clock. Damn! she'd hoped to squeeze in a few minutes to see if she could find anything to confirm Rex's tip about Murphy. She needed to check in with Manny as well. She had purposefully called to let him know about her intention to visit San Fermin, but only reached his voicemail. She'd texted but he hadn't replied.

Whitaker was standing beside a white SUV with a state logo on the door. He caught sight of her and waved. She recognized him from the press conference: thirtyish, tall and red-haired, with the springy step of a gazelle.

"Hi!" He called, bounding toward her. "So glad you could make it. The commissioner is really excited about this project. He wishes he could come himself, but he's running for governor and he's got a packed schedule." It was only when he opened the back door that Digger noticed somebody else was already sitting in the front passenger's seat. It was Izzy. She turned around, recognized Digger, and raised an eyebrow.

"Oh. It's you. Guess we'll be spending some time together."

Whitaker caught the end of her sentence as he folded his long body into the driver's seat.

"Oh, you guys know each other already?"

"Not really," Izzy said, "We just have a friend in common."

Digger left it at that. She remained silent as they drove south on Interstate 25 and turned onto US550 at Bernalillo. Just beyond the town, they passed a billboard featuring a picture of the State Land Commissioner and the message "Chris Lovington for Governor." Whitaker pointed at it and gave a thirty-second speech praising his boss and the mission of the SLO. From the way he talked, Digger figured if Lovington said "jump" Whitaker would go into orbit.

"So, what exactly does he want us to do today?" Izzy asked.

"Oh. Yes, of course. I thought you all had been briefed." Whitaker seemed surprised. "Well. As you know, our office has agreed to lease part of a section of state land to Solar GRX for a very modest amount and kick in some state investment in return for a share of the profits."

"Yeah, well Kramer explained all that to me when we met." Izzy sounded bored.

"Oh. Well then, as you and Miss Doyle probably know, Solar GRX picked the site because it's close to a transmission line which gives them a way to sell the power they produce. But to access that line, they need to cross a portion of pueblo land. The commissioner talked to the governor of the pueblo, and he agreed to meet with us to discuss it."

"Okay. I get that. But why is she here?" Izzy asked, jabbing a thumb at Digger.

That caught Whitaker off guard. He shot a glance back at Izzy. "Actually, the Commissioner didn't explain that. He just said Secretary Montoya requested that she should come along."

Digger interrupted him. "I think I'm supposed to sweet talk them about the cultural sites."

Izzy said nothing, but the look she gave Digger vibrated with hostility. Digger ignored her and stared out the window.

The landscape was dramatic. The land beside the road was

gouged with deep ravines, and the brick-red earth was pockmarked with juniper of such a dark green it looked almost black. In the distance, the Jemez mountains curved slate gray against the bright blue of the sky.

As they rounded a curve, the pueblo finally appeared on the left. They turned off the highway and followed a narrow winding road for about a half mile—before the pavement suddenly ended, and they bumped along on washboard gravel for the next quarter mile into San Fermin.

Normally the pueblos didn't allow visitors. The only time Digger had been into a tribal village was for the feast day at Jemez Pueblo. On that annual day, the street was lined with vendors selling food, souvenirs, and artwork. People thronged the street and crowded around the plaza to watch the dancers. The dances went on all day and into the night. A matrix of men, women, and children moved and chanted to the rhythm of the drums, sweat glistening on their bodies. They danced barefoot for hours until the sand became ingrained in the soles of their feet. The atmosphere was joyous.

Not so at San Fermin today. The dirt street through the village was almost deserted when they drove in. The pale brown, flat-roofed adobe homes looked sad and neglected. Some had chain-link fences that kept a clutter of dusty machinery, old bicycles, and vehicle carcasses from invading the street. A couple of dogs barked hysterically as their group passed, straining at the chains that held them staked to the ground. Two men peered at the SUV from beneath the hood of an old Camaro.

Whitaker stopped outside a large white building that looked like a 1980s rural post office.

"Okay. This is it. The governor's office is inside. His name is José Archuleta. I'll introduce you to him."

Whitaker extracted himself from the front seat, went around to the back of the vehicle and took out a large binder. He led Izzy and Digger through the front door into a small lobby where a middle-aged man with steel-gray hair scraped back into a ponytail greeted them.

He guided them into a conference room hung with black-and-white portraits of grim-faced men. Digger guessed the portraits were former governors of San Fermin—all of whom happened to be men—in contrast to many of the other local pueblos that were governed by women.

The current occupant of the governing position was sitting at the end of a small rectangular conference table. José Archuleta was a short, squat man with powerful shoulders. His hair was mostly silver, and he wore it slicked back. From the deep grooves in his cheeks, Digger guessed he must be nearly seventy. He rose as they entered.

"Mr. Archuleta, thank you very much for agreeing to meet. I'm Andy Whitaker, we talked on the phone."

Whitaker covered the distance between them in two springy steps, leaving Izzy and Digger, who were still standing in the doorway, to introduce themselves.

Archuleta's dark eyes traveled slowly over Whitaker as if he were an apparition from a far distant planet. Then he shifted his gaze to the two women who had been left standing and nodded toward the empty chairs.

Digger kept quiet for the next half hour as Whitaker and Izzy talked enthusiastically about the project and the benefits to the environment.

The San Fermin governor listened without comment, his face inscrutable. Digger was sure he had heard it all before from Lovington. When Whitaker had finished his presentation there was a long silence.

Archuleta let the silence hang, his face still and immoveable, as though carved from stone; something ancient and immutable that had adapted through eons of change. Only his eyes moved, roving back and forth among the three of them. Finally, he took a slow, deep breath. "And what is the benefit to my people?"

Whitaker flushed, his shoulders jerking awkwardly. It was Izzy who spoke in the smooth, practiced, phony tone Digger recognized from years of corporate PR interviews.

"Solar GRX recognizes the value of having an easement through San Fermin land to allow power from the solar array to get to the transmission line…"

Archuleta broke in. "From what you say, the easement is essential."

"Yes, but of course," Izzy said, "And that's why the company is prepared to pay you for the easement. I believe you've already received an offer by email."

Archuleta lifted his head and looked from Izzy to Whitaker, his nostrils flaring. "We received the email. That is a start. We are prepared to negotiate."

Whitaker's eyes widened and he shot Izzy a look. Digger felt like laughing. There was a protracted silence in the room which was finally broken when Archuleta rose from his chair.

"I think you should come with me to see the area," he said.

He called out something in his native language and the man who had shown them in reappeared to open the door. Archuleta gave him some instructions; then in English, he said, "Come, I will show you the land."

They climbed into an old Jeep which bounced along the rutted road for a couple of miles, skirting juniper bushes and cholla until they came to the edge of a wide arroyo. Archuleta braked abruptly and instructed the visitors to get out of the vehicle.

It was by now nearly noon, and the sun was at its apex, making the sky a washed-out blue. Digger guessed the temperature was in the high nineties. In the distance, she could see a line of transmission towers.

"Here," Archuleta said, pointing in the general direction of the land under question.

Digger imagined a sparkling field of solar panels, iridescent blue against the beige terrain. Lovington and Kramer had said the array contained the potential to power hundreds of homes. She knew that right now those homes were depending on the huge power plant near Farmington that burned thousands of tons of coal, and emitted mercury, sulfur, and God knows what other stuff into the air, even as the summers were getting hotter and drier. She herself had seen the anxiety on Abuela's face when the rains were late and her garden withered.

Whitaker and Izzy walked cautiously along the edge of the deep arroyo, leaving Digger and Archuleta standing beside the Jeep. The governor turned to her. "All this time, you have said nothing. Why are you here?" he asked.

Digger admired his directness. "You're right," she said, "I'm with the New Mexico Department of Cultural Affairs. The Secretary, Julia Montoya, asked me to come today because she is concerned that this project should not harm beautiful places like this that are important to San Fermin." She opened her backpack, pulled out the brochure Montoya had given her and handed it to Archuleta. He held it, studying the photo and text on the front for a minute, then he frowned. "I have never seen those places. Thank the Secretary, but we don't need her help."

Whitaker was in a bad mood on the drive back to Santa Fe, complaining to Izzy about the governor's attitude. "From the way he talked with me the other day, I thought this trip was just a formality." Izzy gave a sarcastic laugh. "You don't know much about the way things work, do you?" After that he was silent. Digger's mind was elsewhere. Montoya had made such a big deal about her concern for San Fermin. Now Archuleta was saying the sites she talked about didn't exist. So, who made the brochure? Where was that picture taken? What the hell was going on?

CHAPTER 11

Whitaker and Izzy dropped her off in front of her office. She waved goodbye as the SUV headed down the street. She had to clear her head. Without realizing it, she found herself in front of the Roundhouse—the state capitol building. She sat on a bench near the front entrance and called Maria.

"What's up? I thought you'd still be on the road. Did Izzy do something wrong?"

"No. It wasn't Izzy." Digger gave her as quick an explanation as possible.

"That's weird. Why did Montoya give that brochure to you? Do you think she knew it was faked?"

"That's what I'll try and find out, but I may be a bit late coming home. I've got a lot of research to do."

She walked slowly around the area to Don Gaspar Avenue and headed toward her office building. Her instincts were telling her not to talk to Montoya. She was sure her boss was deliberately keeping her in the dark about why she was interested in the project. It gave her a bad feeling. No, she just needed to ask someone else about the brochure, but she would need to make it casual—to avert suspicion. As she strolled into the building it came to her: Marigold Ellis!

People said Marigold had been at the department since Moses was in diapers. From her office near the front door, Marigold had a view of everyone who entered and left the building, and she happened to be notoriously good at sniffing out gossip. Marigold was at her desk when Digger walked in. A short, plump woman with a cloud of frizzy gray hair, binocular-strength glasses, and melon-sized breasts, she was deep in concentration as she dissected an apple with what looked like a nail file.

"I have a pocketknife in my backpack that might do a better job than that," Digger said. Marigold looked up through her thick lenses. "Oh, it's you. Would you like a slice?"

Digger pulled up a chair and sat across from her. "Thanks. I'm good."

Marigold popped a piece of apple in her mouth and chewed self-consciously. "I'm trying to eat healthier. I always used to have a donut in the afternoon, but my doctor says I need to lose weight."

Digger thought the doctor had a good point, but she didn't comment. Instead, she took the brochure out of her backpack and laid it on the desk close enough so Marigold could read it.

"Do you know who produced this? I found a name inside, Jill Franks. Does she work here?"

Marigold pushed aside the plate with the apple slices. She peered at the brochure, opening it to read the text inside. "Hmm. Franks. The name rings a bell. It'll come to me."

Marigold stared at the ceiling, squinting as if she were trying to read an invisible teleprompter. Suddenly she emitted a sharp huff and her face lit up.

"That's it. Jill Franks. I remember now. She was never an employee. She was hired on a secretarial contract." She leaned forward, lowering her voice. "At the time, I thought it was very strange. The secretary handled it all herself. It didn't go through the regular channels—you know, approvals and all that. I've been here a long time and ..."

Digger broke in. "What was she hired for?"

"Oh—for some kind of research, as far as I know. I only saw her a couple of times, whenever she came by to meet with the secretary."

"You mean Secretary Montoya?"

Marigold nodded.

Digger picked up the brochure and slid it into her backpack. "That's interesting," she said, keeping her voice nonchalant. "I read through this and wanted to know a little more. Any idea how I could reach her? Would there be any contact information for her?"

Marigold gave a mischievous smile. "I'm sure I could find something for you. 'Course we're really not supposed to share that kind of thing, but seeing's how it's you...." She leaned forward. "Plus, I'm retiring soon. I've got my pension, so who cares!" she cackled.

Marigold signaled for Digger to remain seated while she left the office. Several minutes later she returned and slipped a folded piece of paper into the open top of Digger's backpack.

"We never saw this. Okay?" She gave an exaggerated wink and returned her attention to the half-dissected apple.

On the way back to her own office, Digger wondered whether Montoya would even want an in-person report on the San Fermin visit. With all the confused thoughts racing through her brain she didn't really want to see her right now. She decided to send an email. That would cover the bases, give her time to check out Marigold's information, and have a closer look at Solar GRX.

Digger's office mates were engrossed in conversation about some new chain restaurant she'd never heard of. They barely noticed her return. It wasn't as if she had much in common with the two women. They were both married, had sport-obsessed kids, and spent most of their free time ferrying them to practices and games. Apparently, they hoped it would pay off in terms of college scholarships.

Digger retrieved the wad of paper from her backpack and unfolded it. At first, she wasn't sure what she was staring at. She'd been hoping for some kind of official document, but this was just a bunch of handwritten notes. She saw the name R. Garcia crossed out. Next to it was Jill Frank's name and a phone number with an Arizona area code. There were also a couple of dates from earlier in the year, and a dollar figure that made her eyes pop.

Deciding to discuss it with Manny, she pulled out her phone and punched in his number. It rang a long time, and she was about to leave a message when suddenly he picked up.

"Hey there! It's you." He sounded rushed.

"Sorry, are you on deadline?"

"You're in luck. I just filed my story. What's up?"

Digger asked him if he could call the Arizona number. She wanted to know who it belonged to, but she didn't want her own number to show up. "If someone answers and they identify themselves, just apologize and say you got the wrong number. If they don't give a name, ask for Jill Franks, say you thought she was an old college friend or something like that. I'm sure you can come up with something."

"Uh-huh, yeah, no problem," he paused, then added, "Has this got anything to do with that stuff we talked about the other day?"

"Yeah, in a way, but I can't go into it here. I'll tell you about it tomorrow if you've got time to meet. Can you let me know about that number as soon as possible?" Digger thanked him, then looked back at the paper Marigold had given her. She'd said Montoya had handled the contract personally and that was highly unusual. Was this Montoya's handwriting? She began hurriedly searching through the papers and binders on her desk. There must be something that bore the secretary's signature or some stray handwritten marginal note.

A voice distracted her.

"You're just stirring up quite a storm there, girl! Lost your lottery ticket?" Her colleague Tina was standing beside the desk. Embarrassed, Digger looked up, careful to lay an elbow over the handwritten note. "Sorry! Just a memo. I need a better system."

Tina rolled her eyes. "Well, you haven't been here that long. It gets easier."

Digger gritted her teeth. This was one of the times she really missed the newsroom. She wondered if she'd ever get used to these people. She wasn't even "Digger" here. After they'd heard Montoya call her Elizabeth, they'd started calling her Liz. At least Grandma Betty would have been happy. Grandma never liked the nickname they'd given her at The Courier. "Digger! she'd said. "What kind of name is that at all?" Sometimes Grandma just sounded so Irish.

Digger continued her search more carefully. Finally, she came across a report she'd written for Montoya in her first month at the department. Along the top of the page a comment had been scribbled. Digger laid the page alongside the note on her desk to compare the writing. She was no expert but at first glance it looked like the same hand, the elaborate capital "F" and a lower-case "y" with a long tail. She stared at it, trying to make sense of what she had discovered.

Her phone sounded out the Big Ben chime. She picked it up and saw it was Manny. "Well, that was interesting."

"Okay, so how long are you going to keep me in suspense," Digger said, trying to hide her impatience.

"Nobody picked up," Manny said, "But there was a recording that said, 'You've reached Janet Macy, please leave a message.'"

CHAPTER 12

The fire had gone out of the day, and the air had the hint of evening coolness by the time Digger reached the little adobe house in Los Jardines. She squeezed her Subaru into the narrow space at the end of the lane and walked back between the hollyhock-lined walls to the blue gate. She'd grown to love the faded indigo. Inside that gate she'd found peace and a contentment she'd never thought possible.

Maria was working on her laptop at the table that dominated the space between kitchen and living room. She had to make the most of the summer break. Once schools reopened she'd have little time to devote to her campaign, and then November would come all too soon. She looked up as Digger came in and quickly took in the expression on her face. "Rough day, huh?"

Digger nodded.

"Abuela has made posole, but we can eat it anytime. Want a beer?"

Digger shook her head. She'd wanted to go for a run to help clear her thoughts, but it would also be good to walk with Maria and talk things over.

They set off up a familiar narrow lane that ended at a sagging barbed wire fence. They easily slipped through the strands of wire and followed silently followed a familiar path that wound between the cholla cactus and shaggy clumps of Chamisa. Walking in silence for a few minutes, they enjoyed the familiar sound of their feet crunching on the gravelly soil. Digger liked to review whatever stories of her day unfolded and she appreciated Maria's patience. They knew each other well enough now, there was no need to rush into words. Ahead of them, the Sandia mountains were just beginning to glow their sunset pink.

"It's hard to know where to begin," Digger said aloud. She stopped and sat down on a low rock. Maria listened without comment as Digger recounted what she had discovered in the note Marigold had given her.

"So, this Jill Franks is somehow connected to Janet Macy, the woman with Solar GRX?"

"Yeah. Maybe they're even the same person. Marigold said nobody ever saw her interact with anyone in the department other than Julia Montoya, who had also handled the contract personally."

Maria raised her eyebrows, shaking her head. "From what I know about the way state contracts work I'm guessing that all has to be illegal as hell."

Digger shrugged. "Yeah, and I've uncovered a lot more weird shit I haven't told you about yet. After I talked with Manny, I went online and searched Solar GRX. They have a website but almost no information. I found an address, but when I did a map search for them, the only listing was a UPS store."

"Like one of those places where you can rent a mailbox?"

"That's what it looks like. I'm going to talk to Manny about it tomorrow."

Maria looked at her, frowning. "From what you said the other day, your boss was only acting like she cared about the pueblo. Do you think Archuleta was telling the truth?"

Maria's question jolted her. The thought had never occurred

to Digger. Did the San Fermin governor have anything to gain by refusing help from the Cultural Department? None of it made any sense. She exhaled slowly, shaking her head.

Maria bent and put an arm around her, kissing the top of Digger's head. "Come with me to Alma's fundraiser. We can talk to her and her neighbors—see what they think about the solar project. We better go back now. Abuela will be waiting."

Izzy Chavez glared out at the tiny park below her Albuquerque apartment. Daylight was fading and traffic noise was down to a low hum. The park was almost empty except for an overweight woman with baggy shorts who was walking an equally overweight dog. They stopped by a bench while the dog squatted and crapped. The woman shoved a hand in each pocket of her shorts and came up empty. She sneaked a glance all round to see if anyone was looking and walked away from the pile her pooch had left. Izzy opened the window to shout at her, but the woman was gone. She shut the window and looked at her phone again. Damn those people! She'd left two voicemails and still they hadn't called back. She picked up her phone again and stabbed at the screen. It rang twice, three times, then she heard Janet Macy's voice, thick and sweet as the cheap kind of pancake syrup.

"Well, hi there Izzy! Good to hear from you."

"Hey, didn't you get my voicemails? We've got a problem. Archuleta is demanding we double the offer for the right-of-way easement."

"I did, I did," Macy said, unfazed. "I got your voicemails and talked it over with Tony. You see, utilities don't usually have to pay for easements. I know this is a different kind of situation so we're open to negotiating a certain amount. Not the whole thing, but enough to make him happy. You get my drift?"

Izzy exhaled tightly. "Yeah, I got it."

Macy piled on the Southern charm. "You're doing a great job. Izzy. We're just so pleased with everything so far. We'll be in touch with the San Fermin governor and Chris Lovington—and then we'll get back to you. Okay, hon?"

After the call, Izzy went straight to the refrigerator and poured herself a glass of white wine. She considered the remains of a Chinese takeout, then tossed it. Screw Miss Sweet Voice, she was going out to eat.

Abuela ladled a large spoonful of posole into each of her girls' bowls. Corn and red chili soup was Abuela's specialty. Digger couldn't resist a second helping. After the meal, Maria took her laptop to the bedroom to finish the presentation she was working on. Digger made a pot of chamomile tea for the three of them and took a cup out to Abuela who was sitting on the front porch in the old bus seat. The two of them sat for a while in the semi-darkness. The small side street where Abuela lived had no streetlight, and the stars were so much brighter here than in Albuquerque. A half-grown moon was just visible over the mountain crest. Digger could feel the day's heat still radiating off the wall at her back and she caught the scent from a rosemary bush.

Digger still wanted to ask the old woman what she knew about Montoya, but she hesitated to break the quiet spell of the womblike garden. It was Abuela who spoke first: "Querida?" What is it?" the old woman said, "I can tell you have questions."

Abuela's ability to read her thoughts always amazed Digger. "You're right," she said, setting down her cup. "It's about my boss, Julia Montoya. Maria said you knew her family." She felt Abuela's hand on her arm.

"You sound worried," Abuela said.

Digger shrugged.

The old woman sat thinking for a moment. Then she said,

"Julia Montoya," pronouncing the "j" as an "h" in the Spanish way, "Montoya is her married name. She was raised as a Garcia. The Garcia family had a ranch up by Cimarron. I used to visit a cousin of mine who was married to one of the men who worked there. Orlando Garcia, her father, he was in politics. About twenty years ago he ran for governor. He was popular, but there was some kind of scandal. I don't know what it was or how it started. Whatever it was, he took it hard. He died in a car crash a a little while later. There were rumors he'd taken his own life, but..." She shrugged. "Who knows."

Digger did a quick mental calculation. If Abuela's memory was right, Julia Montoya would have been in her late teens or early twenties when her father ran for governor and died. What did that mean? His death? How can it bear any relevance to the present? But a parent's death can cast a long shadow—and Orlando Garcia, head of a prominent New Mexican family, had lost his run at Governor. Maybe it was suicide?

CHAPTER 13

Digger spotted the email from Julia Montoya as soon as she opened her inbox. It was a curt response to the report she'd written about the San Fermin visit. It was short and to the point:

"I think we'd better talk about this. Come by my office at 9:30."

She groaned. There was no way she could avoid seeing Montoya and facing her wasn't going to be easy. She'd described the discussion between Archuleta, Whitaker, and Izzy, making it clear that in his position as Governor Archuleta wasn't at all happy with their offer. But she'd left out any mention of the brochure that was put before him. Montoya was bound to ask about that. She looked at the clock on the wall. Twenty minutes before she had to face the boss.

Montoya was standing by the window with her back to the door when Digger arrived. She knocked gently to announce her presence, and the secretary turned round. Today Montoya was dressed in a sharply tailored deep turquoise suit with a creamy silk blouse and a necklace with inlaid coral. Her plum-colored lipstick had a shine to it like dew on fresh fruit—or at least that's what Digger imagined dew would look like. She'd never lived in the country but the misting machines at the supermarkets gave fruit that same shimmery look. Damn! Why did her boss have to look so elegant and so intimidating this morning?

"You wanted to see me?"

Instead of heading for the cozy sofa nook, Montoya strode purposefully over to her desk and sat down. Okay. It was going to be one of those awkward interviews. She was glad she'd thought to bring a legal pad; it never hurt to take notes.

Montoya put on a pair of reading glasses and fingered the papers in front of her. Digger assumed it was a printout of her report.

"Did the governor give any indication of how much more he wanted?"

"Not at the meeting. He just indicated he was open to negotiation. As I said in my report, the other two at the meeting mentioned that they would be talking to Commissioner Lovington. I assume they'll continue negotiating."

Montoya removed the glasses and set down the papers. She leaned forward slightly, steepling her fingers so that her hands obscured the lower half of her face. Digger could hear her draw in a breath.

"I know you were just there as an observer, but did you have a chance to talk with the governor about my department's interests in San Fermin?"

She'd been dreading this moment, wrestling with whether to tell Montoya about her conversation with Archuleta. If she did, it might mean the rest of her suspicions would come out. She didn't want that. Before she said anything she wanted to figure out what the link between Montoya and Janet Macy might mean. Six months she'd been working for this woman, still not fully knowing what she was supposed to be doing here. Everything she'd been asked to do seemed insignificant make-work projects—at least until the solar thing. It obviously meant something more to Montoya than what appeared on the surface. She looked up, meeting her boss's penetrating stare, and tried to keep her voice flat.

"I showed him the brochure you gave me and mentioned your concerns, but he didn't seem interested. I think his mind was on the easement contract. I didn't press it. It didn't seem the right time." Montoya stared back at her eyes hard. Then she frowned, looked down at the papers, her nails clicking on the desktop. Finally, she looked back at Digger. "Fine," she said, curtly, "Thank you for going with them. I have a meeting with the state governor today, and maybe we'll be able to talk about this project."

Digger took the cue. Interview over. She nodded, forced a smile, and left the room.

Manny was waiting for her where they'd agreed to meet at the Giant gas station on St. Francis Drive near Interstate 25. She'd agreed to meet him there, drive south in his car and talk. Santa Fe was a small town and the last thing she wanted was for Julia Montoya to find out she was talking to a reporter, let alone asking questions about Jill Franks and the phony brochure. She parked and walked over to where he was standing beside an aging battered orange VW bug.

"Nice ride," she laughed.

He replied with a sour smile. "It was my uncle's. I wasn't as lucky as you. I was out of work for a couple months when the paper closed."

"Sorry."

He walked around and opened the passenger door and chin-pointed for her to get in. They got on the freeway and headed south. Digger waited for Manny to talk but he remained silent. She'd meant the comment about the car as a joke, but he was clearly offended. He was right. She'd slid into a new job with a substantial pay increase while colleagues like Manny were left hanging. She realized that she had no idea where he lived and whether he was married or had a girlfriend. He was one of only two Native Americans working in the newsroom. What did that mean for him? Funny how you could spend so much time working together and only know the narrowest slice of each other's life.

His face, in profile to her, could have been cast in bronze. "Hey," she said, "I'm really sorry. I didn't ask for this job, you know, it just came out of the blue, and it's getting weirder and weirder every day."

Manny grunted. He kept his eyes on the road ahead for another couple of miles.

Digger was beginning to wonder whether she should have asked him for help. Finally, he turned and gave her a half-smile.

"It's okay. We all went through some shit," he said. She felt like patting his shoulder, but she knew Manny didn't like being touched. She waited.

After about a minute he sighed loudly as if he'd been holding his breath. "I found out a bunch of stuff."

Another pause. Now Digger could hardly contain her impatience. Were they going to drive all the way to Albuquerque before he gave in?

Finally, he chuckled. "Alright, so, here's the thing. After we talked, I called a cousin of mine. She's married to a guy from San Fermin. She told me the governor, Archuleta, isn't too popular. A lot of people think he's done nothing for the tribe. According to her, the rumor is that he's desperate to look good. That's probably why he's banking on the deal with the solar people and raising the price."

Digger watched the parched landscape slide past. The old car wasn't going very fast, and the engine made it hard to hear Manny's words. She pointed up ahead to a tourist spot beside the freeway and suggested they could stop there and talk more easily. Manny pulled the bug in beside a small RV. They got out and strolled away from the other vehicles to a bench in the shade of a cottonwood tree.

"What you say about Archuleta makes sense," she said, "But what about that brochure? The name on it was Jill Franks and that was on the note with the phone number I gave you."

"Yeah, and the recorded message said 'Janet Macy.' Isn't she the one you told me about? The one at the press conference?"

Digger nodded. She'd been puzzling over it, trying to figure out the connection.

Manny was silent, his head upturned, eyes squinting at the sky. Shafts of sunlight stabbed through gaps in the leaf canopy. It was almost two o'clock, nearing the hottest time of day. The sound of water splashing from a drinking fountain nearby gave the illusion of relief. Digger had the feeling Manny had a lot more to say, but he would talk only when he was good and ready.

Finally, he turned to her. "My cousin said something that might make sense of all that. Her husband has a dirt bike, and he rides it out on the edge of the reservation. A while ago, he saw a jeep out there and a couple was walking around looking at stuff with binoculars. He was kind of suspicious because a few years ago there was talk of oil and gas exploration out that way. He went and asked them for water, just as an excuse. They said they heard there was a cave somewhere there. He thought that was weird too. The land around there is all sand, no rocks."

Digger let out a long, slow breath. "You think those people might have been Kramer and Macy? That they could have been there scouting out the solar site and where they'd need to get the easement for access to the transmission line?"

Manny cocked his head. "I'm not saying it's anything, but it would fit the timeline."

Digger was thinking the same thing. But that still didn't explain the brochure and how Montoya was involved—or Jill

Franks. She'd been hesitating to tell him what she'd discovered about Solar GRX, thinking he might do his own research, but now seemed the right time.

"You're not in a hurry to get back, are you?"

When he shook his head, she told Manny all about the Solar GRX website that lacked any information about past projects, their only probable "office address" listed as a UPS store, and Montoya's request that she follow the project but keep quiet about her interest. She finished their meeting with a comment and a command: "So, now that you know as much as I do, you're probably going to start a news column or write some stories, but you can't name me as a source. That would for sure get back to my boss and I would be fired."

Manny nodded. "I understand."

"I can't afford to lose my job or rock the boat right now—not with Maria running for office."

"Manny shot her a smile and wagged a finger. "Just you and me babe."

CHAPTER 14

Tony Kramer was lying on his back with a sheet half covering his naked body, gazing at the ceiling. "I could get used to this," he said, pointing at the vigas, those exposed wooden beams that made the hotel authentically quaint.

Built in 1936, the adobe-style El Rey Court was one of the few remaining Route 66 motels that had managed to morph with the times and now catered to well-heeled travelers seeking a nostalgic experience.

Janet Macy had just emerged from the shower, one large towel wrapped around her body, another smaller one swaddling her wet hair.

"Are you referring to our 'afternoon delight' or to this charming period establishment?" she said. She gave Kramer a coy glance and sat down in front of the vanity. He let out a roar of laughter.

"Shame on you! And you a man of God!" she teased.

"A 'former' man of God."

She turned 'round, pulling the towel off her head. "Seriously, you know they only want you for your salesman's smile, and I'm the eye-candy. We've got to make this thing work fast because the election is just a few months away."

She and Kramer had flown back to New Mexico after talking

to Izzy. They'd set up a meeting with Chris Lovington to discuss what to do about Archuleta's demand. Kramer sat up and began pulling on his clothes.

"I thought Chris was pretty positive," he said. "Sounded like he could re-purpose some state money by calling it an infrastructure project."

"Of course, he would say that. I'm sure it's not that easy," Macy said, sounding unconvinced.

Kramer walked over and laid his hands on her shoulders. "Look," he said softly, "Chris Lovington is desperate for this to happen. With all the hype about climate change, solar energy is golden. He wants to be governor, and this will look good on his record."

Macy gave a tiny sigh of exasperation and began to inspect her nails. Kramer waited. He was happy with the way things were going, both professionally and with Janet. But if she got cold feet it could screw things up for both of them.

"Don't worry so much," he said.

She stopped concentrating on her nails and looked up at him, frowning. "I got a call a couple days ago from a New Mexico number I didn't recognize. Now I'm wondering if it was a reporter. Don't you think it's weird we haven't had someone asking more about this project?"

Kramer shrugged. "If a reporter calls, we meet them, tell them more or less what we've already said, then refer them to Izzy. That's what we hired her for."

"And what's Izzy going to say?"

"We'll give her a couple numbers in Phoenix to call. Let them handle it." He stood up and went back to where his suitcase lay open on a stand. "Come on, I'm going to take you to dinner at Tomasita's again. Don't you just love their margaritas?"

➤

Maria and Digger were on their way to the fundraising event at Alma's home in San Fermin. As they drove west on US550 out of Bernalillo, they passed Lovington's campaign billboard, but at this time of day the picture was obscured in shadow. The early evening sun had taken on a golden quality. It was softer than the mid-afternoon blaze but still mercilessly bright, and the heat was unrelenting. That morning, before she left for work, Digger had helped Abuela water her squash plants.

"We need rain," the old lady had said, fingering the leaves of the plants. Abuela was always worried about the lack of rain—but especially now, given the worries over climate change. All through the spring and early summer she had labored in her vegetable garden, watching over the young shoots and carrying water from the barrel which had caught very little of the precious precipitation.

"When I was a girl, we used to have snow. It was right up to here," Abuela said, pointing at a spot halfway between her knees and her thighs. "The rains always came by mid-July. It rained every afternoon for an hour. You could set your watch by it. Now, it's all different. You never know from year to year." She shook her head.

Digger thought about Abuela's words now as she looked at the sky that was obstinately free of clouds. Maria was silent at the wheel, and she could tell how nervous she was by the jerky way she handled the old Rav4. The fundraising event at Alma's home was the first she'd attended since winning the primary. Maria was worried about finances. She needed to pay Dillon, and there would be bills for fliers plus all the other publicity necessary for the campaign. More than that, Maria needed to garner as much support as she could from communities outside the city of Las Vistas. A lot of people living in the city were retirees who came from outside New Mexico, and they tended to be suspicious of anyone that didn't look like them. As a reporter, Digger had seen how positively people had reacted to Maria when she led a protest against a new road development project that threatened the site of a historic chapel. Now she was up against Danny Murphy—exactly the kind of glad-handing guy that incoming Las Vistas voters would love.

Alma's house was near the entrance to the pueblo. Her flat-roofed adobe-walled home looked similar to all the others on the side street. Inside the chain link fence, a swing set and a small red bicycle hinted at a house full of children.. A clump of pink hollyhocks bloomed along the front wall. Alma welcomed all her visitors, one by one, at the door. "Come in, come in. They're waiting for you inside."

Digger guessed there were maybe fifteen or twenty people crammed in the small living room. Most were young women, and some had a man in tow. Some were parents of students at the school where Maria taught.

An old couple was sitting on a sofa that had been pushed against the wall to create more space. Alma guided Maria to a corner from which she could address the crowd. Digger carefully made her way toward the back of the room and sat next to the old couple.

Alma clapped her hands for attention to silence and then introduced Maria. "I think a lot of us here already know Maria Ortiz in her role at San Fermin Elementary where she has been teaching our children for several years. I know my girls always come home excited to tell me about their art projects and all the other exciting things they've learned with her. Maria has been a passionate advocate for our children and now she wants to take that dedication to the state capitol. She is running to become the next representative for our district, and she deserves our support."

Alma patted Maria on the arm, then stepped back and leaned against the wall. Maria smiled, pulled her shoulders back, and gazed around the room. Her hair was tied back in a loose twist, revealing the slender silver chain at her neck. She wore one of her favorite loose tops, magenta with white embroidery, cinched with a woven leather belt over a dark mid-calf skirt. Digger saw her shoulders rise briefly as she breathed in before starting her speech. "Thank you, Alma, for your trust in me, and thank you all for coming." He nodded at everyone, turning her smile on as many shouters and clappers as possible in the room of her supporters.

Digger had helped Maria prepare for this moment, going over and over the speech. As she listened to it now, hearing the intensity in Maria's voice, she knew why she had fallen in love with this woman. Maria's dedication to a cause was white-hot, a pure unadulterated flame that burned from her heart.

"If I am elected," she said, "I will make sure your voices are heard in Santa Fe. For too long, traditional communities have been ignored while those in power listen only to corporations and property developers. It is time that the leaders in this state pay attention to the people who inhabited this land long before corporations and property developers existed."

Digger let her eyes roam over the faces in the room, gauging the reaction. She saw a few heads nod, a slight smile here and there. A couple of small children, sitting on their mothers' knees, stared at Maria, eyes large, mouths open in wonder. The grownups clearly liked what they were hearing. Digger was relieved. Tonight's meeting was an important step in building Maria's confidence.

After the speech, Alma and her daughters brought out snacks, and conversations broke out around the room. Digger wanted to know how much people in the community knew about the solar project. She let her eyes roam over the old man seated on the sofa next to her.

Despite the heat, he was wearing a red checked shirt in a thick cotton material. She knew now from living with Abuela that old people experienced the heat differently. She leaned toward him.

"Is Governor Archuleta here? I didn't see him," she commented.

"He would not come to this." The old man said without moving his head.

"No?"

The old man turned then and regarded her for several seconds without answering. His dark eyes seemed to look right through her toward a far distant future, or maybe a distant past. When he spoke again, his voice was so low it sounded as if it came from the bottom of a deep well. "He has no trust in what they do in Santa Fe. This young woman speaks with a heart full of fire, but it will be tempered. I have seen many of these young people come and go, heard many promises, but we have seen little change. Governor Archuleta does what he can, but what is there here to offer our young people a future?"

Digger decided not to ask about the solar project. She took a different tack. "But aren't there opportunities for other businesses, tourism maybe? I heard there was a cave, and some petroglyphs. People would be interested to see them."

He looked at her warily, glanced around the room, and then, speaking slowly, choosing his words, he said, "When I was a boy, I heard stories about the ancestors. One of the stories was about a cave. But the people who told those stories are long gone. We have no interest in tourists here."

Digger nodded, thanked him, and eased off the sofa. She was more puzzled than ever. Either there was no cave, or Archuleta shared this guy's attitude about tourists. Or maybe the search for so-called "sites of special interest" was just a cover story that Jill Franks, Janet Macy, or whoever she was, put out there while looking for the best access route across San Fermin land to the transmission line.

She spotted Alma and her young daughter coming in from the kitchen with more plates of cookies and threaded her way through the room toward her. She'd met Alma once before at the first of Maria's protest meetings that she had covered as a reporter. When she caught sight of Digger, Alma set down the plate and greeted her again. "Maria always speaks so well. She would be so good for this community."

Digger smiled. Alma's enthusiasm was a welcome shift after the old man's bleak forecast. Alma had been one of Maria's staunchest supporters during the road protest. If anyone had strong opinions about the solar project, it would be Alma.

"Have you heard anything about a solar array being built near here?" She asked the question as carefully and precisely as a fly fisherman casting a line.

Alma took the bait instantly. She leaned in so that her face was just inches away from Digger. "We've heard some rumors. If they're true, it could be very good for us. It might mean jobs, so people wouldn't have to go to Albuquerque to find work. Who knows, maybe we could even get our electricity that way." Her earnest tone carried a hint of desperation. Of course, thought Digger, eyeing Alma's daughter who was hovering shyly behind her mother.

"You work in Santa Fe now," Alma said, "What have you heard?"

"I've heard the same thing," Digger answered carefully. She didn't want to tell Alma about her encounter with Archuleta. She caught Maria's eye and tilted her head toward the door.

It took them nearly twenty minutes to say their goodbyes and thank all those who showed up. Alma was almost tearful as they left. Digger put her arm around Maria as they walked the short distance down the dark street to where they'd parked. They stopped at the car and looked up. Out here, away from the glare of innumerable city lights, the sky blazed with stars. Maria slid her arms around Digger and traced her lips across her forehead, down her cheek, and nuzzled her mouth. They kissed, oblivious of everything around them. A clamor of voices erupted from Alma's house as guests chatted with each other. The enthusiasm brought them back to the moment. On the way home, Maria could hardly contain her excitement. The gathering had fueled her competitive spirit and she bubbled over with ideas about the meetings she planned for the coming weeks.

Digger was only half listening. Alma's hopes for the solar project, what it could do for the pueblo, wasn't that exactly the rosy vision Kramer was painting in his speech that day at the State Land Office? But what if it never happened, like the great billowy clouds that loomed over the desert with the promise of summer rain, only to fade to nothingness before a single drop reached the parched earth.

Ahead in the darkness, she could see the outline of the mountains, lit by a nearly full moon and the glow of lights from Albuquerque off to the south. She worried about Maria too. Tonight's meeting had gone well, but there was so much that could get ugly as the race continued.

Her phone hummed from the pocket where she'd stuffed it during the meeting. She pulled it out and saw it was Manny.

"Hey babe. You got a minute?"

"Yeah, what?"

"I'll be quick, I had to work tonight, and I'm supposed to be on a cigarette break."

"You don't smoke. What's going on?"

"I think I've found out how Kramer got into the solar business."

Digger sat bolt upright. "No shit, what?"

"I haven't got time now. Can you meet me tomorrow at that bookshop cafe at noon? Okay, I gotta go."

CHAPTER 15

Tony Kramer held the spoon above his cappuccino, unwilling to disturb the creamy white pattern the barista had created with the froth. The front desk clerk at the El Rey had recommended the café. He'd talked it up as one of the funky hip places in the Santa Fe Railyard development. Who would have thought a view of railroad tracks could be charming? Granted the tracks weren't that scenic, but from the direction he was facing, Kramer could see the dark blue outline of the mountains. Sangre de Cristo, Blood of Christ. This city was a whole lot nicer than Phoenix.

"What are we going to say to this guy?"

Janet Macy's question interrupted his daydream. He plunged the spoon into the foam, stirred vigorously, then looked at her. "We follow the plan we discussed last night. So long as we stick to the script, we'll be alright. You clear?"

Macy's lips puckered. She'd had a second margarita last night after dinner and looked a little rough this morning despite the sunglasses. He had to keep her on track. He'd always admired her corporate sheen, the right look, the right words, steely confidence. That's why they made a good team.

"Okay." She frowned briefly, made patting motions on her hair, and took a sip of coffee. Kramer took hold of her free hand and gave it a reassuring squeeze.

"Look," he said, "We both knew coming into this that the job would only be for a few months, until November at the latest. We just do the front-man stuff and Randy is going to handle the rest. Besides, don't you like these trips to New Mexico? We get to spend more time together."

Macy rolled her eyes, squeezed his hand and made a kissing motion with her lips. She was about to say something more when they saw a young Native American man ride up on a bicycle and proceed to lock it against the railings at the edge of the deck. He took off his helmet and peered around as if looking for someone.

"That's our guy," Kramer said, tapping Macy's shoulder. They stood and hailed him.

Manny Begay introduced himself, shook hands with each of them and slung his backpack on the floor beside the chair.

"Coffee?" Kramer offered. Manny shrugged, "Thanks, just a regular coffee, whatever's the house blend."

While they were waiting for Kramer to get the coffee, a train pulled in, its side decorated with a red and yellow swirling image of a bird.

"I just love these trains you have," Macy gushed, "who'd have thought of decorating them like that."

"It's the Railrunner. You know, like the bird in the cartoons—Railrunner, roadrunner—beep beep!" Manny said.

"Oh, I get it now," Macy said, laughing.

As soon as Kramer returned with the coffee, Manny opened his backpack and pulled out a notebook and lighter-sized recorder. "You okay with this? I want to be accurate."

Macy shot Kramer a glance and waited for his nod. "Fine," he said, "Where would you like to begin?"

"How about we start with some background. You said you'd

been involved in solar projects in Arizona. What has Solar GRX done?"

Kramer put on his Gospel-sincere smile and launched into his prepared statement. He explained that Solar GRX was a new venture started by people experienced in the construction and solar industries. They'd been looking for opportunities to diversify and New Mexico seemed like an obvious choice. They'd been put in touch with Chris Lovington as someone who might assist them with obtaining land for the project.

"Who was it who put you in touch with Lovington?"

"It was one of the partners in the construction business I mentioned, he has some connections to New Mexico."

"Does this company and this guy have a name?"

"Jeff Chalmers, you can look him up. He's prominent in the construction industry in the greater Phoenix area."

The reporter jotted down the name, appeared to be thinking for a moment, then looked up. "How about the financing for this deal?"

Kramer had been expecting this line of questioning. He and Lovington had been over this ground several times. "The State Land Commissioner has assured us we should be eligible for state incentives such as the high wage tax and job training funds, plus we are expecting to land several million in state investment money."

"Several million? Exactly how much?"

Kramer cut him off. "We're still negotiating with state entities on the amount."

"But you're installing a solar array to generate power, not a manufacturing facility. So why the money for jobs?" Manny's face was neutral, but his tone was skeptical.

Kramer ran a hand over his well-coiffed hair. "True," he said, "But we estimate the construction and installation will generate up to one hundred jobs and then there will be ongoing maintenance and supervision. So, we're very confident that there will be lots of opportunities for long-term employment. And, don't forget, this is in an area where jobs are scarce."

"Uh, huh." Manny looked from Kramer to Macy and then down at his notes. Café noises clattered all around them, another Railrunner chugged slowly into the station, blasting hot air into the already warming day. A few passengers got off. Manny was flipping through his notebook. Finally, he looked up. "So, are you working with any other investors? Seems like you would need a lot more capital."

Kramer laid his hands on the table. "Yes, we're working with a few private investors in Arizona and in LA."

"Private investors? Can you be more specific?"

Kramer pushed his coffee cup aside. "I'm not at liberty to disclose their names right now." He smiled.

Manny pressed on. "What about the easement to get access to the transmission line? I heard there was an issue with San Fermin Pueblo? And do you have a purchaser for the power you produce?"

"I'm really sorry, but I'm afraid we've run out of time," Kramer said firmly, and stood up. "We have an appointment elsewhere in Santa Fe in about twenty minutes. But here's my card and it has contact information for our public relations representative, Isabel Chavez. I'll make sure she answers the rest of your questions."

Kramer laid a hand on Macy's shoulder and stood up. "Well, it's been real nice talking to you," he said, extending a hand to Manny. "Please feel free to reach out to us again, or you can talk to Ms. Chavez."

Izzy Chavez put down her phone and pounded a fist on her desk. "Fuck, fuck, fuck!" She yelled at the kachina doll perched on the filing cabinet. She wanted to throw something but finding nothing conveniently to hand, she opened a drawer, yanked out a stapler and flung it at the wastepaper basket by the door. She'd just gotten off a call with Janet Macy, who was all sweetness and steel, as usual. Apparently, they'd just talked to some reporter who'd asked a lot of questions and they "ran out of time," so could she call him back today. They'd email her the information in half an hour. If she had any more questions, she could call their office in Phoenix.

Ran out of time! Yeah right! Just let Izzy handle the tough questions. Why the fuck couldn't they handle it themselves. She'd asked Macy that, in more polite language, and received some bullshit answer. If she was such a professional, how come she couldn't answer a few questions from a reporter? Thinking about reporters brought up thoughts of Maria and that skinny white girl she'd married. She'd been a reporter before she worked at the Cultural Department, hadn't she? And she'd come on that trip to San Fermin Pueblo—why?

She rocked back in her swivel chair and stared at the ceiling. Suddenly, suspicion prickled like the brush of tiny cactus spines. Was it Maria's woman who'd sent the reporter chasing after Kramer and Macy? The prickle became a slow burn and resentment stirred in her gut. She'd wanted to get back at Maria ever since they'd split. Make her feel the same hurt. Rejection was a mother! Now, as her eyes drifted over the swirled stucco patterns on the ceiling, she thought of a way. Maria was running for office...if she won, she'd be in her element, making all those self-righteous speeches. Izzy was not going to let that happen.

On impulse, she picked up her phone and scrolled through her contacts until she found the name she was looking for. Cindy was in the same group of friends she and Maria hung out with at UNM for a while. Cindy had left before graduating, marrying, and having a couple of kids right away. Izzy knew the older kid was at one of the schools where Maria taught. She tapped in the number, hoping it was still good. It rang so long she figured she'd have to leave a voicemail when a woman's voice answered.

"Hey, Cindy! It's Izzy, here. You got a minute?"

"Um, oh, Izzy, sure. It's been a while."

Izzy got straight to the point. "Listen, I heard something yesterday that worried me. You have a kid at Arrow Elementary, don't you?"

"Yeah?" Cindy answered suspiciously.

Izzy tried to put more anxiety into her voice. This had to sound genuine. "Well, it really worried me. You remember Maria Ortiz? We all used to hang out together. She's now teaching art, and Arrow is one of her schools."

"Uh-huh?" Still suspicious.

"Well, I heard from a friend of mine that there was cocaine hidden in some of the art materials she took to the school this week. Apparently, she's into it big time. As soon as I heard it I thought of you and your kids. Maybe you should check with the school."

"What! That's crazy! I can't believe Maria would ever...I mean how did you hear this? The school never contacted me."

Izzy softened her tone. "Well, I hope you're right. I'd hate to think that about Maria too. But I know you care about your kids. Listen, Cindy, I have another call I have to pick up, but let's get together real soon. I'd love to see you."

Chapter 16

Digger silently thanked Manny for being late. He'd suggested they meet at Collected Works, the old bookstore and café on Galisteo, just a short walk from the Plaza. Waiting for him gave her time to browse and even sink deep into an antique sofa while she read a Kathy Reichs mystery. A tap on the shoulder and a familiar voice roused her.

"You got time to talk, or do you want me to wait while you find out who did it?"

Manny was standing at one end of the sofa, looking very much as if he'd like to take some bookworm time too. Digger gave him a look and put the book down reluctantly. "You were the one who was late. I had to find some way to distract myself."

He twisted his mouth toward the café tables, pointing in the Navajo way. "Let's go get coffee, I've got a lot to tell you."

Digger sprang for the coffee and added a couple of cinnamon rolls. She knew Manny had a sweet tooth. Manny took a sip and a generous mouthful of roll while Digger waited impatiently.

"Okay, so how long are you going to torture me?"

"Mmph. Let a guy eat, no?" He grinned at her and chewed through two more sugary bites. "Okay. Here's the deal. I remembered what you said about that guy, Kramer, that he looked and sounded like a preacher, and he talked about Phoenix. That's where I started."

Manny had searched for Kramer's name associated with churches in the greater Phoenix area. He'd finally hit on one in Mesa. Manny swiveled his tablet around so she could see a Google image showing a complex of tan buildings the size of a small community college. He went on, saying he'd scoured newspaper records and found a story in the East Valley Tribune, the paper that covers Mesa and several other area communities, about a fundraising event the church held. The story listed several of the big donors.

"It mentioned this guy, Jeff Chalmers. He runs a construction company that specializes in solar-powered custom homes for people who want to live off the grid. He's got two niche markets, and you can probably guess one of them."

"Crunchie-granola environmental types—with money. And the other?"

"Survivalists. You know, the guys who want nuclear-proof bunkers filled with weapons and enough food to last them through the next millennium."

Digger thought about it for a minute. Of course, they'd be in Arizona. If they were in New Mexico, the first group would be living in yurts in Taos County and the survivalists would be in the mountains of Otero County.

"No shit! So how does Kramer fit into this picture?"

"I'm getting to that." Manny finished his roll and took another gulp of coffee. "I called the church and struck it lucky with some gossipy old lady. According to her, Jeff Chalmers and Kramer got to be real friendly. Next thing you know, Kramer is starting to incorporate messages about solar power into his sermons: 'Bring the power of sunshine into your life,' and 'let God's sun be the power of your world.' Pretty soon, Chalmers has hired Kramer to do some ads and publicity."

"How'd you find out that last piece?"

"My church source said people weren't happy with Kramer doing the ads, and there was some other unspoken stuff. I think there was a scandal."

"Janet Macy?"

Manny waggled his eyebrows. "Probably." He went on to describe his unsatisfying interview with Kramer and Macy at the cafe by the Santa Fe Railyard.

Digger sat back and stared at the book display in front of the fanlight windows that looked out onto the street. Manny had done a lot of work. She should have been doing this—would have been doing were she still a reporter. She told herself to stop making excuses. She had to keep moving forward. She looked at Manny, shaking her head.

"So, now we know how Kramer can claim he's been involved with solar projects and how, supposedly, Solar GRX was founded. But we still don't know if this thing is for real."

Manny shrugged. "Yeah. I got the brush off when I pressed them on the financial details. They told me to call Isabel Chavez. Is that who I think it is?"

"It's her alright. Maria's ex. She's doing PR for them."

"I've heard she's a real peach, right?"

"Yup," Digger said, standing up. "I've got to get back to work, but let me know if you hear anything, okay?"

Digger walked down Galisteo Street deep in thought. Why would an Arizona construction company decide to branch out and build a solar array in New Mexico? She was so engrossed she barely remembered to stop and look both ways at Alameda before continuing to her building. She had just settled in at her desk when the phone in her backpack chimed.

"Are you somewhere where you can talk?" Maria sounded on the verge of hysteria. Digger glanced around her office and decided to head for the corridor. She didn't want the department soccer moms eavesdropping.

"What's going on? You sound upset."

"Oh my god, oh my god! I don't know what I'm going to do." Maria was barely coherent.

"Calm down, and tell me—what is it?"

There was the sound of a long slow breath. "Someone called the school claiming I had been bringing drugs onto school property hidden in my art supplies. The principal just called me into her office. I think I'm going to be investigated."

"Do you know who it was who called?"

"They're not telling me anything. The police are coming to search through all my stuff."

Digger thought about it. Having the police search would probably work in Maria's favor. She could also offer to take a drug test to prove there was nothing in her system. She told Maria as much, then added, "Can you think of any reason someone would do this?"

The response at Maria's end was an angry snort. "I'm guessing its politics. Someone's trying to sabotage my campaign. You said things would get ugly."

Digger couldn't argue with that.

CHAPTER 17

Digger was worried when she didn't hear back from Maria during the afternoon. But when she arrived home, the sight of Abuela's blue wooden gate was always reassuring. And there was Abuela herself, napping in her favorite spot, the old broken-down bus seat she used as a garden chair. Lady Antonia lay curled asleep in her lap. It appeared that Abuela's tuna charm offensive had won over the cat. As Digger bent to kiss the top of Abuela's head, she was surprised to hear music coming from the kitchen. On going inside, she found Maria chopping onions. The chill sound of "Suavecito" oozed from the iPad on the table. Digger stopped just inside the doorway, and took in the scene.

"Am I missing something here? Weren't you in crisis just a few hours ago? Now you're ready to rumba?"

"Ah, *preciosa!*" Maria said. She put down the knife, turned off the music, came over and flung her arms around Digger. "You gave me good advice. I'm obviously no criminal."

Maria said the police had arrived at the school and thoroughly searched the classroom and all her supplies. "Of course they didn't find any drugs," she said, waving a hand dismissively. Maria said she'd then insisted on taking a drug test to prove her innocence. They'd finally agreed and made special arrangements with a lab in Las Vistas. Turnaround on the urinalysis would be 48 hours at the most, she said, returning to her work with the onions.

"In the meantime," she said, waving the knife in the air, "I'm going to find out who the hell called the school." She stabbed the knife into the cutting board.

"Right," Digger said. "Did the principal at least apologize?"

"She was very apologetic. We've worked together for a few years, and she always counts on me, especially at times like this, at the beginning of a new school year. She wouldn't go into detail, but she indicated that the call came from a parent."

"Any ideas?"

Maria shook her head. "None."

Although Maria was playing it down, Digger knew she was rattled, by the way she talked obsessively about her campaign as they ate their meal together. Digger caught Abuela's eye a couple of times, but the old lady just shrugged. As soon as they had finished dinner, Maria dug out a pile of paperwork and started making phone calls. One was to the chair of the county Democratic Party, Mary Coates. Mary had supported Maria's effort to preserve the Spanish chapel and had helped her recruit volunteers for the primary campaign. Digger was doing kitchen cleanup and only heard half the conversation, but when Maria mentioned Chris Lovington's name she turned around to listen. From what she gathered, Lovington himself would be holding a campaign rally in Las Vistas the next week, and Maria would be able to speak at the same event. Digger saw that as an opportunity for herself. She wanted a chance to talk to Lovington, maybe even get him to answer a few questions about the solar project.

The next morning, Manny texted her a link to his story. Digger heard the text come in when she parked by the office. She stayed in the car and read the story on her phone. The article appeared with a map of the proposed site and a head-shot of Chris Lovington. Manny had covered his bases and got a comment from the State Land Commissioner about the easement through San Fermin Pueblo land. Lovington just stated that they were "still negotiating a deal." The story pointed out that the Solar GRX website was thin on details, just saying that it showed photos of generic solar arrays but none of the company's actual work. Manny quoted Kramer as referring him to his "public relations consultant" Isabel Chavez, who then referred him to a number in Phoenix. A voicemail at the Phoenix number said "You have reached the offices of Solar GRX" but messages were not returned, Manny's story said. As she read it, Digger wondered what Montoya's reaction would be. She was expecting a summons and it came within the hour. The secretary was peering at her computer screen and barely glanced at Digger as she walked into her office.

"Have you seen this? I just read it. Do you know this reporter?"

"We used to work together at The Courier. So, yes, I do know him. "

Julia Montoya swiveled around, took off her glasses, and stared hard at Digger. "Did he contact you about this project?"

"No." Technically this was correct. Digger had been the one who first contacted Manny and shared her misgivings. But Manny had done most of the homework and his work was solid. Digger wasn't sure if Montoya believed her, but the secretary's expression softened. Digger decided to elaborate, it might give her more credibility and she didn't want Montoya getting suspicious. There was a lot more she wanted to probe.

"Manny used to cover the police beat at The Courier. I guess he's doing business stories for the Daily Post. I don't know him well, but he was always a good reporter—very thorough."

Montoya switched her attention back to the story on the screen. Digger noticed one hand was rubbing the silver cuff on the other wrist. She knew that meant Montoya was agitated.

Something about the story had upset her, but Digger didn't know what.

"So, okay," Montoya said finally, "As I said before, please keep an eye on this, quietly. And let me know if you hear anything about any other articles. I don't like surprises."

"Got it," said Digger. She smiled and left.

Digger was walking across the Plaza on her way to Santa Fe's famous Institute of American Indian Arts Museum of Contemporary Native Arts to pick up information on the upcoming exhibitions when her phone pinged. Maria. She looked around for a bench and sat down.

The text said, "I know who it was."

Digger messaged back, "Who? How did you find out?"

Maria messaged, "It's easier if I call you." A moment later the phone rang. "I called the principal back and I finally got her to give me a name," Maria said.

Digger wasn't surprised Maria had succeeded. When she wanted something, she could be relentless.

"The person who called was Cindy Lopez. We used to hang out together at UNM and she has a daughter in one of my art classes." Maria paused. Digger could hear her breathing hard as if she could barely contain her fury. "So, I called my old friend Cindy and asked her—not too nicely—why the hell she would do something like that. I told her about the police and the drug test and she was completely apologetic. Then she told me it was Izzy who'd called her, saying how worried she was and all that bullshit."

"What the fuck?"

"I told you she was nuts. She's getting back at me because she's jealous of you. You need to watch out."

CHAPTER 18

The Chris Lovington rally was held in a meeting room at a Holiday Inn hotel in Las Vistas. Digger had attended similar events as a reporter, and she expected a lot of forced jolliness and snide digs at the opposition. Looking around at the people who were showing up, Digger figured Lovington's campaign must have talked up their guy's stance on renewable energy. They were mostly middle-aged or older folks, dressed in the kind of casual clothes that carried hefty price tags at REI. She wondered how receptive they would be to Maria.

Mary Coates greeted Maria and Digger enthusiastically and guided them to the front row where she introduced them to Chris Lovington. He shook hands and smiled, briefly. Digger was relieved he showed no sign of recognizing them from their being at the press conference.

Mary Coates picked up the mic and started the event with a brief speech about Lovington and his background, growing up on a ranch in Eastern New Mexico, his involvement with the agricultural products industry, and his role at the State Land Office.

"And now my good friend Chris Lovington is going to bring that wealth of knowledge and experience to his role as the next governor of New Mexico!"

The crowd in the room responded with polite applause. Lovington shook Mary Coates's hand and waved at everyone. In his neat gray suit, thick glasses, and pencil mustache he reminded Digger of the funeral home director at her old friend Halloran's service.

"Thank you everyone for coming here tonight," Lovington began in his high-pitched, fussy-sounding voice. "I want to tell you about my vision for New Mexico. But first, I'll tell you what I do now, and why that makes me the best person for the governor's job."

Lovington took a couple of steps closer to the front row, mic in hand, and looked around before he launched into a well-rehearsed speech. "As some of you may know, the State Land Office manages millions of acres across New Mexico that were designated as state trust land more than a century ago. The mission of my agency is to use that state trust land to raise money for schools and hospitals and the like. And the way they do that is by leasing state land for all kinds of business purposes—things you're familiar with like oil, gas, and mineral exploration, agriculture, livestock grazing, and outdoor recreation. But in this day and age, when we're looking at the serious effects of climate change right here in New Mexico—I'm talking about the increase in drought and wildfires—renewable energy projects like wind and solar are the way of the future. That's why my agency is leasing out land for a solar array that will generate power for New Mexicans and help pave the way for a better future for this wonderful state."

Lovington went on in this vein for a few more minutes, adding some talking points about what he planned to do as governor. Digger found herself grudgingly impressed by his sincerity. At the news conference, when she'd heard him speak before introducing Kramer, she'd been skeptical. But now he sounded as though his concern for the environment was genuine.

When Lovington had finished, Mary Coates stood up from

the front row and led a round of applause. Digger, glancing around the room, noticed a familiar white-haired figure leaning against the back wall. Danny Murphy. She wondered if he'd come to hear Lovington or whether he'd found out Maria would be speaking and was using the event as an opportunity to size up his opponent. She nudged Maria and cocked her head in Murphy's direction. Maria's eyes widened as she recognized him. She was about to say something, but Mary Coates' voice cut in, "And now for our other speaker." Maria put on a smile, rose, and went to shake hands with the party chair. "I'd like to introduce Maria Ortiz," Mary Coates began, "Maria is the candidate for our legislative district. Some of you may remember her from last year when she led the campaign to preserve the Spanish chapel. I'm happy to say that her work paid off and the chapel has now been honored with a plaque commemorating its history."

Digger had been concerned about how the well-heeled outdoorsy types who'd come to hear Lovington would react to Maria, but the speech she gave dovetailed closely with the points he'd made: care for the environment, jobs in rural areas, boosting education, water conservation. Maria knew how to read a crowd.

Mary Coates wrapped up the speech portion of the event, by pointing out a table near the door where everyone could sign-up to volunteer for the candidates or make campaign donations. "Now, this is going to be very informal," she said; instead of holding a question time, I suggest everyone can mingle and talk to the candidates individually."

There was a general scraping and shuffling of chairs as people in the room began to migrate toward one of the speakers or head for the door. Three older women sporting League of Women Voters pins swarmed around Maria. Digger nodded at her and indicated that she was going to talk to Lovington. Digger hoped she could get a minute with him away from eavesdroppers, but a huddle had already gathered around him too. She was halfway across the room when she felt a tap on the shoulder. Danny Murphy. He moved in close, so close she could see how the pale blue of his golf shirt matched his eyes.

"Well, well, Miss Doyle, I see you're here with Miss Ortiz. Guess you gals got friendly over the road protest last year."

Clearly Murphy hadn't learned of her change in marital status, and she wasn't about to break the news to him. "I'm following her campaign, yes. And you? I hear you're interested in some land west of Las Vistas, near San Fermin, not far from that solar array Chris Lovington talked about."

Murphy gave her a sly smile. "Still the newswoman, I see. Yes, I'm interested in some land out there." He didn't elaborate.

Digger's curiosity was piqued. "What do you plan to do with it?"

"Oh, I'll think of something." Again, the sly smile. "Well, it's been nice seeing you again. Piece of advice. Tell your friend she should cut her losses now. Politics is a rough game." He thumped her on the shoulder and left. Digger was so angry she wanted to yell after him, but at that moment she spotted Lovington standing alone, free of his entourage. This was her chance.

Digger plunged right in, asking him how he'd chosen the Arizona company for the solar development project. His account confirmed what she'd heard from Manny about the Arizona connection, so she pressed a little harder. "But how was it this company approached you? Seems like they would have gone to one of the utilities rather than the State Land Office."

Digger expected him to be evasive, but he looked at her straight on, his protuberant eyes slightly moist behind the thick lenses.

"I'm not sure if you know this, Miss Doyle, but I'm a Christian." He paused and Digger groaned inwardly. There was a lot of baggage that usually came with that declaration, but what he said next came as a total surprise. "I believe we all have a duty to do best by our fellow humans and part of that duty is to take care of the earth. I see solar energy as taking one of the gifts God has given us and using it to serve our needs in a way that respects our planet."

Was he really saying all these things? Digger wondered. Did he actually believe this?

"So, you see," Lovington continued, "when I had a phone call from Jeff Chalmers telling me about his work, his collaboration with Tony Kramer, and their interest in doing a project in New Mexico, it seemed like a call from God. And it came at the right time for my campaign. I can take this state forward on the strength of our solar power."

Digger decided to play Devil's Advocate. "But you are running against a Republican who has strong ties to the oil and gas industry," she said, "and that has brought a lot of money to New Mexico's economy. Your agency has relied on those leases to bring in revenue for all the things you talked about a little while ago."

Lovington raised his chin so that his eyes focused above her as if he were peering into some distant point in time. "I believe I am being guided in this mission. Sometimes you have to do the right thing now to make up for the mistakes of the past. Now, if you'll excuse me, I have a few more people I must talk to. It's been a pleasure."

Digger watched him make his way back toward the exit door where Mary Coates was shaking hands with people as they left. Lovington's words left her stunned. She still hadn't moved when she felt Maria's arm slide around her shoulder.

"You planning to stay here all night?"

"No," Digger said, shaking her head as if to clear it. "I just had the weirdest conversation with Chris Lovington. Turns out he's had some kind of come-to-Jesus experience, and that's why he's pushing for this solar project." She frowned, puzzling over Lovington's remark about something in the past.

"You worry too much about that, Mi Amor. Come on, I've got lots to tell you."

The evening had re-energized Maria, dispelling the lingering anxiety over Izzy's interference. On their way back to the car, Maria talked excitedly about the people who had volunteered for the door-knocking campaign she was planning.

"We're about to get crazy busy!"

"I thought we already were."

"You were a reporter. You know what campaigns are like." Of course, Digger knew. Campaigns took on a life of their own, and she had a niggling feeling they would hear more from Izzy, and from Danny Murphy.

Chapter 19

They had just walked into the little adobe house when Digger's phone buzzed. She saw it was her grandmother's number. Odd to get a call mid-week. They usually talked on weekends.

"Nana, what's up?"

"Elizabeth, dear. It's your granddad. He's had a heart attack and I'm with him here in the hospital. I just had to call someone. Do you think you can . . . ?" Her voice caught.

"Of course, I'll come," Digger said immediately. Her grandparents had de facto become her parents when her own mother and father were killed in a car crash. Grandma Betty was a stern old Irishwoman not given to showing emotions. If she was this upset, it must be serious.

Digger dreaded having to call Montoya to ask for the time off, she'd felt a distinct cooling in their relationship since the visit to San Fermin. But there was no way around it. She tapped in the number and waited, heart thumping.

Montoya answered, clearly surprised. Digger apologized for calling in the evening and explained the urgency of the situation. Montoya's response was swift and calm. "That's no problem. Take the time you need. Families are important."

The Southwest Airlines flight was delayed taking off, and Digger worried that her grandmother would be kept waiting at a time when she already had enough on her plate. The last message she'd had was brief. They'd operated on Grandpa Jack and put in two stents. Digger had to trust that no more information meant his condition hadn't deteriorated.

The plane dipped through thick clouds as they descended toward Hobby Airport, the vast city freeways swirling beneath them like a snake fight. Moments after they bumped down, Digger grabbed her bag, squeezed into the aisle, and waited impatiently for the line of passengers to move. The wait seemed to take forever. Why did these people take so long to get their shit together? Anxiety knotted in her chest. She hadn't heard from Grandma Betty since the night before. Did that mean good news or bad?

During the flight, she'd found herself thinking about the accident that killed her parents. Bad news triggered those memories. They were always lurking in the back of her mind. The accident was the atom bomb that changed her world, propelling her here to Houston, the hot damp city, and the silent darkened house of her grandparents; all of them holding in their shared grief.

Grandma Betty was waiting for her in the arrivals hall, dressed in a pale blue linen suit. Casual clothing was never her style. Digger waved and ran the last few steps, gathering her tiny grandmother in a hug that nearly swept her off her feet. The hug was an excuse to hide the tears that threatened to stream down her cheeks.

"How is he?"

"Better, thank God." Her grandmother pinched her lips together in the way Digger knew meant she was "getting on" with what had to be done. But there was fear in her eyes. Digger laid a hand on her arm, wanting to reassure her. It was as if their roles were reversed and she had become the caretaker, the protective one, the one keeping bad news at bay.

Once outside the terminal building, she felt as if she'd opened a dishwasher and stuck her head in it. Within seconds, the hot humid air fogged her sunglasses and had her T-shirt sticking to her back. Grandma Betty was so distracted they spent twenty minutes wandering around the parking lot trying to find the car. When, at last, they found it and got in, the air conditioning blasted the smell of freon and dampness.

Traffic was heavy as they drove across the city, heading for the calmer streets of her grandparents' home in the Bunker Hill neighborhood. Huge trees hung with clumps of Spanish moss shaded the attractive homes set among neatly cut green lawns and lush flowerbeds. A young woman in running gear waved at her grandmother as they passed. A little further on, an older man was walking a tiny dog.

"Is that Mr. Bauer?" said Digger, "I remember he always used to walk the dog in the mornings."

Her grandmother nodded. "Yes, same man, different dog though. The other one died last year. He took it hard."

After she'd moved to New Mexico, Digger used to come back to Houston to spend Christmas with her grandparents. Last year, however, they had gone on a cruise, and she had just met Maria. Abuela had invited her to join the family's tamale-making get-together. Now, as she followed Grandma Betty into the kitchen, she noticed the faint familiar cooking smells and the familiar electric kettle on the counter. Sure enough, her grandmother immediately filled it with water and set it on to boil.

"You'll have a cup of tea?" She said, her back still to Digger. It wasn't a question. Tea was what happened when you entered Grandma Betty's kitchen. She had boxes of Barry's tea bags sent over from Ireland.

Digger studied her grandmother over the rim of the tea mug. Strange how older people gradually look older, she thought, the familiar creases deeper, a host of new lines networking across the cheeks. What would my mother look like now? She wondered. She reached out a hand and laid it on her grandmother's arm.

"Are you going to be okay, Nana? I've got a couple of days off, but I could stay longer if you need me to."

Grandma Betty's blue eyes moistened, and her pale eyebrows drew down, as if conflicting thoughts were rippling through her mind. "He's strong. When I went to see him last night, he held my arm and promised he'd be home soon." She looked down and the line of her mouth drew tight. Digger knew it was not the time to ask anymore.

While her grandmother made lunch, Digger went down the hall to the bedroom that became hers when she was twelve years old. In the doorway she stopped and set down her bag. It was a guest room now, as it had been before her grandparents took her in. She stood, wondering again what life would have been like if the accident had never happened, if her parents had reached their work that morning like every other morning. So many nights she'd stared at the ceiling in this room asking that same question.

The newspaper stories she'd read so obsessively fueled the rage against the driver who hit them. He'd gotten off with a slap on the wrist, thanks to some string-pulling by his father, a retired sheriff. When she'd finally met him last year, he was so pathetic she'd had to walk away. Like the therapist said, sometimes it's possible to let it all go. Rage wouldn't bring her parents back.

"Memories?" She felt Grandma Betty's hand on her shoulder. Digger nodded, without looking around at her.

"I used to worry about you so much when you came to us. You were such a sad, lonely little thing. And Jack and I—well, we'd just lost our son."

Frank, Digger's father, was the youngest of their children and the only boy. Digger remembered the nights when she awoke to the sound of her grandmother's barefoot steps up and down the creaking hallway, followed by the soft sound of her weeping. She turned to face her grandmother. "Did you know about me…" She searched for the right words, "about me…and women?"

Grandma Betty was silent for a few moments, then she patted Digger's shoulder. "Of course, I did, but I didn't want to say anything. I thought I'd let you figure it out in your own way. And you did well for yourself, Lizzie," she said, using Digger's childhood nickname, "And you've married a fine woman. Your parents would be proud of you. I'm proud of you."

After lunch, Grandma Betty drove them the short distance to Memorial Hermann hospital. Grandpa Jack was in a room by himself, propped up in a bed surrounded by machines with blinking lights. His eyes were closed, and his face was paper pale. Grandma Betty quietly pulled up a chair to the bed and bent over towards him. When she murmured his name, his eyelids fluttered open and he peered around, gradually regaining consciousness. The corners of his mouth stretched upward in a faint smile.

"Hi," he croaked, "I see you brought one of my favorite people—yourself. You ready to move back to Texas, Lizzie?"

Digger leaned over the bed and kissed the top of his head. "I'm a married woman with a wife to think about now," she teased. "But I'm always glad to see you, Grandpa."

Grandma Betty fussed over him, straightening the bedclothes, and asking about his nursing care. Grandfather's voice grew stronger as he made token protests, throwing a wink in Digger's direction. "So, what are you up to these days when you're not visiting an old man in the hospital?"

Digger gave an overview of her activities within the Cultural Department. When she mentioned the solar project, he looked around, frowning. "Tell me more about that."

"It's a kind of a long story. Do we have time?" Digger glanced at her grandmother. She nodded.

Digger described the initial news conference and the feeling she'd had in Lovington's office and then detailed everything she'd found out since then. "To me, there's something off about this whole thing. But when I got a chance to talk to the State Land Commissioner, he sounded as though he completely trusts these guys. He's making this part of his campaign, and a lot of people support that kind of thing as a way to combat climate change."

When she'd finished, her grandfather nodded slowly, his fingers tapping on the bed sheet. He looked over at his wife as though sharing a thought. "Does this sound familiar, Betty?"

"Troy?" she offered. He nodded.

Digger could have kicked herself. Her grandparents' company dealt with oil and gas leases. They'd probably come across all kinds of speculators. She hadn't even thought of asking their advice, they were just her grandparents.

The door to the room swung open and a tall nurse in lilac scrubs breezed in. "Hi Mr. Doyle, how are we feeling?" Without waiting for an answer, she flashed a smile at Grandma Betty. "I'm afraid I'm going to have to ask you to step outside, I have to check a few things."

Grandpa Jack squeezed his wife's hand. "It's okay. I'm starting to get tired. Lizzie, so good to see you. Thanks for coming."

Once they were back at the house, Grandma Betty took Digger into the converted garage they used as a home office and booted up the computer. Half an hour later, she crowed with excitement. "Here it is. Look at this! No, wait, I'll print it."

Her grandmother pointed at the documents. "These are from about four years ago. This company came to a small community near Temple, Texas. It's mostly farming around there, but there had been a lot of interest from solar companies wanting to lease land. They were wanting to take advantage of a tax break that is legally available. That sort of thing stirred a lot of push-back from local farmers. But this crowd said they didn't need the tax break. They were offering to pay taxes to help the school district, hire local people for some of the construction jobs, and on and on. County officials loved it. You can imagine, they just saw dollar signs and they approved it in no time."

"How come you know all this?" Digger said.

Grandma Betty glanced up from the papers in her hand. "Your grandfather and I kept an eye on trends in the industry. We'd talked about shifting away from oil and gas. We thought there could be a good future in renewables. So, we started looking at solar opportunities. We'd looked at a few prospects by the time this one cropped up. This deal sounded different, and that made your grandfather curious." She shot Digger a familiar look. "You know how curious your grandfather can be—I think you inherited that from him—anyway, he started asking around, people he knew in the circles that invest in solar, that kind of thing. He couldn't find anyone who'd heard of these people, let alone buyers committed to investing. Then he started poking around among the supply contacts he's dealt with in the past. He couldn't find any record of anything being purchased or sent to that location. It just didn't add up. Sure enough, the construction date came and went, and nothing happened at the site."

Digger was intrigued. "So, who were these guys?"

Her grandmother scanned through the printouts again and handed her one. It was a copy of a document from the Texas Secretary of State's office showing corporation information about the company, including names of company officers, along with an address in Dallas. Digger noticed that one of the names was

Randy Garcia. Nothing odd in that; it was a common Hispanic last name, but something about it jogged a recent memory.

"Did you ever find out anything about the company? Or the people?"

Grandma Betty shook her head. "No. The whole thing sounded bad, so we dropped it."

Just then, her grandmother's cell phone vibrated on the desk. She'd put it in silence mode while visiting the hospital.

Grandma Betty picked it up, noticed the number, and held up a hand. "Sorry, but I'm going to have to take this. It's Tess."

Tess Jardine was the office manager who'd been with her grandparents' company as long as Digger could remember. Her grandmother's face showed irritation. "Of course, Tess, I'll be right over," she said, then hung up. "Always something. Nothing big, but I've got to go. Later that afternoon, while Grandma Betty drove Digger to the airport, she asked again about the solar company.

"I can't remember, dear. Maybe when your grandfather is better, he'll have something."

Chapter 20

A shard of sunlight sliced through a gap in the curtains, cutting a line across Izzy's face. Gradually aware of the brightness, she opened first one eye and then the other, swimming slowly back into consciousness. She heard breathing that was not her own and eased her head around to see the woman in bed beside her. Cheryl. She closed her eyes again: remembered going to Frankie's, dancing, kissing in the parking lot, and then here. The warmth of Cheryl's body had felt good. She slid an arm over and trailed her fingers down the creamy pale skin of her back.

"You're so bad," Cheryl murmured. Raising up on one elbow, she gave a mischievous smile and said, "You want more?" Without waiting for an answer, she rolled her body over onto Izzy, kissing first her neck then working slowly downward.

Almost as soon as they had finished, Cheryl slipped out of bed and began dressing. Izzy pulled the sheets up around her neck and watched. "What's the hurry? It's Saturday."

"I have to work this afternoon and I need to get ready."

Izzy pouted. "What about tonight?"

Cheryl flashed her a smile. "Maybe you could meet me where I work, and we could go somewhere after."

Izzy tried to remember if Cheryl had talked about her job. "Remind me. Last night I wasn't thinking about work."

Cheryl smirked. "Admit it, you forgot. Just like a butch!"

"Oh, come on! I remember the important things, like the lizard tattoo on your left shoulder blade."

"You're good at this," Cheryl raised an eyebrow. "Okay. I'm a server at the golf club. You can come by for a drink and meet me there. I get off at eight."

Izzy nodded. "Just one more thing." She climbed out of bed, walked over to Cheryl, and pressed her body against hers, as she held her in a kiss.

The Las Vistas Golf Club wasn't exactly Izzy's idea of a date. The place was too straight and too white. She spotted a sign pointing to the bar and headed for it. At least she could have a drink while she waited for Cheryl.

The bar decor was faux pueblo: rawhide furniture, walls hung with Native American rugs and desert landscape paintings. There was even a kiva style fireplace in one corner. A few men were gathered around a table on the far side; other than that, the place was almost empty. The guy behind the bar, a preppy-looking type in a kelly-green golf shirt, looked bored. Izzy took a seat at the bar counter and ordered a Modelo. He blinked a couple of times then seemed to register what she'd said.

While she waited for her beer, she took out her phone and messaged Cheryl.

"Just got here. Having a drink in the bar. See you soon."

She'd just tapped "send" when she noticed the man sitting next to her in a turquoise golf shirt with the club's name embroidered on the chest. "Hi, he smiled. You don't mind if I join you."

It wasn't a question and Izzy figured she couldn't say no. Preppy Guy had just deposited her Modelo in front of her. His attitude seemed to have changed. The polite smile he gave the newcomer reminded Izzy of a dog waiting for a treat.

"I'll have one of those, Ricky," the newcomer said, pointing at Izzy's beer. Izzy noticed wavy white hair and deeply tanned skin. She assumed he must play a lot of golf.

"Sure thing, Mr. Murphy." When Preppy Guy went to get the beer, the newcomer held his hand out to Izzy. "By the way, I'm Danny Murphy, I'm the manager of the golf club. I'm always glad to see new people here."

Izzy realized why his face seemed familiar. She'd driven past yard signs in her neighborhood. "Oh—you're the guy who's running against Maria Ortiz."

"I'd prefer to think that Maria Ortiz is running against me. I think I'm a much better candidate to represent this district." He grabbed the beer Ricky had just set in front of him and held it up in a toast.

Izzy played along. "You know much about her?"

Murphy shrugged. "Just what I saw last year when she was protesting that road. I think she's too radical for people in Las Vistas. Have you met her?"

"We were at college together."

"Oh yeah?" Murphy suddenly looked more interested. Izzy took another sip of beer, thinking about what she was going to say next. This was an opportunity she hadn't expected.

"We were pretty close at one time," she said, casually. "But...you know, people do their own thing. I heard a rumor she got into trouble recently at the school where she works."

"What kind of trouble?" Murphy was definitely hooked. Izzy shrugged, trying for the concerned but slightly bitchy tone she remembered from middle school. "It might have been something to do with drugs, I don't know really. It was just something I heard."

From Murphy's expression, she imagined he was mentally filing away the detail to fuel a negative campaign flyer.

"So. . . . Anyway, she said, wanting to change the subject. "What made you decide to run for office?"

Murphy gestured toward the huge picture window that looked out over a putting green where a flag flapped in the evening breeze. "I manage this place," he said. "But my real interest is in development deals, and politics seemed a good way to further that interest. Right now, I'm looking at some land west of here near where they're talking about putting in that solar array. You know about that?"

"Yeah—as a matter of fact, I do public relations and the guys behind that project are my clients."

Murphy leaned in again, interested. Izzy was enjoying this.

"So, how soon do you think it's going to get off the ground?"

Izzy thought for a moment. She probably shouldn't have mentioned her work with the solar people. The last time they'd talked, Janet had referred her to the Phoenix office. All those people would say was that they were pursuing different sources of financing and things were looking "promising."

"They don't have a hard date yet, but I think there's going to be an announcement soon," she offered.

Preppy Guy Ricky reappeared at the other side of the bar, as if anticipating another order of drinks. Murphy glanced at Izzy. "You like Buffalo Wings?"

Izzy had stuffed down the leftover half of a Subway meatball sandwich she'd found in her refrigerator before coming out, but she was getting hungry, and Cheryl wouldn't be free until after eight. Not knowing if dinner would be in the cards, she shrugged. "Sure."

Murphy waved a hand at Preppy Guy. "Ricky, ask the restaurant to send us over an order of wings, will you?"

A few minutes later, Cheryl appeared carrying a tray with the order of wings. She was dressed in a Kelly-green blouse and skirt that made her look like a Barbie Doll. Izzy coughed to disguise her laugh.

"Thanks Cheryl," Murphy said, as Cheryl set the tray down between them. Cheryl caught Izzy's expression and shot her a look, eyebrows raised. "Oh—you're having the wings? I thought you were a vagi-tarian.," she said, messing around with the pronunciation.

Izzy grinned back. "Oh, you know the expression about being on a diet and looking at the menu."

Murphy glanced between them, trying to navigate the signals. "You two know each other?"

Izzy shrugged. "We met recently."

"Yeah, very recently," Cheryl said. She made a show of setting out plates and paper napkins. "Anything else, Danny?"

Izzy slid a glance at her phone. It was almost eight. "Oh," she said, looking at Murphy apologetically. "You know what? I'm going to have to go. I've got an appointment to call a client just after eight, and I left their file in my car. Thanks a lot Danny, it was nice meeting you." She shook his hand and nodded at Cheryl, hoping she'd take the hint.

She did. About ten minutes later Cheryl emerged from the club house. She had ditched the green uniform for tight blue jeans and a white V-neck T-shirt that showed off the shape of her breasts. She walked slowly across the parking lot to where Izzy was waiting beside her car.

"Well, that was a fun little charade," Cheryl said.

Izzy moved to kiss her, but Cheryl brushed her away. "Not here. Danny might be watching out the window."

She grabbed Izzy's hand and pulled her around a corner. Cheryl's car was at the far side of the parking lot, with an unobstructed view over the golf course. She unlocked the doors and motioned for Izzy to get in. Once inside, Izzy turned to her, eyes questioning. "So, it's 'Danny' huh? You sleep with him?"

Cheryl rolled her eyes. "No. He tried it on, but I said no. I just want to keep on his good side. I've been volunteering for his campaign. If he wins it could mean opportunities for me."

"You think he will?"

Cheryl tossed her head. Her voice was sarcastic. "He doesn't give a shit about politics. He's just in it to get money for his development plans. Actually, it's the money, plus he wants to get back at the woman he's running against. He lost a lot of money because of her, and his business partner, a guy who goes by "Johnny Raposa" is in jail."

Izzy pretended to listen. In the evening light, the golf course was a Rorschach blot of dark green against the tan desert landscape. The mountains had turned the pink of an infected wound. She thought of Maria dancing with that woman. Her wife! She'd given Maria everything and it had never been enough. Even when she held her in her arms, she could feel Maria straining away, like a child reaching for someone else. She was always so righteous! She could never see that she hurt people. It infuriated her how much she hurt and still wanted Maria.

Blue-gray shadows seeped over the mountain. Bruises on the wound. An idea stirred, she could almost feel it, like the germination of a bitter seed. That woman Digger, Maria's wife, was the reporter whose stories had stopped Raposa's road plan and exposed his tax fraud. Danny had his reasons for getting back at both of them. Well, so did she.

She slid an arm around Cheryl. "I think I know a way you could help Danny's chances."

Cheryl brightened. "Yeah? How?"

"Maria and her girlfriend—her wife, actually—are at Frankie's most Friday nights. You could go along there, come on to her, make the wife jealous, really throw her off her game."

Izzy gave Cheryl a grin. But the response wasn't what she'd expected. Cheryl stared at her, nostrils flaring as if she'd opened a Tupperware full of leftovers gone bad.

"Listen, I don't sleep with men, and I don't sleep with other women's wives. Now, get the hell out of my car."

CHAPTER 21

Digger parked her Subaru and slung the messenger bag with the campaign fliers over her shoulder. She stood looking up the street, remembering the day almost two years before when the monsoon storm had struck. The sky had turned to ditchwater brown, and rain pummeled the soft sandy earth like mortar fire, blasting new channels across the desert hillside. Every home on the street had been flooded as water from the road, high on the steep hill outside of town, poured down into the new community. Digger had slogged through the wet sand to interview the bedraggled residents. When the mayor showed up, she demanded he explain why the city allowed the homes to be built on unstable ground.

Poor old Jack Kimble. As mayor, he'd promised to come up with a fix, but nobody wanted to pay for it, and he'd gone on to lose his bid for re-election. She noticed that there were still no gutters alongside the street. So, the next time a big storm hit, the houses would surely be flooded again. Oh well. As Sally Jenkins, one of the most vocal residents said, they could take care of themselves.

As luck would have it, one of Maria's campaign volunteers hadn't shown up to go door-knocking tonight, so Digger had stepped in. The first house from the corner was a sprawling custom home with a semi-circular driveway and a front yard planted with desert willow, clumps of red yucca, and lavender. Her stomach fluttered as she approached. Asking questions from strangers was one thing when you were a reporter. You felt like you had invisible armor. Making cold calls for a political campaign risked a slammed door in the face. That was hard to take.

The front door looked like the entrance to an old church—dark wood decorated with bands of black forged iron. A wastebasket-sized brass bell hung beside it. She rang and waited until finally she heard footsteps The door opened and a large woman in a Texas Tech tank top and saggy shorts eyed her expectantly. Her expression quickly changed as she registered that Digger was not there bearing Amazon packages.

"Oh," she said, one hand ready to close the door.

"Honey, is that the UPS guy?" The voice came from the man of the house.

Digger pulled out one of Maria's fliers. "Hi," she said brightly. "I'm here on behalf of Maria Ortiz. She's the candidate running to represent this district and she'll be holding a town hall-style meeting in Las Vistas next week. She wants to hear what people think legislators in Santa Fe should do for them." She held out the flier to the woman who stood there looking confused.

"Who did you say you represent?"

"Maria Ortiz. She's a teacher at San Fermin Elementary and...."

"Oh, was she the one that was protesting that road? I remember her. It was all over the news." She frowned. "I have a sister who bought a house over in the Los Sueños subdivision and when they stopped building that road, the rains ran down that hill into her street. The value of her house dropped like a stone. No, we don't need people like her. No way." The door made a heavy thud as it shut.

Digger stepped back and gazed up at the street. One down and about twenty-five to go. She stuffed the flier back in her bag and headed on to the next house, which happened to have had a "For Sale" sign out front. She nearly walked past it, but the sight and whirr of hummingbirds clustered around the bird feeder drew her in. She hit the buzzer. The woman who opened the door was Sally Jenkins, or at least she used to be. The past two years had clearly not been kind to her. She'd lost about thirty pounds and the feisty expression she'd displayed as she harangued city councilors about the flooding, property taxes, and dog feces in the local parks was gone. Her face was drawn, her eyes clouded with worry. She stared at Digger for a few seconds, then recognition dawned.

"You're that reporter gal, used to come to city council meetings, right?"

"Yeah, that's me. Elizabeth Doyle. I was with The Courier. I saw your sign out front. Are you...are you having to sell the house?"

Sally expelled a heavy sigh. "Yeah. My husband had a stroke a couple months ago and we've got medical bills out the wazoo. We're going back to Long Island to live with our daughter. She's gonna help me care for him."

Digger opened her mouth, trying to think of something appropriate to say. "I, uh, I'm really sorry to bother you. I'm campaigning for Maria Ortiz, she wants to represent Las Vistas."

Sally leaned against the doorframe as though she were immensely tired. "Yeah. I remember her. She stuck up to those council idiots and that asshat Raposa. So, she's running against that jerk at the golf course? Sure, gimme some of those fliers and I'll hand 'em out to my friends at church."

Forty minutes later Digger had circled back to the car. Only two doors in the face, and the rest of the encounters were a mixed bag. Half of them had either never heard of Maria, or they said they didn't follow local politics, or thought all politicians were corrupt, so what was the point of voting anyway. One young woman, who had answered the door with a baby in her arms, said she'd be happy to take a flier. The baby grabbed the paper and stuffed the corner of it in her mouth.

"I'm sorry. she's teething, the woman smiled apologetically, but when Digger went to hand her another flier, she waved it away. "It's okay. We'll read it later. Sorry, but I have to go now. She needs changing."

Digger shrugged, disheartened. At this rate, Maria's chances weren't looking good. What would she do if she lost the election? She didn't even need to ask herself the question. Maria would find a new goal, a new cause, it was in her DNA. And what if she did win? The state legislature was only a part-time gig; thirty days one year, and sixty days the next. But there would be committees, meetings with constituents, events to attend, and dealing with harangues from the people who disagreed with things she did and said. How would that affect them? How much would it intrude on the safe little burrow that was Abuela's home—that place where she could feel safe, snuggling beside Maria in the night while the coyotes yipped outside, and the bitter cold of midnight ate at the Moon.

The phone in her pocket sang Maria's tune. "Are you done? We're at Mojo's. can you meet us here?" Her voice sounded weary. Getting votes was only half the battle. Raising money was an even bigger headache. Maria had borrowed money from her father and an uncle for the campaign and she had no idea how she was going to pay them back.

Mojo's was the downtown cafe a short walk away from the old Courier offices. Digger used to grab a latté there mid-mornings or meet sources if she wanted to interview them away from the newsroom. The tiny parking lot looked out on the street, and she could see the outline of the Courier offices—windows blank and "For Lease" sign still out front. Her throat tightened every time she saw it, remembering all the people who worked there, all the stories, a way of life, gone.

Maria's group had taken over a table in the far corner of the cafe. There was Alma and her sister and a couple of women who'd worked with Maria on the road protests. They looked glum. Digger pulled up a chair, leaned in, and kissed Maria before greeting the rest of them.

"Dare I ask how it went?" she said hesitantly.

Maria blew air through her lips. She opened her mouth, but Alma cut in. "Somebody has been spreading that rumor about Maria bringing drugs to the school. We know it's not true. I went to the principal, and she agrees. But look at this."

Alma shoved a flier across the table. It showed a picture of Danny Murphy swinging a golf club, with the slogan, "For-ward with Murphy." A paragraph underneath the photo listed his accomplishments. So far, it looked innocuous. Digger looked up at Alma, puzzled.

"Look at the back."

On the back, Murphy claimed he was working to help young families in Las Vistas, "Unlike my opponent," it went on, "who thinks it's okay to bring banned substances to an elementary school, putting your kids at risk!"

"Shit!"

"That's what I said. Actually, what I said was a lot worse," Maria admitted. She put her head in her hands, shoulders slumped. "You know who's behind this. I can't believe she's so jealous she would do something like this."

Digger knelt beside Maria and gently lifted her chin. "Look at me," she said softly. "Remember when they yelled at you at city council meetings, when you thought the stopping the road was a lost cause? Don't let them get to you. This time, I'm with you. We're all here with you."

Maria's dark eyes glistened, and she gave a tiny nod. "Thank you," she whispered.

Digger studied the flier again, her brain racing. She'd covered a ton of campaigns as a reporter and a lot of them went negative. If this guy was going to throw dirt, Maria had to fight back fast and hard. Who could she call? Wait, there was the blond TV reporter who she'd bailed out a bunch of times when the reporter showed up clueless. Digger reckoned she was owed a return favor.

She glanced at Alma. "You said the principal agreed that there was no truth to that whole drugs story, right?" Alma nodded. She looked back at Maria, "And you insisted on being drug tested the day the rumor came out?"

"Yeah. You know I did," Maria said.

"Okay," Digger said, looking around the table. "Here's what we do. Call the principal and get her to agree to back you up. Have her meet us as soon as she can outside in the parking lot. Then call Carla Stevens at the TV station, mention my name, and say you're going to hold a press conference, and have the principal with you when you go on camera."

Maria was already dialing the TV station before Digger finished speaking.

CHAPTER 22

Digger was running late for work, her mind still on last night's press conference. Luckily, Carla had been decent enough to remember Digger helping her out. She showed up, true to form, in a tight-fitting dress and killer heels. School principal Florencia Ortega had arrived flustered and out of breath just as they were about to go live. Digger was proud of Maria's performance. She looked confident and proud as she denied the drug rumor, backed up by Ortega who spoke enthusiastically about all Maria had done for the children and the school. Maria carefully denied any knowledge of where the rumor had started.

When the interview aired on the late evening news, they'd cut to Danny Murphy standing outside the golf club. Instead of answering Carla's question about the "banned substances" remark, he'd sidestepped it with a brief speech about his commitment to education and family values. Carla had pressed him, but he just shrugged and walked away. Digger guessed Maria had probably been the winner in this round, but the fight wasn't over—not by a long shot.

The next morning, Digger was hurrying across the entrance lobby when she heard her name called. Julia Montoya was standing in the doorway of a small conference room. "How is your grandfather, Digger?" she asked. "I haven't seen you since you went to Houston." Her voice was full of concern.

She was wearing a fuchsia-pink linen dress, that showed off her olive skin. Montoya was always so well put together; it made Digger feel acutely aware of her much-worn Dockers and scuffed loafers. "He's much better, thanks," she answered. "My grandmother expects he'll be home soon." Digger thought that was the end of the conversation, but Montoya lingered. "You're very close to your grandparents, aren't you?"

Digger knew when Montoya was probing her private life, and it increased her sense of discomfort. She gave the details as briefly as possible. "Yes, I went to live with them when my parents were killed in a car accident," she said, adding, "I don't like to talk about it."

When she told the story people usually murmured platitudes like "I'm so sorry," but Montoya just looked thoughtful. "Yes," she said, at length, "I know what you mean. I felt the same way when my father . . . ." she hesitated, her voice faltering. Digger tried to read her pained expression—sadness with a hint of anger. "When he passed away," she said, finally finishing the sentence.

Then she gave a tight smile, turned, and walked back to her office. Digger stood watching her, wondering if Julia Montoya had loved or hated her father. Or maybe she was angry at the way he died? Abuela had once hinted at something tragic in that family.

Digger was able to leave the office early and found Abuela outside when she arrived home, sitting in her favorite place on the porch. The porch gave just enough shade so that a person could escape the paralyzing heat of the August evening sun. Even Lady Antonia had decided it was too hot in her normal sunny spot by the birdbath and had taken refuge curled in Abuela's lap.

"Hola Cowgirl," she said, greeting Digger with the nickname she had given her. "You're home early today?"

Digger eased down next to her on the low wall that surrounded the porch. Normally, Abuela would be out there in her vegetable garden, checking for squash bugs and filling the earthenware jugs she used for irrigation, to help conserve water. But it was still too hot to work in the garden.

"Want some lemonade? I made some," Abuela offered.

"Thanks, in a minute maybe." Digger said.

They sat for a while in silence. Digger wanted to soak in the stillness that reigned within the adobe walls—the vivid pink hollyhocks beside the gate, the peeling indigo paint on the gate itself. She wanted the best for Maria, but she also hoped her campaign would not destroy the peace they shared here.

"What is it?" Abuela's roughened old voice broke into her thoughts.

"You always know when something's bothering me," Digger chuckled. "Remember when you told me about Julia Montoya's family? About her father?"

"Orlando Garcia."

"Yeah. I had the oddest conversation with her today. She mentioned him dying, but she said it in such a weird way."

Abuela stroked her chin, as if considering her words. "Maybe those old stories are true."

"Stories? About how he died? You think he was murdered?"

"No," Abuela said slowly, "but some people thought he killed himself." She crossed herself, then fixed her dark deep-set eyes on Digger and nodded. "You know how to find things out. You should go looking."

When Maria arrived about an hour later, Digger was at the kitchen table, deep-diving into Google for information on

Orlando Garcia. Maria set a sack on the counter. "I brought enchiladas from Rosario's. It's my turn to cook tonight but I'm tired and I didn't want to put it on you or Abuela."

She leaned over Digger, nuzzling her lips into the back of her neck. "Hola, mi amor, I'm afraid I have to go out again to meet Dillon. He's going to help me plan the town hall meeting."

Digger pulled Maria down onto her lap and kissed her, taking in the scent of her skin, her hair. When they finally broke apart for air, she said, "Sometimes I worry for you, and for us. Things could get ugly. I've followed elections, and I've seen people twist the truth and even make threats. Maybe I should come with you tonight."

Maria sighed. "It's okay, love. Remember how I told you once that I don't break easily? It's still true." She leaned in and brushed her lips on Digger's forehead. Then she stood and smiled. "I know you can't stand Dillon. He can be a pain in the butt. You sure worked a miracle last night getting that TV reporter to interview me. I got so much support at school today," Maria kissed her again. "Can you tell Abuela I've got dinner?"

Maria left almost immediately after they'd finished eating, and Abuela went to her room to watch her favorite TV mystery. Digger went back to her laptop, still searching for anything she could find about Julia Montoya's father. The way her boss had looked when she referred to him puzzled her and then what Abuela said about him stirred up dark feelings. She still had flashbacks about her parents' deaths.

It was hard to sift through all the hits she got on "Orlando Garcia" because it was such a common name. Using her library card, she trolled the archives of the Santa Fe Daily Post, the Albuquerque Journal, and a couple of smaller newspapers before finally coming upon his obituary in the Daily Post: "Orlando J.

Garcia, of Santa Fe, passed away on July 11, 1998. He was born in Cimarron, New Mexico, and grew up there with his three sisters, surrounded by a large, loving family. He served in the U.S. Navy in the Vietnam War and afterward received a Bachelor's Degree from UNM. He went on to earn his Juris Doctor degree at Colorado State. During his distinguished career in law, he spent several years in the Attorney General's Office, after which time he pursued his own career in politics. He is survived by his wife of 27 years, Ana Elena Sanchez Garcia, his son Raul (Randy) Garcia of Dallas, Texas, his daughter Julia Elena Garcia, of Santa Fe...."
Whoa! Digger stopped reading.

Could the son that was living in Dallas in the late 1990s possibly be "the" Randy Garcia that appeared on the document Grandma Betty had shown her? It was a long shot, but worth a try. She pulled out her phone and dialed her grandmother's number.

"Hi, Nana."

"Oh, Elizabeth, what a nice surprise! I was just telling your grandfather that we should call you. He came home from the hospital yesterday and he's doing so well."

"I'm so glad," Digger said. She held her impatience to solve the Garcia mystery of Raul vs. Randy at bay while she caught up on her grandfather's condition, spoke a few words with him and gave him a run-down of her own activities. Finally, she got her grandmother back on the phone and steered the conversation around to the subject she had called about.

"Nana, you know those papers you showed me about the solar deal in Texas—Troy, Texas, was it? Could you go find them again and tell me the name of the business and the names of the company officers."

"Is this to do with that stuff you were talking about? Sure!" She sounded excited to help with the mystery. Give me a few minutes to go find it." She hung up.

Five minutes later she called back. "Okay, I've got the papers

I showed you. The name of the company was TexRaySol and the people listed...." Digger heard papers rustle, and her grandmother muttering through them, and then she was back on the phone. "There's quite a few names here. Do you want all of them? I could take a picture and message you."

"That would be great! That way I can see them all. Thanks Nana!"

"Wait! Don't hang up. Looking through this stuff made me remember something I meant to tell you when you were here."

"I'm listening," said Digger, her curiosity aroused.

"Remember I told you the whole deal was a little odd. It was the way the company representatives played up to the mayor and councilors, talking about jobs and all the projects it would bring to the community. The local mayor at the time jumped on it. He was running for the state legislature and something like that would boost his chances. The TexRaySol guys really played up to that. There was supposed to be a groundbreaking about a month before the elections, then suddenly, they were 'gone.'"

"What do you mean, gone?"

"Gone, as in, the groundbreaking didn't happen, nobody could reach anyone about it, phone numbers didn't work, or people didn't answer—that kind of thing."

"So, what happened?"

Her grandmother gave a short sarcastic laugh. "As you can imagine, the mayor lost in a landslide. The local papers described it as a scam. But if you ask me, I think somebody in that company targeted him. It was like they wanted him to fail. But why? I have no idea and since they disappeared, no one ever found out."

Digger's mind was whirling. Parts of this sounded so familiar, yet it all seemed so far-fetched. And if the "Randy Garcia" involved with TexRaySol was in fact Julia Montoya's brother, what on earth did that mean?

CHAPTER 23

Tony Kramer stood by the window of the hotel room enjoying the view of the city—how the windows twinkled in the morning light. The room on the fifth floor of the Albuquerque Doubletree faced east toward the Sandia range and the mountains formed a great deep-blue protective wall just beyond the city's edge.

"I could sure get used to living here," he said to Janet, who had just emerged from the bathroom, fully made up and her hair sprayed into a smooth helmet around her face.

"Well, I prefer Santa Fe," she said, "Albuquerque has a dangerous reputation. Why did you want to stay here anyway?"

Kramer frowned. He'd explained it all to her before they flew back to New Mexico, but apparently, she didn't appreciate the details. He needed her to keep her eye on the ball. The meeting he'd scheduled with the power company people was critical. Lovington was starting to pressure him, asking awkward questions. He walked over and put his arms around her.

"We're meeting the guy from HDPL—that's High Desert Power and Light—to talk about connecting to their transmission line and getting a purchase power agreement. Those were the things the reporter was asking about, and now Chris is bugging me too. They have to know we are serious. HDPL's offices are in downtown Albuquerque and the only time he had available was nine o'clock. I figured it would be easier if we stayed right here. Then we can take that cute train up to Santa Fe to meet Chris. The station is, like, a five minutes' walk from the hotel, I looked it up."

Macy looked at him as if he'd lost his mind. "Walk? Train? Honey, I have never ridden on a train."

He grinned. "I figured you'd say that. Don't worry, I got the hotel to book us a rental car to get to Santa Fe, and we'll even take a taxi the five blocks, or whatever it is, to the meeting."

When Tony and Janet arrived via taxi at the HDPL offices on Gold Avenue, the security guard promptly took their names and details, issued them with badges, and made a phone call to someone upstairs. Minutes later a dark-haired young woman in a striped dress walked out of the elevator and greeted them. "Good morning, I'm Sandra Rivera with the HDPL communications team, I'll take you up to meet Mr. Cantrell."

Charles Cantrell was a tall bulky man who looked as though he had once been an athlete, but a few years and several pounds had softened the contours of his frame. He shook hands and led them into a small conference room. Sandra followed and offered them bottles of water. Kramer accepted one, Macy declined. They sat facing each other on either side of a broad, gleaming conference table. Cantrell fished business cards out of his breast pocket and slid them over, one to each of them.

Kramer made a show of picking up the card and read aloud, "Charles Cantrell, Senior Vice President of Operations." Kramer realized he should have had cards. He'd asked Jeff Chalmers to organize that, but nothing had materialized. He looked up at Cantrell and gave him his best Sunday service welcome smile. "Thanks for meeting with us today Mr. Cantrell."

"It's Chuck," Cantrell said, leaning forward on his elbows, his eyes fixed on Kramer.

"In your email you indicated you wanted to discuss the possibility of connecting to the transmission line, and talking about a purchase power agreement?"

Kramer nodded.

Cantrell rubbed his jaw with one hand. "We don't usually deal with those things together, but I read over what you sent me, and I talked with the state land commissioner. He told me that he and the governor are strongly in support of your project."

This was exactly what Kramer had been hoping for. Randy's instructions had been to play up the political angle. The current governor had announced early in the year that he couldn't run again for family reasons. Lovington was hell-bent to replace him, and he had a pretty good chance of winning because his opponent was facing a harassment accusation from a co-worker. If Lovington became governor, he'd be looking at a lot of investment in energy projects. "Make sure you play that card with the power company guys," Randy had said.

Kramer looked straight at Cantrell, nodding slowly. "Yes, the governor. And probably the next governor, too. I'm very confident that Chris Lovington will win the election."

Cantrell met his gaze and it seemed to Kramer that the other man understood the subtext of what was being said. Kramer took it as a cue to continue and launched into the outline he'd prepared, detailing the precise location of the project, the size of the photovoltaic array, the projected output, and the estimated timeframe for the scope of work. While he spoke, he picked the map out of the pile of papers and pushed it across to Cantrell.

"So, that shows the orientation of the array and the access road across state land. As you can see, it's ideally situated to connect to the existing transmission line. That was one of the reasons the state land commissioner has been so enthusiastic about the location. And, as you know, he is campaigning on boosting renewable energy in New Mexico."

Cantrell studied the map for a couple of minutes. "It looks to me as though you'd have to cross pueblo land right here if you want to connect at the closest point."

Kramer had been expecting this. "Yes, we've been fully aware of that, and we've been in talks with the San Fermin governor, who is by the way very supportive. He realizes the potential value of the project for the tribe. It can mean a lot of jobs."

The meeting lasted another forty minutes while they went over the details. Kramer left feeling confident. Cantrell had seemed satisfied. He'd shaken hands with them, hadn't he? And he'd said he would be in touch within a couple of days.

They asked the security guard to call them a taxi and told him they'd wait outside. While they'd been in the meeting the temperature had been steadily rising. Heat radiated off the buildings and the street. Even the air itself seemed to Kramer like the blast from a giant hair dryer. They hadn't waited outside two minutes before Macy turned on him furiously.

"Just how long do you think we're going to be able to keep this up if the investors don't come through?"

Kramer took a deep breath. "Calm down. Jeff said Randy is close to having it wrapped up."

"Randy, always Randy!" Macy snapped. "Have you even met the guy?"

Kramer set down his briefcase and laid his hands on her shoulders as thoughts whirled through his head. He'd lost a lot because of Janet but he wanted her. It was like an addiction; every time they were together it got better, and he wanted more. Had it only been six months ago that she'd shown up with her husband at his Sunday morning fellowship service? He'd spotted her there among all the other faces and he couldn't take his eyes off her.

Afterward, they'd met and talked during the coffee social, and the attraction was instant for each of them. A week later they were in bed. Somehow her husband found out and it led to him being ousted from his position at the church. Thank God for Jeff and his support. He'd offered him the job to promote the solar installation part of his development business. Janet had left her husband, but he was still making life difficult for the both of them. If they could move out of the state it would solve so many problems.

He knew he had to reassure Janet because if she got cold feet now it could ruin all his plans. "Look," he said, gently, "We could make a new life here. I could find another church to pastor. You'd be away from your jealous ex and get back into a good sales job."

Macy scowled. "Do you ever wonder where the money is coming from? And why we're doing this?"

Kramer huffed impatiently. "Look, these guys have got deep pockets and as long as they're paying us, we've got to go along with it. This is a big chance for you and me. Let's not blow it."

"But what happens if this whole thing blows up?" Janet asked, shaking her head.

"We let Izzy handle it," he said, as the taxi pulled up alongside the curb. "But now, we go back to the hotel, get our stuff, drive to Santa Fe, and tell Chris the good news about all the progress we've made this morning.

CHAPTER 24

Digger sat hunched over her computer, eating a burrito while she peered at the screen. The other two women in the office had gone out for lunch and she took advantage of being alone to use the photos her grandmother had sent for her to look into information about TexRaySol. Prowling around the Texas Secretary of State's website she found the company's name and saw it had listed a registered agent at an address in Dallas. However, the agent's name wasn't one of those that appeared on the document Grandma Betty had shown her, and the listing was shown as inactive. Apparently TexRaySol hadn't been doing any business for almost two years.

Using Google Maps and Google Earth, she searched for the address. What she found appeared to be a residential area rather than an office building or park. She tried the phone number listed but heard a recorded message saying it was no longer a working number. She tried looking for the agent's name on Facebook, LinkedIn, and Twitter, but there were so many hits it was impossible to pin them down. She looked at her watch. She could maybe sneak over to the library and use their computer for more research.

The library was on Washington Avenue, she guessed it was

about a brisk fifteen-minute walk. Once there, she logged in to a website that collated archives from papers throughout the country. After a brief search of Texas papers, she found a short article about the project near Troy that Grandma Betty had talked about. It didn't mention a "Raul" or "Randy" Garcia, but she noted the name of the mayor. A little more searching and she found a contact number for him. Maybe it was worth a try. She walked outside the library, sat on the nearest bench, and punched in the number. She was about to give up when a man's voice answered.

"Hello, this is Terry."

Digger did a quick mental ethics check and decided to go for it. "Hi, this is Elizabeth Doyle with the Daily Courier in New Mexico." She had been a Courier reporter, so maybe it was only half a lie. She figured he wouldn't bother to check that The Courier had ceased to exist almost a year ago. "I wondered if you had a minute to talk about the TexRaySol project. I contacted you because there appears to be a similar situation happening here in New Mexico."

The silence at the other end stretched on for what seemed like an eternity. "The thing is," Digger prompted, "here in New Mexico a company showed up a couple months ago saying they plan to build a big solar array outside of Albuquerque. They're promising jobs and all that kind of thing, but I can't find any information out there about any other projects they've done. I was doing some background research and read about what happened in your area. I wondered if it might be the same people behind it, only using a different name. That's why I'm like to talk to you."

The man let out a long sigh. "Okay," he said, "That was a few years ago. What did you want to talk about?"

Digger's heart thumped. At least he hadn't hung up. What could she ask him that wouldn't prompt him to cut her off. She hadn't prepared for this. With her mind still racing, she dug out the recorder, which she used to use for interviews, from her backpack and put the call on speaker. "Well," she said, "I was hoping you might be able to tell me a bit about the contact you had with TexRaySol. I've got a couple of names from official sources, and I learned that the company is no longer active in Texas. Could we talk about the people with whom you worked on that project?"

Again, a long pause. "If you've got the company records, I think you can get the names."

Digger wasn't ready to let it go. "Why do you think they approached you? It was just before an important election, wasn't it? And I understand you were running for a seat in the state legislature. Do you think there was a political motive?"

Another long sigh. This time it sounded angry. "Looking back on it, the timing, it sure did seem suspicious. The guy running against me was a partner in a small oil and gas outfit. Those guys are dead set against solar or wind energy and they always go around riling up the ranchers against that kind of thing. When the TexRaySol folks showed up, they made this big splash, got me on board hook-line-and-sinker, then just disappeared. It was the danged-est thing! 'Course it left me looking like some kind of snake oil salesman and I lost the election big time."

"Do you know of any way to contact them?"

"Like I said, they just disappeared. I wasn't going to throw money at hiring someone to track them down. I was hurting enough as it was. I still don't know whether somebody had it in for me personally or whether it was the oil and gas guys that run 'em off."

"I'm really very sorry to hear that," Digger said. Thanks for talking with me, Terry." She ended the call and stopped the recording.

As soon as she got back to the office, she messaged Manny and asked if he could meet her later. He agreed. She thought for a few moments then texted him the location. When she left work, she noticed huge dark gray clouds billowing overhead. The monsoon rains had been fickle so far, but this looked like real rain might hit soon. She'd arranged to meet Manny in the parking lot at Museum Hill on the outskirts of the city. She figured they could find a bench to sit on or duck into one of the four museums or the cafe to talk. As she pulled in, she spotted his elderly Beetle. He saw her, got out of his car, and waved. She had parked about twenty yards from him and gotten out of the car when she felt the first drops hit. They jabbed like icy needles on her bare arms, soaking her shirt within seconds. Just as she reached Manny, they heard the first ominous roll of thunder.

"Quick!" he yelled.

They scrambled up a few steps, then halted, looking wildly left and right through a curtain of rain.

"This way! She grabbed Manny's arm, and they ran splashing through the downpour toward a line of red umbrellas on the cafe patio.

By the time they'd hustled inside, their hair and clothes were dripping wet. Digger wiped a hand across her face to dry her eyes. People squeezed in around them, giggling and giddy with the sudden arrival of rain.

Manny pointed to a table near a window, far away from any of the other customers.

"You find the weirdest places to meet. Next time you'll probably have me sitting on the top of Mount Taylor," he said.

"Sorry about the weather. If we had met someplace downtown, somebody I work with might have seen us talking and I didn't want to risk that."

Manny shrugged and ran his hands through his glistening wet hair. A young Native American server appeared at their table, and she gave Manny a quick appraising glance. He nodded and grinned and they exchanged a few words that Digger didn't recognize. It struck her how good Manny looked with his hair slicked back. She wondered if he had a girlfriend or was married. Without bothering to ask, Manny ordered a coffee for them both. The server smirked slightly, shot a look at Digger, and left.

"She comes from Crownpoint, where I grew up," he said simply. Then he cocked his head at Digger. "I suppose you've got something new to tell me. And you want to know if I've found out anything more. Shall we toss a coin for who goes first?"

"Heads!" Digger said. She pulled a quarter out of her pocket and flipped it. "Okay, you go," she said as it landed tails up.

Manny leaned his elbows on the table and pressed his hands together, covering his mouth. Digger waited. He exhaled, spread his hands in front of him, and bent in close to her. "I've seen a copy of the contract," he said, almost in a whisper.

"No shit! How'd you manage it?"

Manny gave her his slow, self-satisfied smile that told her he was not going to reveal his source. She knew what his next words would be, and she was right.

"I've got my ways," he said, nodding.

She could barely contain her impatience. "Okay, hotshot, so are you going to tell me what's in it or not?"

He pulled a notebook out of his messenger bag, flipped over a few pages, and began reading. "The basic deal is that the Solar GRX guys are agreeing to pay the State Land Office four bucks an acre for a half section—that's three hundred and twenty acres—so, you can probably do the math on that."

He continued outlining the details. It turned out that the company was also going to pay the SLO a percentage of the revenue earned by the sale of power produced by the solar array. There was more language about responsibilities and duties and timelines.

"But here's the real kicker," Manny said. "The state is agreeing to pony up money for wages and a bunch of other incentives, but there's no clawback." He stopped, looking up at her to see if she understood what that meant.

"You mean, that if they don't perform, the state could be out all that money?"

"Yep, and get this," Manny said, shaking his head as if he couldn't believe what he was about to say. "They can get the money as soon as they break ground."

"Holy shit!" Digger gasped. "Why the hell would Lovington—or anybody else in their right mind—agree to that?"

Manny shrugged. "Beats me."

She leaned back in her chair, staring out the rain-smeared window and could just make out the huge statue of Apache Mountain Spirit Dancer. A year ago, she wouldn't have known anything about the statue, she could credit her new job for the name.

So much else just didn't make sense.

CHAPTER 25

Maria looked beautiful in the late afternoon sunlight as she posed for Rex, dark hair shining, wide sincere smile, eyes bright with promise. He was taking a new series of photos for her campaign flyers. He had suggested shooting the head-shot in Abuela's garden with the soft contours of the adobe wall and the outline of the mountains as a backdrop.

Watching her as Rex worked, Digger's heart ached with joy. Sometimes she found it almost miraculous that they had been able to overcome so much to be together. Sometimes she had to fight back the fear that still lurked within her, that this happiness would be taken away. In the depth of the night, she had to push away those thoughts and press her head against Maria's warm back.

Finally satisfied, Rex set the camera down on the patio table, fished his cigarettes from his vest pocket, and lit one. "Okay, one down and two more to go. What time do we have to be at the town hall?"

"It starts at seven and it'll probably take twenty minutes to get there. Maria wants to be there early to check if everything's been set up properly. I'd say we ought to leave in about half an hour. You want to ride with me?" Digger said.

"Sure, and if you're driving, I'll take a beer before we leave. You got any?"

Digger left him putting away his camera gear and went to get the beer. She'd been shocked at Rex's appearance when he'd shown up. Even since the last time they'd seen him he looked like he'd put on weight, and the skin beneath his eyes was pink and puffy. She knew he hated his job, but maybe there was more going on. She opened a bottle of Modelo and took it out to him. Abuela was at the other end of the garden, watering her rose bushes.

"I just have to help Maria, I'll be back in a minute," she said. She left Rex and went back into the house. Maria was in their bedroom gathering her notes and a bundle of flyers for the meeting. Digger walked up behind her, slid her arms around Maria's shoulders and kissed the back of her neck.

"This is an important night for you," Digger said.

Maria turned around, her eyes searching Digger's. "I know. Sometimes this whole thing scares me. But I feel that I must keep going. When I see the kids at the school, listen to their parents, and hear the struggles they have, I know I want to find a way to fight for them."

Digger held her close, and they said nothing—just stood together listening to each other's breathing and the faint sound of an old dog barking somewhere down the street.

Rex sat silent, looking out the car window as Digger drove. She glanced at him periodically, but he seemed far away. Finally, she said, "What's going on with you, Rex? It's more than the job, isn't it?"

He blew air through his lips, his shoulders slumping. "It's Karen. She wants to go back to Wyoming. She says it's because of her mom being sick, but I know it's me. Just the way she looks at me. I ... I don't know what to do."

They were stopped at a traffic light and Digger looked over at him. He was staring down at his lap, tiny rivulets of tears glistening on his cheeks and dripping from his chin. She took a hand from the steering wheel, reached over and rubbed his shoulder. "You've been through a lot, Rex. Halloran dying—and I know you and he had been friends for years—and then the paper closing. How long had you been there?"

"Twenty-eight years."

"If you want to talk about it some more, call me, Okay?" He nodded. The light changed and they drove on.

The room at the Community Center had a tired look—scuffed floors, plastic chairs smell of stale coffee—but the minimal charge to use it made it ideal for Maria's cash-strapped campaign. Maria, Alma, and the rest of the volunteers were already busy with last-minute details when Digger and Rex and the first attendees arrived. Maria's team had called and emailed voters, and they had canvassed some of them, going door to door. Digger steered Rex toward the small podium where Maria would speak. The posted time arrived and passed, as people were still trickling in.

Dillon had recommended using the community center on the northern edge of Las Vistas in order to draw voters from surrounding areas as well as from city residents. Digger surveyed the crowd and smiled when she saw José and Ana, neighbors in Los Jardines, sitting at the end of one row, next to Abuela. The old couple spotted her and waved shyly. A couple of rows away she saw Florencia Ortega, the school principal. She was looking Digger's way and their eyes met, Florencia nodded. Digger gave her a thumbs up sign.

She went to tell Maria, but just then Dillon gave Alma a signal and walked toward the entrance door. As he reached the door, three more people walked in. Digger recognized the burly form of Larry Martinez, and behind him Tony Apodaca. The two Las

Vistas city councilors had supported Maria's campaign against the road. The third man was Jack Kimble, former mayor of Las Vistas. Kimble remained in the doorway for a moment, looking slightly lost as he gazed around the room.

The last time she'd seen Kimble was when he'd dramatically emerged from the woods as a powerful rainstorm destroyed the foundations of the mountain-side road Maria had campaigned so hard to stop. It was six months after he'd lost his election and he'd let himself go. Standing on the edge of the woods that day he'd looked like a homeless man, with ragged hair and beard, rain-soaked clothes hanging off his gaunt frame. Today, he wore an open-necked dress shirt, pressed pants, and his hair and beard were neatly trimmed.

"Hello Mayor," Digger said, walking up to him. His eyes focused on her, and he gave a grateful-looking smile. "Ah! I'd hoped to see you here. I came to listen to Maria. She deserves my support."

"Well, since two of your former councilors are here too, let's go get a picture before the meeting starts," Digger said. She waved to Rex, beckoning him to follow her to the podium. Maria's face lit up as she saw Kimble and the two councilors, and she rushed to shake hands with them. "So glad you came. I really didn't think I'd get such a great turn-out."

They chatted and smiled for a few minutes while Rex snapped a few publicity shots, then Dillon came and spoke to Maria, while keeping an eye on his watch. Digger led the three men toward a half-empty row of chairs near the back of the room and sat down next to Martinez.

The mic screeched briefly, and Dillon looked embarrassed, "Sorry folks, we seem to be having a slight technical problem."

Conversations filled the room again while Dillon, Alma, and Maria huddled over the equipment on the podium.

Digger was distracted by the sound of Martinez and Apodaca murmuring to each other beside her. She heard Apodaca's gruff voice say, "I think she'd be better for the city than the other guy."

"Murphy? Yeah, he was too tight with Johnny Raposa. I don't think you could trust him," Martinez said.

Apodaca lowered his voice even more and Digger had to strain to hear what he said.

"You know he's bought that land on the west side of the city. I heard he might be trying to build a hotel out there, next to the reservation."

"Why would anyone want to stay out there?"

"Beats me. Maybe he thinks he can get permission to have a casino. But being in Santa Fe might help him get whatever he wants," Apodaca said.

Digger reached around for her backpack to jot down notes on what she had just heard. She was still writing when Alma's voice came over the mic and the murmuring around her hushed.

"Hello everyone, thank you for coming tonight," Alma said. "Maria Ortiz, our candidate, is eager to talk about her vision for this district and she wants to hear from all of you as well."

Maria took over the mic and began by welcoming Kimble, the Las Vistas councilors, and school principal Florencia Ortega. "And of course, I couldn't be here tonight without the two most important people in my life, my grandmother Conchita Chavez Ortiz and my wife, Elizabeth Doyle, whom everyone knows as Digger." There was a buzz of conversations, and then waves of clapping as the name of each guest seated around the podium was announced. Digger found herself blushing.

Finally, Maria stepped up to the podium, adjusted the mic, and launched into a speech about her growing up in the area, her ambitions as a young girl, the challenges she faced, and her career as a teacher. Pretty standard stuff, until she began to talk about the Spanish chapel. At that point, her voice became charged with passion, and she spoke fervently about the need to preserve the unique culture of the area while encouraging the kind of growth that would benefit the people and the land.

During the early part of the speech, people in the audience were still whispering among themselves, but gradually they fell silent, captivated by Maria's energy. When she finished, there was another wave of clapping, even louder than before. Once the room quieted, Alma invited the audience to ask Maria questions. One woman asked about Maria's stance on early education.

Maria's face lit up. "I believe investment in early education is vital to all New Mexico families, and my goal, if elected, would be to seek ways to use money from the Land Grant Permanent Fund for early childhood education initiatives."

The next question was about a proposed change to the way property taxes were calculated. Digger closed her eyes, remembering just how insufferably tedious some of the public meetings she used to attend could be. She knew Maria knew hardly anything about the minutia of property taxes, but she admired the way her wife fudged the answer to sound at least as intelligible as a lot of public relations people.

Halfway through her response to the next question, Maria's voice faltered. Digger looked up and noticed the direction of Maria's gaze. She swiveled her head and saw Izzy appear in the doorway, walk to the back row, and take a seat. After a brief hesitation, Maria continued speaking. She answered a couple more questions, then a woman's voice hard and shrill rang out: "What do you say about the allegation your opponent made that you brought a banned substance to the school where you teach?"

Digger could almost hear a collective gasp around the room. Maria's face blanched and her eyes widened. Digger saw her shoulders slowly rise and fall as if she had taken a deep breath. Then her voice rang out loud and firm. "The purpose of that allegation was not political, it was a personal vendetta, and the source of that rumor—because that is all it was, an unfounded rumor—the source of that rumor is sitting at the back of this room." She pointed to Izzy. "I know it started with you so admit it now!" she cried out, eyes blazing.

A chair screeched on the floor. Digger looked back to see Izzy leap to her feet, face twisted with fury, then she spun round and stormed out the door.

A hubbub swept through the room. Florencia Ortega was on her feet now, rushing to Maria's side. Hands waving, voice raised she shouted, "I want you all to know that I have worked with this wonderful woman for five years and she is as dedicated as they come. Vote for Maria!"

People in the room echoed the call. Rex was in the thick of it, snapping pictures of Maria, Florencia, and others who now stood crowded around them, everyone clapping for Maria. Relief flooded through Digger. For now, at least, Maria's little ship of hope had survived Izzy's sabotage attempt and it was still afloat.

CHAPTER 26

The night chill had not yet invaded the garden of Abuela. The smooth adobe walls still radiated the heat of the day. Digger and Maria stood wrapped in a silent embrace while above them a full moon moved imperceptibly on its nightly journey. They breathed stillness. Digger closed her eyes, drank in the scent of Maria's skin. She wanted time to stop, to hold this moment, when she felt in balance, no regrets for the past and no longing for the future. Then, from the distance came the yip of a coyote, and Abuela's voice.

"Mija? Are you there?" The silhouette of the old woman appeared in the doorway, backlit by the living room lamp. She stepped carefully toward them, and Digger saw that she was wearing her old yellow nightgown. Maria eased her arms from Digger and held out a hand.

"We're here."

Abuela stood before them now, and her face, lit by the moon, was streaked with tears. Digger had never seen the old woman cry. It was like seeing an oak tree weep.

"What is it? What is it?" Maria asked, anxiously. She put an arm around her grandmother.

Abuela bent her head toward Maria and groaned. "Mija, I'm afraid for you. That woman saying those things about you. I worry."

Digger had been afraid of moments like this when the ugly side of a political campaign hit home. She'd been worried about the effect it would have on Maria, and their relationship, but she hadn't counted on the impact it could have on Abuela. Everything that Maria had ever said about Abuela spoke of the woman's courage against a world where she was abandoned by her husband, with four children to care for.

In her youth she had traveled to California to support Cesar Chavez and Dolores Huerta in their fight for farm workers. Abuela had seen the dark side of politics and now she was afraid for her granddaughter.

"Abuelita, I'm okay," Maria murmured, caressing her grandmother's hand. "You're the one who inspired me to do this work, remember? Juntos podemos, right? together we can do this," she smiled, taking her arm.

"Let's go inside," Digger said, gently taking Abuela's other arm. Together, they guided her toward the open door. Maria talked softly to her grandmother while Digger found herself reverting to her own grandmother's eternal remedy for trouble, putting the kettle on and making a cup of tea. Lady Antonia was curled on Abuela's lap when Digger set the steaming tea mug down beside her. "I see all that tuna bribery paid off. That cat loves you. I'm jealous."

Abuela's lined face softened into a smile. "Thank you for sharing her with me Cowgirl."

Maria hugged her grandmother again. "Remember, Labor Day weekend is soon, and we've got the family coming. I'll take some time off and we can all be together."

The next morning, Digger called Rex. He was in a sour mood

and let her know right away that the photo shoot he'd just finished was a huge pain in the ass. "I'm about ready to jack in this for-shit job. People can't make up their minds and they think they know more than I do about how to get a good picture."

She decided a little flattery might smooth his ruffled feathers. "They don't know Jackshit, Rex. You were always my favorite photog at The Courier because you knew what you were doing. Like those pictures you took for Maria—they turned out great. I picked the stuff up at the printer's yesterday. The flyers and yard signs are just what she was aiming for. And you saved her a bundle. I can't thank you enough. I've got to be in Albuquerque this afternoon. Can you possibly squeeze in twenty minutes of your time to have coffee somewhere?"

He hesitated, blew air through his lips, then agreed. "Sure, how about the old place?"

She knew he meant the cafe near the Courier offices. He must be feeling nostalgic. She glanced at the folders on her desk and calculated how long it would take to make the UNM visit.

"Think you can make three o'clock?"

"I'll make it happen. See you there."

Shortly after three, Digger pulled into the tiny parking lot that served the cafe and a cluster of small businesses. Rex was already seated, coffee in hand, at an outside table shaded by a faded red umbrella. She hailed him and went in to order a chai latté for herself. When she sat down, she studied him a bit, trying to gauge his mood. "Want to talk about the stuff you said the other night?"

He eyed her, shrugged, and gave a long sigh. "I shouldn't have said all that. Karen and me, we go through these patches. Something or other happens at work and she gets upset, and all of a sudden, she wants to go back to Wyoming. We've been here half a lifetime and we've been together for thirty-five years. We get through it. Power of habit, I guess. We'll be alright in a while"

He sighed again, thrust his chin out in a determined smile and nodded.

Digger tapped a fist on his shoulder. "I just wanted you to know—."

"Yeah," he broke in. "I know. So, what about you? That scene the other night must've rattled Maria, and you too, I bet?"

Digger looked up at the umbrella, thinking about the conversation she'd had with Maria in bed after they'd soothed Abuela's fears. She'd felt the shake in Maria's shoulders, and she'd held her for a long time while she sobbed wordlessly. Digger knew all too well about the times when the internal storm made words impossible. She turned back to face Rex. "I know it did. It rattled both of us, but she had to act strong in front of her grandmother. That old lady is tough, but she was really 'shook up' about it."

Rex looked down the street toward the old Courier offices. She followed his gaze. The building was full of memories for both of them. Rex sighed. "Elections can turn shitty," he said. "It's not simple, and you know that. We've been through a bunch of them around here." He patted Digger on the shoulder. "Right now, I'd say Maria's chances are iffy, Danny Murphy can tap into a lot of big donors. What do you think she'll do if she loses?"

Digger leaned back, folding her arms. She'd thought about the possibility of a loss, and the answer was always clear: "Maria will find a new cause," she said. That's who she is. That's why I love her; because she's always all-in. She never sits on the fence."

Rex laughed. Then his face grew serious. "And what about you? I get the feeling your new job's not going that great. Want to tell me about it?"

She sighed. "How much time do you have?"

He pushed the empty coffee container away and pulled out his cigarettes. "I can make that stick-up-her-ass realtor wait a little."

As briefly as she could, Digger told him what she'd learned

about the solar project. "There's just a lot of it that doesn't add up and there's some weird stuff that smells off."

Rex rubbed a hand along his jaw as if preparing his response. "So, our old pal Manny has been helping you deep dive on this? Does your boss know?"

Digger shook her head. "I got the feeling recently that she suspects what I've been doing. I also think she's somehow involved with it, but I don't know how or why." Rex frowned, shaking his head. "Not good. Watch your back, Digg, and maybe start looking around. You've got your future to think of and you might not be as lucky as you were when the paper closed."

CHAPTER 27

Tony Kramer checked his phone again. No message. They'd agreed to meet at two o'clock and it was nearly two-fifteen. If the man didn't show up pretty soon, they wouldn't have much time to talk before he had to go meet Janet. They just had one more day in Santa Fe before they had to fly back to Phoenix, and he'd suggested she go shopping. He wanted to check out this guy Murphy on his own before he upset her anymore.

Last night Izzy had called him with the message that a guy called Danny Murphy was interested in the solar project and wanted to talk with him. She filled him in on a little of the guy's background. He'd been involved in property deals in Scottsdale before he came to New Mexico a couple years back to take over as manager of the golf club in Las Vistas. Now he was running to be a state representative. She'd suggested he call Murphy right away.

Normally he'd wait till the next day, but something about her tone—a hint of urgency in her voice—made him decide to follow her advice. So here he was, on a Monday afternoon, sitting on one of the tall chairs covered in dark red leather at the bar of the Inn of the Governors. He'd ordered a local beer and sipped at it slowly, wishing it was something stronger, but mindful that he had to keep a clear head. The glass was almost empty, and he was about to get up when a tall, deeply tanned man with a shock of thick white hair walked in. The man looked round, eyed him and immediately came and sat down in the next chair.

"Tony?" Kramer nodded. "Hi, I'm Danny Murphy. We spoke on the phone last night." Murphy was wearing a turquoise golf shirt with a club insignia embroidered on the collar. He held out a hand and Kramer noticed how the hairs on his arm caught the afternoon light, glowing like golden fur.

He shook Murphy's outstretched hand. "Isabel Chavez told me you'd talked. She said you were interested in the solar project."

Murphy grinned, then turned to signal the bartender, a skinny guy with a droopy mustache that looked like a throw-back to the seventies. "Vodka on the rocks. Grey Goose if you've got it." He switched his attention back to Kramer. "Yeah, I don't know if she told you, but I've got some land out near the solar site, and I thought we might have some interests in common."

As Murphy filled him in on the details of the land, where it lay near the Indian reservation, Kramer was fascinated by the man's face. The eyes, pale blue like the ocean shallows in—where was it? Cancun? Cabo? And that smile. A salesman's smile. Kramer had the weirdest feeling. It was as though he were looking at a mirror image of himself.

A few months ago, when Jeff had offered him the job, he'd jumped at it. Jeff had introduced him to Randy who'd handled everything from then on. He didn't question why they'd hired Janet through a different state agency in New Mexico. They'd been directed to scout out the land before Randy put them in touch with Lovington. At the time, Kramer thought that's just the way they did things in a backward place like New Mexico. Plus, he was desperate, the church had kicked him out because of Janet, and her husband was making life unbearable.

But in the middle of the night, with Janet tossing restlessly beside him—they'd given up taking separate rooms—he felt his conscience stir like the onset of heartburn. He was, after all, a man of God, or used to be. In the morning, to prepare for the meeting, he'd called Randy to ask if he'd heard about Murphy's Arizona business interests. "Murphy? You mean Danny Murphy?" Randy had sounded enthusiastic. "Sure. He was in with some big money here. If he wants to talk to you, go for it. Whatever it is, I'd like to hear about it."

Now, he studied Murphy as the man took another slug from his glass and then swilled the ice around appreciatively. "So, here's the deal," Murphy said, "The plan is for an exclusive subdivision for custom homes and a boutique hotel. You know, one of those retreat center spa places that attract high-dollar clientele that want to be pampered out in nature. That's why I think there could be a good tie-in with the solar power thing. It would give it the right eco-vibe."

Kramer wasn't sure where the conversation was leading but kept his expression positive. "Yeah, I get it," he said, nodding. "I think that angle would appeal to Chris Lovington too. You know he's running for governor and he's really pushing this project."

Murphy slapped his hand on the counter and grinned. "That's exactly the way I hoped you'd see it. That's why I think I've got a proposal that's a win-win for both of us."

Hope stirred within him. Was this an answer to his prayers, a glimmer of light after the dark night of the soul? "Let's hear it," Kramer said.

Murphy talked at length about his background in development in the greater Phoenix area, mentioning names Kramer had heard of or heard Jeff refer to. He kept using phrases like "what I'm going to be telling you." Kramer quickly realized he was getting the sales pitch, but he kept silent. Finally, Murphy said he'd talked to "people in Arizona" and found they were interested in investing in the solar project. Murphy stopped talking then and eyed

Kramer, as if waiting for a reaction. Kramer had played poker in college, before he found his calling to the Lord, and this moment felt like the turning point in a hand. "What's in it for you? And what about your own campaign?" he asked. Murphy laughed, bumping a fist on the counter. "Look, I know Chris Lovington has staked his reputation on this project, he's campaigned hard on the whole green economy thing. Me, I'm running for more personal reasons, so if I don't win it won't kill me. But if this solar thing happens it could be a real boost for the plans I have for this land. That's what I'm really interested in."

Kramer considered. Murphy's offer to invest in the project was tempting. He still didn't have any firm answers from Jeff or Randy on how the financial negotiations were going. If Murphy could do what he said ... well, it remained to be seen. "What if Lovington doesn't win?" Kramer asked.

Murphy leaned in close. "Look, he's up against a guy who's got oil and gas interests behind him. People with deep pockets. But the way I see it, is if this solar goes through, it doesn't matter if Lovington wins or loses, we still win. You get me?" He let the sentence hang.

Kramer exhaled slowly. "Okay. I'll report back to my people in Phoenix. How soon can you give me the real numbers? We've got less than two months till the election."

Murphy tapped him on the shoulder. "You'll have an email by the end of today." He drained the last of his drink and stood up. "I'd like to stay and chat but I've gotta go now. Nice meeting with you, Tony."

Kramer watched Murphy head out of the bar and saw him walk past the windows that looked out onto West Alameda. He felt shaken. He'd connected with Chris Lovington as a fellow Christian. He respected the man's vision and his faith in the project. He wanted to have that same faith, not these nagging doubts.

He looked around at the warm colors of the bar, the view out to the tiny Santa Fe River. He wanted this new life, and he wanted it with Janet.

As if on cue, his phone rang, and it was Janet.

"Guess what?" she said, excitedly, continuing without waiting for his reply. "I just got an email from Chris. He said Archuleta, the San Fermin governor, has agreed to the easement. It's a go!"

CHAPTER 28

Two Months to Election Day

The soft prodding of a cat paw woke Digger—Lady Antonia's way of letting her know that it was Tuna Time. Lady Antonia might accept Abuela's advances, even allowing her to scratch her ears when she curled in the old lady's lap. Still, old habits die hard, and Digger was the cat's feeder of choice in the mornings. Habit dictated that she get her a quarter cup of Iams and one teaspoon of tuna, to be set out in a dish at exactly six o'clock, weekends no exception.

Today was Saturday, the first day of the long Labor Day weekend and Digger was disinclined to yield to Lady Antonia's demands. She lay motionless, hoping to fool the cat while she listened to Maria's soft sleep breaths beside her. Digger hadn't slept well—waking sometime in the middle of the night, her brain kept ratcheting back to thoughts about the contract Manny had shown her. Sure, there had been other cases with no claw-back requirements where state funds had been pledged to support an enterprise that promised to bring jobs. Say the words "economic development" to a government official in New Mexico and they would practically fall over themselves in their eagerness to win the favor. But the risks inherent in the Solar GRX contract seemed like insanity. Without any performance or clawback requirements, the Solar GRX people could start work, then pack up their tools and leave and the state would be out all that money. She wondered if they'd even ordered equipment. She wondered if her grandfather still had the contacts he'd used to find out about the Texas project. She wondered, what was their game here?

Ouch! cat claws reminded Digger none too gently that someone wanted breakfast. Digger climbed out of bed and padded barefoot into the kitchen to fill Lady Antonia's bowl. The clock on the stove showed it was just past seven. Figuring it would be an hour later in Houston, she retrieved her phone from the bedroom and called her grandparents. Grandma Betty answered, surprised to hear from her so early, but when she explained the reason for her call, she handed the phone over to her husband.

"Hey Grandpa, how're you feeling today?"

"Oh, just dandy. They've got me on a bunch of pills and I'm feeling a hundred percent again. Thanks for asking."

"Great. Hey, I really wanted your help with something. Remember the Troy deal?"

Digger briefly outlined what she was hoping to find out, pausing while he took notes and made sure he had names and locations spelled correctly. "Thanks, Grandpa. I hope it's not too much trouble."

"Not at all. Glad to help. Since it's a holiday weekend, it may be early next week before I can get back to you. You girls doing anything special for the weekend?"

"We've got a thing tomorrow. Maria's family. At least it's a break from her campaign gigs. The pressure is on right now."

She heard sounds from Abuela's room and moments later the old lady appeared. "Ah, Cowgirl, you're up so early! I was going to make breakfast for you. It's Saturday, you can take it easy. Maybe go somewhere. You girls work too hard."

Digger sank down on the worn corduroy-covered sofa. Going somewhere sounded like a perfect idea, if only she could persuade Maria to take a few hours away from her campaign planning. "I'll go ask the wife," she said, laughing.

Digger climbed onto the bed beside Maria, bending to kiss her forehead, then traced her lips down her cheek to her mouth. Maria moaned, flung back the covers, slid an arm around Digger, and pulled her down so their bodies fit together. "Mmm, I woke up and you weren't here. Don't leave me like that in the morning. I miss you."

The smell of frying bacon and coffee finally lured them out of bed and into the kitchen. Digger had pulled on a sweatshirt and shorts, Maria a thigh-length T-shirt printed with stars. When she suggested the proposed solar site, Maria was eager to go. They set off after breakfast while it was still cool. A couple of recent rainstorms had awakened dormant life in the desert, giving the slopes of the low hills that they drove beside a tinge of green. September brought so many changes. Just yesterday Digger had noticed patches of gold on the higher flanks of the mountain where the aspen trees had already begun to change color. For days the smell of roasting green chile had wafted around the supermarkets. Abuela had been busy preparing and freezing it for the winter.

Maria sang as she drove. They'd decided to use her car because it had four-wheel drive if they needed it. Looking out of the car window at the blue outline of the Jemez mountains in the distance, the red earth sides of an arroyo, and the immensity of the blue sky above, Digger wanted time to stop. Let this moment continue, just Maria and I traveling together. She still had flashbacks sometimes, and for just a few seconds she would relive thoughts of the day her parents were killed. There was the time before the crash and the time after when everything changed. Time hadn't stopped the morning of the crash and it didn't stop now.

The car sped on and soon they reached the turn-off to San

Fermin. From the center of the pueblo, they turned east, following the dirt road that Archuleta had used the day she visited with Izzy and Andy Whitaker. They bumped along the washboard surface, trailing a huge cloud of dust. Digger scanned the landscape, trying to recall the place where Archuleta had pointed out the easement route. After a couple more minutes of bone-shaking travel, she recognized a clump of juniper and told Maria to stop at that spot. They got out and walked around, hearing nothing but a whisper of wind in the branches. Here and there the breeze stirred up swirls of dust. Digger squinted in what she recalled was the approximate direction and spotted the transmission line in the near distance.

On the visit with Archuleta, they hadn't gone to the solar site per se, but Whitaker had indicated the location, saying it was about half a mile east and slightly north of where they'd stopped to discuss the easement. Digger took out her phone. She'd never used the compass app but now seemed like a good time to put it to use. She studied it for a minute then looked up and pointed. "It looks like we should go this way," she said.

They set off again by car, following faint trail marks over the uneven land. Maria was worried that their vehicle might get bogged down in the sand, so they decided pretty quickly to continue on foot. The trail was challenging. They had to wind their way through sandy depressions and scramble down and back up the sides of arroyos, while always keeping an eye out for snakes. Eventually, they came to the edge of a bluff. Below it was a large flat area where they could see a line of stakes in the ground. Digger noticed a sign affixed to one of the stakes not far away. They scrambled down the final arroyo, clutching at rocks protruding from the red earth. Maria slipped just before she reached the bottom, scraping her hands and forearms.

"Damn, whose idea was this anyway?" Maria said.

Digger untied the bandanna from around her neck and dabbed at the scratches. "Sorry. I didn't know we were going to be rock climbing."

They walked over to one stake that bore a sign: "Property of Solar GRX. Keep Out."

"That's rich," Maria scoffed. "It isn't even their property. It's still state land. Can we go back now? My arms hurt!"

Digger helped Maria as they picked their way back up the slope. At the top of the bluff, she stopped to study the site again, trying to imagine it covered with iridescent blue photovoltaic panels. According to Whitaker and Lovington, the proposed array was intended to produce twenty megawatts—enough for several thousand homes. The contract Manny showed had shown Digger said the amount of state land set aside for the site was 320 acres. Based on her research, the size of the planned array would need two hundred acres. So, why the extra land? Yet another piece of this puzzle that didn't seem to fit.

Maria was already heading back toward the car, and Digger was about to follow her, when she noticed what looked like a road on the far side of the flat area. In the contract, the state had agreed to put up funding, through the sale of bonds, to put in infrastructure for the solar array. As she looked around, it hit her that "infrastructure" would require, at the very least, an access road.

"Come see this!" Digger called.

When Maria came back, Digger indicated the road. "I'll bet that connects with the highway, So, that's how they'll get access for the construction. Let's look for it on the way back. I'm wondering if they've started bringing in equipment yet." If they had, it could mean things were going to move fast.

Digger looked around again, eyes sweeping from left to right. Something in the distance to her right glinted in the sun. Houses?

"What's that over there?" She pointed.

Maria stared, squinting. "Probably the outskirts of Las Vistas. You know how the city keeps expanding to the west."

Somehow, Digger had never realized how close the solar site was to the city. So, where was the land that Murphy was planning to develop? She needed to check with Rex.

Once they got back on the highway, they drove slowly on the shoulder, scanning for the road to the solar site. Sure enough, about four miles from the turn-off to San Fermin, Digger spotted what at first glance looked just like a widening of the shoulder, a place where a car could turn around. But when they stopped, they could see it led to a dirt road. Maria parked and they got out and walked about fifty yards until they came to a gate. It was padlocked and a sign bore the same message they'd seen on the stake. Up ahead they could see some kind of heavy equipment and separate piles of what looked like sand and asphalt.

Digger looked at Maria. "Well, it Looks like construction's about to get started here."

CHAPTER 29

Abuela's Labor Day barbecue was an excuse for the extended family to gather, grill meat, drink beer and—Digger hoped—avoid airing old grievances. That hope went up in smoke on the morning of the holiday when Abuela mentioned over breakfast that Maria's mother would be coming.

"She what!" Maria yelled, jumping up from the table. "How could you let this happen. You know what she's like! How she treats me, treats my wife!" Chest heaving, olive-toned cheeks dark with rage, she stormed out of the house.

Digger looked across the table at Abuela, wondering if the next thing she would hear would be the sound of Maria's car roaring down the narrow street. Instead, she heard the slam of the studio door.

Digger raised an eyebrow, inviting Abuela to explain. The old woman pursed her lips and let out a long sigh. "You know her father has lent her money for the campaign."

Digger nodded. She guessed what was coming next and she didn't like it. Maria wouldn't like it either, she and her mother hadn't spoken in at least two years. But the campaign costs never stopped, and Maria was constantly hustling for contributions.

The next campaign finance report was due in less than two weeks and Maria's father, Humberto Ortiz, had been a big donor.

Digger thought about the Christmas Eve when Abuela had invited her to join the family in making tamales. She remembered the way Abuela had greeted her son; the warmth between them and the chilly way the old woman had greeted Maria's mother, Consuela. No love lost there. Consuela made it clear she had no use for Digger either. What did her father say? Digger asked.

Abuela poked her fork at the remains of the egg congealed on her plate, her lips puckered together like a drawstring bag. "He asked me if Consuela could come. He hates that they don't talk. He loves Maria and he wants her to be part of the family again."

"I guess that depends on Consuela, but I wouldn't bet on it," Digger said.

As she expected, she found Maria in the studio. She was working on a painting of the landscape near Abiquiu; great geometric slabs of brick-red rock, vivid blue sky, and swirling clouds. Digger walked up behind her and laid her head on Maria's shoulder, resting her hands on her hips. She felt the tension ease from Maria's body in a soft sigh. She wanted to say something reassuring that wasn't trite and shallow, but she couldn't think of anything better than, "It's going to be okay." She repeated this over and over, as she breathed close to Maria's ear.

"I'm scared," Maria said, the words barely above a whisper.

"Of her?"

"Not just that. This whole thing. The campaign, running for office. The responsibility. What was I thinking? Putting you through this. What will it do to us?"

Digger circled her arms around Maria, holding her close, shutting her eyes. An idea came to her. They had a few hours before the guests would arrive. Everything was more or less ready for the barbecue. They could slip away.

It had been nearly a year since they visited the Spanish chapel, the place Maria had fought so hard to protect. Her efforts had stopped the road from being built, but in the initial construction dozens of huge old cottonwood trees had been ripped out, leaving the land bare and raw. The city had eventually turned the area into a parking lot and erected signs for the trails that criss-crossed the bosque. One of the signs said "Capilla de Nuestra Señora de los Sueños, Chapel of Our Lady of the Dreams." The name referred to an old legend that the chapel had been built by a Spanish explorer who was lost and dying of thirst when he had a vision of the Virgin Mary in a dream and awoke to find a stream.

Maria stopped by the sign and shook her head. "I wanted them to honor the place, not turn it into a tourist attraction."

They set off along the path that wound through the trees. The sun shone through the canopy, making the leaves glow coppery gold against a denim turquoise sky. After several minutes Digger saw it, the low adobe-brown chapel building with the arch that held the bell. When they reached the chapel, Digger could see the ragged cracks in the walls had been repaired and the door repainted.

Maria studied it silently. Digger knew she must be feeling a mix of emotions. She had fought fiercely to protect this place, she used to say that it was the one place she could always find peace when life got tough.

"Remember how it looked when you first brought me here," Digger said. She laid a hand on Maria's arm. "It was practically falling down. Now it looks cared for. You made this happen. People believed in this. People believe in you." Digger waited for her to say something and when she didn't, she gripped Maria's hands. "Look at me! The election is just weeks away. You've got the debates coming up. Saving this place was what got you started, you need to talk about it, take pictures, make people understand why this is important."

Maria's eyes lit up and she smiled. "Oh my. I created a monster.

Remember when I used to accuse you of sitting on the fence because you wouldn't commit."

Digger shrugged. "That was when I was a reporter. I had to be that way."

"I like the new you better."

Digger kissed her and turned back to the door. "Come on. Let's go inside."

She reached down, turned the iron clasp, pushed, and the door yielded. Inside the air was cool and still, smelling of old wood and dry earth. Part of the ceiling had been replaced with new beams. The windowsills were clear of pigeon droppings and the wooden benches that Digger remembered had been moved from their spot along the walls to form two rows of pews. The statue of St. Francis still stood on the spindly wooden table in front of the altar rail and there was the small glass vase filled with wilted golden flowers. Marigolds.

"She still comes here," Maria said softly.

A sound startled them, and they turned round to see the door slowly opening. Jack Kimble stood there, mouth open—evidently as surprised to see them as they were by his appearance. He looked down at what he was carrying and seemed embarrassed. In one hand he held a plastic jug and in the other a bouquet of yellow flowers.

"I can come back later," he said and made as if to leave.

"No, it's okay. Really," Maria said.

Kimble stepped forward gingerly, as if he were afraid the old floorboards wouldn't bear his fragile weight. The old tan shirt he wore, stained with sweat and forest grime, hung off his narrow shoulders.

"I suppose you wonder why I'm here with these," he said. He held up the flowers, sighed, then continued in a low voice. "Last year, after I lost the election, I came here to pray. I didn't know what I was going to do with my life. Each time I came, I saw this old woman. She always brought flowers. It was months before we talked. I finally found out her name and she told me she put them here in memory of her husband who died in Korea." He paused, frowned as if recalling painful memories. "A couple of months back I came here, and found the flowers were dead. The same thing the next week. I realized Mrs. Ortega must have died. So, I started coming here. It seemed important to remember her too."

Kimble eased down on the wooden bench nearest them and set the jug and flowers beside him. Maria reached out her hand and touched his shoulder. "Thank you for your kindness. We should be going."

He looked up, his face alert now, as if he'd shrugged off a burden. "I should thank you, Maria. You and your fight for this chapel."

"Well, I hope I can do a lot more, that is, if I am elected," she said.

Kimble nodded slowly, "Yes, I'm glad you're running. I think you could do a lot of good." He hesitated, looking thoughtful. "I think I should warn you about something. I am on the Planning and Zoning Board for the city now. I get to hear of things long before they go public. You should know that your opponent, Danny Murphy, is trying to get permission for a new development out near the San Fermin pueblo."

Digger was instantly alert. "Yeah, we'd heard something about that."

"From what I saw," Kimble continued, "It's supposed to be a small, very exclusive subdivision with some kind of fancy retreat center, and it's close to where that solar array is supposed to be built."

"How close?" Digger said.

"Maybe two miles, not much more."

A thought struck Digger. "We were just out there, and it looks like they're getting ready to start work on a road to the solar site.

Do you suppose it would provide access for Murphy's development too?"

Kimble gave a wry smile. "If it does provide access, and someone else is paying for part of it, that would be Murphy's style."

They arrived back at Abuela's to find Maria's older sisters, Ana and Cristina, busy in the kitchen. Abuela was outside supervising their two husbands as one scrubbed away old grease from the barbecue and the other swept dust off the outdoor table.

"Man, gramma, don't you never clean this thing. Looks like you never done used it," Fernando said. Cristina's husband was short, beefy, balding—and outspoken.

Abuela swatted him away with a dustpan. "Mijo, just because you married my Crissie don't give you the right to tell me how to run things. It suits me like it is. Here, put this cloth on the table and even your mother-in-law will be happy."

Ana's husband Juan guffawed. "Oh, man, she's like never happy 'cept when she's had a few."

He waved at Digger and Maria as they approached. "Hey, sister, Digger, how you guys doin'?"

Everyone hugged all around. Digger could smell the alcohol on Juan's breath, as though he'd already drunk his share of beer. They spent a few minutes together, the men teasing Maria, and winking at Digger as though they shared an understanding.

As an only child, and then a teenager living with her grandparents, Digger had often felt awkward among classmates at school. At college, even though she knew she was attracted to women, she'd palled around with the guys, playing pickup games of soccer in local parks. She'd looked at families from the outside with curiosity and longing. Being drawn into Maria's family soothed the longing but she was still finding her way, testing what was okay, and what pricked her sensitivities. At first, she could tell

Fernando and Juan weren't sure how to react to her. Over the months though, they had settled into a comfortable, almost bro-like, camaraderie.

Abuela grew impatient. "If you don't get that fire going, we won't have nothing to eat. Mija, go help your sisters."

Maria rolled her eyes, but she headed obediently back to the house. Digger followed. She'd had enough bro jokes. In the kitchen, Cristina was stirring something in a large pot watched by her six-year-old daughter. Ana was keeping an eye on Cristina's younger daughter, while she sat at the table shucking corn. Ana's own child was dozing in a baby carrier next to her. When Digger and Maria came in, the sound of their voices startled the baby who stirred and began crying. Maria immediately reached in, picked her out of the carrier, and cuddled the baby in her arms.

As Maria held the baby, her body swayed gently from side to side. She looked so natural, so comfortable. Watching her, Digger wondered if Maria wanted children. She'd seen Maria hold the baby before, but it never occurred to her until that moment. They'd never even talked about it. She supposed they could find a way, women she knew were doing it. Did she herself want children? She didn't know. She found the thought oddly troubling.

They heard an old man's voice from outside the gate. "Hola, hola!"

"It's Señor Jose. Abuela always invites him." Maria handed the baby to her sister and went to let the neighbor in. The old man and his wife brought a small basket of piñon nuts they had picked. They were still exchanging greetings when the gate opened again and a tall young man with wavy black hair strode in. "Hey!" He called out, and seeing Maria, he rushed over and grabbed her in his arms.

"Hey cousin! You're looking so good! Being married suits you!"

"Luis!" Maria laughed, freed herself and gestured to Digger.

"Luis, this is my wife, Digger." Luis raised his eyebrows, grinning. "Digger? Is that really your name?"

Digger shrugged. "It's actually Elizabeth, but everyone calls me Digger. Nice to meet you."

Luis had brought an old-style boombox and he set it up on Abuela's bench by the front door. Soon the sound of salsa music filled the yard, and they continued drinking beer while Fernando and Juan began grilling. No sign of Maria's parents. If Maria was nervous about confronting them, she didn't show it. She and Luis began dancing on the small concrete pad beside the outdoor table. Digger leaned against the side of the house, beer in hand, watching them. They danced effortlessly, their bodies moving in synch with the rhythm; Luis's arm on Maria's back as she turned, his hands leading her, arcing, draping over his head.

A stab of jealousy made her teeth clench. She wanted to leave, not see them, be away from here. She felt an arm on her shoulder. Abuela was right beside her. She'd seen the look on Digger's face. "You wish you could be dancing with her like that, don't you?" Abuela said, nodding at Luis and Maria.

"Of course, I do." Digger couldn't keep the hurt out of her voice.

Abuela took her hand. "Don't let it eat at you, Cowgirl. They were children together, they started dancing almost as soon as they could walk."

"I guess I didn't grow up in the right family." She knew she sounded bitter.

Abuela leaned close, so close her lips nearly touched Digger's ear. Her voice was low. "You're part of this family now. Isn't that what you were looking for?"

Digger couldn't answer, couldn't meet Abuela's eyes. Her throat was tight, and she was fighting back tears. Abuela was right. Being wrapped into this family had eased the fire; the anger, the resentment about the car crash, her parents' death, Armando not going to jail—and deep down, it still simmered.

"I'm going to go get another beer," she said roughly, heading towards the kitchen. She had just pulled a bottle out of the refrigerator and was looking for an opener when she heard a car horn outside. She set down the beer and went out onto the porch. She heard car doors closing, and moments later the blue gate opened.

"Hola! Hola a todos!" It was Maria's father. They were standing just inside the gate. Humberto, dressed in white guayabera over shorts, beamed at the gathering. Beside him, Consuela stood stiffly, her salon-dark hair scraped back from her face, and her yellow linen dress flawlessly unwrinkled.

The music was still playing, Luis and Maria were still dancing, unaware. Someone, Digger guessed it was Abuela, turned off the music. Luis's arms fell to his sides, Maria turned abruptly and saw her parents. No one spoke for what seemed like an hour but what must have been only a few seconds. Digger's eyes darted from Maria to Consuela. They were like adversaries in an ancient legend embodying long-held grievances. Consuela's anger, disappointment, and rage, over a beautiful daughter who chose to openly love women, Maria armed with fury from the rejection, the endless humiliations. To Digger, it felt like they were all sliding toward the edge of a cliff face, a train wreck in slow motion.

Digger knew this was the moment she had to rescue Maria. She walked swiftly over, put an arm around Maria, and held out a hand to Consuela. "Hi, I'm Elizabeth, I've been looking forward to meeting you." They'd encountered each other once before, Christmas Eve when Consuela had screamed at Maria in a drunken fury. Today she was sober, her dark eyes clear as she studied Digger. Seconds passed. Digger could hear Consuela breathing, see beads of sweat forming on her upper lip.

It was Maria who finally broke the tension. "Mama," she said, leaning forward to hug her mother. They hugged for a long, long time, then Maria turned to Digger, "Mama, this is my wife."

More seconds passed, then Consuela's face softened into a slow, hesitant smile. She put out her hands, clasping Digger's in her own.

"Mucho gusto," she said.

CHAPTER 30

The first thing Digger saw on Monday morning was an email alert from the Daily Post on Manny's story. She slipped out of bed and padded to the kitchen where she skimmed through it online. Damn. He'd laid it all out, everything they'd uncovered so far; the company's almost content-free website, the office address in a UPS store, how the state could be at risk because of the incentives, vague responses from Kramer and Izzy, and Lovington's reassuring optimism. It was all there. It would be a bombshell for Lovington. She could just imagine that his opponent, Tom Sears—the so-called "Rancher from Roswell"—would be salivating as he read it. Sears' main ranching activity was more about nodding donkeys than steers. He had no use for any kind of energy that didn't involve fossil fuels.

Thank God, though, Manny hadn't mentioned her or the Cultural Affairs Department. Still, Digger had a nasty suspicion Montoya would be gunning for her the minute she went back to work. Well, maybe it was time to confront her. There was plenty about this whole deal that smelled like a dead skunk.

She called Manny. It rang and rang. She was about to give up and leave a voicemail when a sleepy voice answered. "What the fuck? It's seven-thirty in the morning, Digg!"

"Oooh, big night out? Am I interrupting something?"

"Screw you."

"I read your story. I have a hunch my boss is going to be grilling me when I get back to work."

"I didn't mention you. Anyway, you just pointed me in the general direction. I did my own poking around."

"Yeah, I appreciate it, but she's already asked me about you, and I suspect there's a lot she knows that she's not telling me."

She heard a series of unidentifiable noises at the other end of the call, and wondered if Manny was alone. "You sure I'm not interrupting something?"

"It's my dog, okay? He scratches a lot in the morning." He sounded irritated.

"Oh, someone's wormed their way into your heart. What's this four-footed cutie's name?"

"Rusty. He was a rescue."

"Rusty the Rescue Dog, it has a certain ring to it."

"Cut the crap, Digg. What do you really want to know?"

"Well, I notice you didn't put anything in about the Jill Franks contract."

Manny made a frustrated sounding grunt. "I couldn't get anywhere with that. Can't you turn up anything else? You're the one working in that department. Someone there must know something—some kind of paper trail besides that note."

"Okay, sure. I'll keep sniffing around, but I'm sure the story's going to stir up the shit. Let me know what kind of reaction you get," she said. "Oh, and hey, I do have something else for you. Maria and I went out to the solar site on Saturday, and we found an access point off US 550 where there's a "keep out" sign posted. We snooped a bit and saw what looks like road construction material piled up near the entrance. If I remember it right, the contract said money could start flowing to the solar folks once building starts."

Manny was suddenly wide awake. "No way! I'll take a drive out there this morning. Thanks Digg. I'll get back to you, okay?"

Chris Lovington stared at the newspaper laid open on his kitchen table. He'd read it over and over as his coffee grew cold. Sunlight was streaming through the window. Outside, another glorious fall day was unfolding, but inside the tiny adobe house he'd rented in the Acequia Madre neighborhood of Santa Fe, it was icy cold. Or maybe the cold was coming from his heart.

He got up and walked slowly to the living room. The place was stark, barely the minimum of furniture. After Christine died, he'd taken down the pictures, the ornaments, everything with brightness and color, and put it all in the spare bedroom with her clothes. He needed to focus on his work so he could keep that part of his past life shut away.

When Sheridan had asked him to run for governor, it was as if a beam of sunlight had penetrated that cold dark place. He had thought he had a chance to overcome the past and atone for the blindness that had once gripped him. Now, this article could sink his whole campaign. With the election now only two months away, this was a disaster. He thought he'd convinced the reporter that everything was under control, that it was just a matter of time, and they'd see the array under construction. What was he thinking?

He sat down at the table again, head in hands. How had he let this happen? What would Joe Sheridan be thinking? Had he read the story yet? As far as he knew, Sheridan's wife was going down fast, he rarely appeared in public anymore, Sylvia Sanchez was handling most of his duties, Lovington hadn't seen him in weeks. Sheridan had put his trust in him, and he had put his trust in Tony Kramer—the former pastor.

Why had he ignored the warning signs? Yes, he'd noticed

them, the lack of hard answers, the delays; the tomorrow, tomorrow, and tomorrow promises. But sometimes things worked like that. In public life you had to be patient, take risks, believe in goals, and survive the hardships. And he had done his best to do all of that. Driving around the state, noting the dryness of the land, and living through months and months without rain, the days—more of them each summer—when the temperature nudged 100 degrees. He knew he had to do something, and this was his chance to help the state.

He picked up the paper, shaking his head. This was a gift to his opponent. Tom Sears would be laughing out loud. He could just imagine the attack ads. He looked at his watch, nine o'clock. Whitaker would probably be calling him any minute now. Before that happened, he had another call to make. He put down the paper and punched in Tony Kramer's number.

Tony Kramer was back in Phoenix and not at all happy about it. He hated the apartment with its cheesy Eighties' decor, and he couldn't stand the faint odor of chicken tenders that wafted over from the KFC on the corner. He'd had to downsize and downgrade his living situation when the church kicked him out. In this place, his living room window looked out on a parking lot and a six-lane boulevard. Janet didn't like staying here with him. "It's too noisy and there's too many weird-looking people," she said. She'd found an apartment in a nicer part of town where she had a view of the South Mountain. He wanted to see mountains, but his apartment faced the wrong direction. Maybe his life was facing in the wrong direction too, he thought.

His phone rang.

"Have you seen the article?"

Kramer struggled to refocus his brain and recognize who was calling. "Uh, Chris? What article, what are you talking about?"

"Clearly you haven't," Lovington's tone was clipped. "Get out your laptop and look up Santa Fe Daily Post. It's on the front page."

Lovington was silent while Kramer opened the laptop on his kitchen counter and typed in the newspaper's web address. Moments later it popped up. The lead story began, "Questions continue to swirl around a solar company that plans to build a huge array on state land near Las Vistas." As he scanned the article his throat went dry. He knew the newspaper would be doing a story, but he'd hoped they would have time to get out in front of it with more positive news.

"Well?" Lovington sounded impatient on the other end of the line.

"I, uh, see what you mean …." His eyes darted around the apartment. He wished Janet were here. It seemed everything was starting to unravel. He paced back and forth at his window view of the parking lot below. The words of a Psalm ran through his head. "Out of the deep have I called unto thee, O Lord."

Lovington went on. Now he sounded angry and desperate. "You realize this could sink my whole campaign? I trusted you, Tony!"

Kramer rubbed his face with his free hand, took a deep breath. "Ok, Chris. Listen, we've got stuff we can hit back with. We've got the agreement from the tribal governor, Archuleta, and we've got the electric utility company on board. And, I haven't brought you up to date on this, we've got supplies at the site ready to start putting in a temporary access road."

Lovington fell silent for a moment, letting the details sink in. "But what about the investors?" he asked. "You keep telling me you're lining things up, so when can I give people a date?" What Lovington didn't say out loud, the one thing that was really twisting his stomach, was knowing that soon as construction as would start up, the contract stipulated the state had to start paying on the incentives, and at that point he would have almost no leverage over Solar GRX.

"I've got some investment news too, Kramer said, "Something cropped up just before the weekend and I was planning to tell you about it right after the holiday, just to make sure it was all firmed up."

Kramer had spoken with Jeff and Randy about Murphy's offer. When he talked with them he learned Jeff and Randy had also been in touch with Murphy directly and the paperwork was moving ahead. According to Jeff, Murphy told them he wanted to keep the deal "at arm's length" so he was setting it up so the investment money would be paid by a company he owned in Arizona.

"So, what's the deal? What's firmed up?" Lovington asked, "I'm going to have every media organization in New Mexico contacting me during the next twenty-four hours, and I need all the good news I can get."

Kramer told him about Murphy's proposal, without mentioning the man's name. When he had finished, he heard a long sigh.

"Okay," Lovington said, "Can you call that reporter and fill him in? I have a lot of damage control to do here."

CHAPTER 31

As if the end of the Labor Day weekend triggered a shift in the weather, Tuesday morning dawned overcast and was threatening rain. While commuting to Santa Fe, Digger was racking her brains for a way to get the paper trail on Jill Franks/AKA Janet Macy that Manny wanted without raising Montoya's suspicions. Her mind was still gnawing on this dilemma when she got to work. She sat in her car for a minute thinking maybe she could try Marigold Ellis again. The woman had been able to slip her a handwritten note about Jill Franks, so maybe she knew of a way to produce something more. It was worth a try. First, she needed something sweet to bribe her.

Instead of going straight to the office, she detoured to a nearby cafe she knew that specialized in donuts. Purchase in hand, she headed to her own office to check in before going in search of Marigold. Her office mates, Tina and Gabrielle were already at their desks, coffee mugs in hand, chatting about a movie they'd seen over the weekend.

"Hi all! Good weekend?" Digger asked. They barely looked up at her before continuing their conversation. Digger thought for the umpteenth time about how much she missed the friendly Courier newsroom. She opened one of her desk drawers and took out the brochure Montoya had given her the day she went to San Fermin, then went off on her mission.

Marigold was bent over her computer shielding the screen so that casual observers couldn't see she was playing Candy Crush.

"Hi, have a good weekend?" Digger said.

Marigold looked around guiltily. "Oh, hi. Yes, thanks. How can I help you?"

Digger slid the bag of goodies onto the desk and opened it. "Would you like one?"

Marigold blushed. "Oh, I really shouldn't. I'm really trying to stick to my diet."

"All the calories are in the donuts. These are just the donut holes. Totally non-fattening."

"Oh, get out of here!" Marigold laughed, helping herself to one.

Digger moved in close. Speaking in a low voice, she asked, "Remember a while ago you helped me out with some information about the woman that did the research for that brochure? Do you think you could find me anything else on that? I know you said it was a little unusual, but I thought she did good work. I'd like to get in touch for a project I'm planning."

Marigold eyed her, then slowly put her hand in the bag and took another donut hole. "No calories, right? I think I might be able to find you something. Give me a few minutes. Wait here."

Digger took the chair beside the desk and waited. Marigold had said Montoya had handled everything about hiring Jill Franks herself, saying that it was very unusual. Marigold seemed confident she could find something, but what if she couldn't? What would that mean? It could mean a lot of things. None of them good.

Marigold returned about fifteen minutes later and slipped a sheet of paper into Digger's waiting hand. "Like I said before, you didn't get this from me, okay?"

Digger nodded. "Thanks. I owe you one."

Marigold dipped her hand in the bag and popped another donut hole in her mouth. She closed her eyes and munched slowly, a look of serene enjoyment on her face. Finished, she opened her eyes, peered straight at Digger and said, "You were a reporter with the Courier, weren't you?"

Digger's heart fluttered, but she answered evenly, "I was," emphasizing the second word.

"I used to enjoy reading your articles," Marigold said. She gave a little chuckle then took another donut hole.

Digger took the paper to her desk. Scanning it quickly, she saw it was some kind of contract, made out to "J.Franks" for "Specialist Services." There was no address, but Digger recognized the Arizona phone number. The description of the work merely said, "research and related tasks." What caught her eye was the dollar amount. It showed $5,000 not the $30,000 she'd seen on the handwritten note. Reading further down, she realized the figure referred to a monthly payment, not the total. She noted the dates. Apparently, the contract began in early May and was for a period of six months. Her heart jumped. Hastily she took a picture of the contract and sent it to Manny with a message asking him to call her ASAP. Then she went out to the parking lot to wait for his call. She didn't want anyone overhearing them. Ten minutes later he rang back.

"Terrific work," he said.

"Yeah, it was easier than I thought. Did you notice the dates?"

"Yeah, what about them?"

"Six months. So, if the project started in May, that gets you to November, right? And what is happening in November?" she said.

"The elections? You think there's a connection?"

Digger's brain was racing, and her words tumbled out. "Think about it. The press conference Lovington held was in mid-June. If Jill Franks or Janet Macy or whatever she calls herself, was hired in May, and did the research, she could have finished it and given a report to Lovington so he could make the announcement. Since then, it seems like they've been stalling. They haven't made any more major announcements. Now we're in September."

Manny made a sound, almost a low growl. "Yeah. You're right. But why end the contract in November if this Jill/Janet woman really is connected to the solar project?"

"I'm not sure. I have a call to make, but I think there might be a connection with something that happened in Texas a few years ago. They ran a scam that seems quite a bit like this one."

"Okay. I'm going to be running around till late this afternoon, then I'll be on deadline. Message me if you find out anything."

Digger was about to head back into the building when she caught the faint, but unmistakable smell of roasting chiles. At this time of year, the supermarkets usually had a roaster—a big drum filled with green chiles rotating over a propane stove—in their parking lots to tempt buyers. Odd, she thought, no supermarkets near the Bataan building. Someone must be roasting chiles as a gimmick. If they were still there later, she'd buy some to take home. Abuela would love it.

She hadn't even reached her desk when Tina commented drily, "Your boss is looking for you, and she don't look happy."

Julia Montoya was standing by her window when Digger walked in. She was wearing a severely tailored dark gray dress with a scoop neck and a silver necklace with the kokopelli pendant she'd been wearing the first time Digger met her. Whether it was the color of the dress or the overcast skies, Montoya's face looked washed out. Her brows knit in consternation when she saw Digger.

"Thank you for coming. Please sit down." She pointed to the stiff upright chair in front of her desk. Today's conversation evidently wouldn't be a cozy armchair chat.

She held up a copy of the newspaper with Manny's story. "What do you know about this article?"

Digger had been expecting this moment and she'd rehearsed dozens of replies in her head. Now, faced with Montoya's accusing expression, her mouth went dry. It was like trying to recall the name of a well-known movie actor and getting stuck on the first letter. She swallowed, took a breath, then, said agreeably, "Yes, I read that too. He makes some good points, don't you agree?"

Montoya blinked, clearly not expecting this kind of reply. "Yes. I would have to agree," she said tightly, "however, I need to remind you that we are not the lead agency on this. I asked you to keep an eye on it, but I do not want the Department of Cultural Affairs to be dragged into this controversy in any way. Do I make myself clear?"

"Absolutely." Digger said cheerfully, though anger stirred in her chest. "I just wondered if you registered the part in the article where it said the contract allowed the company to start receiving the financial incentives as soon as it started construction, and that there's no clause allowing the state to demand repayment." She stopped there. No need to hammer it home by asking if Montoya realized what that could mean. The secretary's face flushed, and her lips tightened. That's done it, thought Digger, now she's going to fire me. Montoya's next words shocked her.

"That is a problem Chris Lovington will have to deal with. He wants to be governor—but this won't do his campaign any good." Her expression was hard to read, but Digger could almost swear there was a hint of a smile as she spoke, or maybe it was the slightly sarcastic tone. She'd had the feeling before that Montoya had animosity toward the state land commissioner, now it was nakedly obvious.

Montoya stood up. "Thank you for your work on this. I believe you have another project you are working on."

That was not a conclusion, but a reprimand to get back to work. Digger understood the interview was over. She nodded and started toward the door. She had almost reached it when a framed photo on the credenza by the window caught her eye. She'd never noticed it before. The frame was elaborate tinwork, the kind souvenir shops sold to tourists. She recognized a younger Julia Montoya standing beside an older man she guessed might be her father, and a young man—a brother perhaps? Later, she couldn't remember what had made her stop at that moment and turn around.

"The photo, your family?"

Montoya looked momentarily confused, then she saw where Digger was looking.

"My brother Raul and me with our dad before he…." she hesitated, "before he died."

"Very nice," Digger said, leaving the secretary's office.

CHAPTER 32

Six Weeks to Election Day

Abuela was feeding Lady Antonia when Digger arrived home. The old lady was asking the cat's opinion on the latest tuna choice. Lady Antonia, sensing her owner's presence, deserted Abuela's offering to come and rub herself around Digger's ankles.

"So fickle!" Abuela commented with a laugh.

"Sorry, I broke up the love fest. Lady Antonia is a one-woman cat, but guess what? I have a surprise for you," Digger said.

Abuela's eyebrows shot up. Digger handed over the bag of freshly roasted green chile. Abuela's face brightened as she inhaled the fragrance. "Ahhh, perfection."

Digger glanced around. "Where's Maria?"

"Oh, didn't she let you know? She's gone to meet that Dillon fellow. He's helping her prepare for the candidate forum next week."

Digger looked at her phone and saw she'd missed the text. She'd forgotten about the meeting. So many calls. So many meetings. But the forum would be critical. It would be the first time Maria would face-off in public against Danny Murphy. She'd seen a Tweet from Murphy earlier in the day—a snide remark about Lovington and the solar project. He put out a steady stream of campaign Tweets daily. Thankfully, so far, none of them had been outright negative about Maria. Izzy's attempt to smear Maria with the phony school drugs story had backfired, but there were always risks.

She set down her backpack, scratched her head, and looked around the kitchen. "Hey, I know it's my turn to make dinner tonight, but first I've got to make a phone call, okay?"

Abuela was already unpacking the chile. "Don't worry, Cowgirl. I've got it all under control. You go make your phone call."

Digger went to the bedroom and closed the door. She was hoping her grandfather had news for her.

"Hey Grandpa! How's it going today?"

"Better and better. They've got me going to a special gym for heart attack patients, so apparently, I'm going to live." He cleared his throat. "I'm guessing you probably want to know what I've found out. Well, I can tell you this, I've been pretty damn busy. I called all the folks I talked to before, and a bunch more names that were given to me. Not a one of them had heard of any orders or shipments to that site you're talking about. But, and here's the thing, there's a helluva lot of interest in New Mexico. Seems like a lot of companies are looking at the solar potential there."

Digger considered this. If there was as much interest as Grandpa Jack said, why hadn't Solar GRX moved ahead? Kramer had told Manny they were still putting together an investment deal. He'd referred him to Izzy, who'd told him to call the Phoenix office and he'd gotten nowhere. She put the question to her grandfather, summarizing the situation so far.

"Hmm. Well, could be that they just don't have a track record. That's how I'd look at it," he find anything on them? I tried the newspaper archives but didn't find much. Grandma said you had at one time considered investing." It was a long shot, but she wondered if he might have collected more information about the people behind it, something with photos if possible. She could not get rid of the feeling that there was some kind of connection with Solar GRX.

"Well, I don't know. That was a while ago. I'll have to go look through my files. Can't promise anything. How's Maria doing?"

Digger sighed. "Busy as hell. We're getting into the home stretch and it's going to get rougher."

"Hang in there, girl. I'll get back to you soon as I can."

It was after seven when they heard Maria's car pull up outside. Moments later she appeared, looking flustered and tired. She lifted the messenger bag strap off her shoulder and plopped it down on the table with a shake of her head.

"Rough meeting?" Digger said, planting a kiss on her forehead.

Maria let her head fall on Digger's shoulder briefly as she relaxed. Then she reached for the bag and pulled out a flier. "Look at this! Murphy's been spreading them all around Las Vistas." She held the paper up for Digger and Abuela to see.

The flier showed two contrasting images. One half of the flier had a black-and-white sketch of a donkey and cart on a winding road to what was obviously meant to be the Spanish chapel. Under it, the text read, "Maria Ortiz only cares about the past." The other half showed a colorful image of several new buildings in the city beneath a bright blue sky, with the mountains in the background. The text beneath it was, "A vote for Danny Murphy is a vote for YOUR FUTURE!"

Digger shook her head slowly. "Well, it could be worse." She knew it could get a lot worse. Maria was resilient, but she'd also seen her wounded and when she was wounded, she could be impulsive. Digger looked at Abuela to gauge her reaction.

Maria read their cautious response to the fliers and grinned.

"And *this* is what Dillon and I came up with tonight." She pulled another flier out of the bag and handed it to them.

The flier showed a brilliant sun rising over the mountains, bathing Las Vistas in rosy golden light, with a silhouette image of young children and their parents in the foreground. The text read, "Vote Maria Ortiz: for a brighter tomorrow, for you and your family! All of us together!"

Digger regarded it, nodding slowly. "I love it, but don't you think you could have slammed him for some of the shady shit he's been involved with in the past?"

Maria shook her head impatiently. "That's the whole point! I'm doing this because I want to bring benefits to the people of this area—all of them! If I go negative on him, he'll respond in the same way, and everything will get vicious. That's not what I want. I want to feel like I have integrity. You used to tell me how important it was to you to hold to your principles as a reporter. Isn't that why you keep questioning things that don't seem right? Isn't that why you're obsessed with this solar deal?"

Maria's voice rose with each sentence, her eyes blazed, her hands shook. Digger stepped back. Stunned. "Woah! Are we having an argument?"

Maria sat down and exhaled slowly, the air making a sound like an old cushion being squeezed. Digger stood looking at her, saying nothing. It was getting more difficult to weather Maria's mood swings. The campaign was eating at them; night after night of meetings, wheedling support from know-it-all volunteers, trying to come up with new ways to beg for contributions, the endless paperwork, the nasty emails. What would it be like by election day?

Maria hung her head. "No," she said wearily, "Not an argument. A plan. I didn't mean to take it out on you." She reached out a hand.

Digger took it. "I know you want to take the high road," she said, "but Murphy and his crowd are not nice people. They don't care about anything but winning."

Later, before she went to bed, Digger decided to check her phone for messages one more time. Maria, exhausted, had already fallen asleep. She tapped the email icon, scrolled, and saw her grandfather had sent something with an attachment. Excited, she went to the living room to look at it on her laptop. When she opened the email, she saw he'd sent two photos. She clicked on the first one and saw it was some kind of prospectus. She guessed it was the solar company in Texas. The next photo showed a headline that read "Our Team" above a picture of four men. She looked at it closely. There was no mistaking it, the face of the man second from left was the same face she had seen in Montoya's office, her brother Raul! Except that the caption under the photo called him Randy Garcia!

She picked up her phone and texted Manny. "Guess what? I think I've made an important connection. Talk to you tomorrow."

CHAPTER 33

Lovington pulled up outside the governor's mansion and found Sheridan waiting for him outside the front door. He walked toward the car and greeted Lovington, standing in the sunshine, with a wave of his hand.

"Hello Chris, good to see you. If you don't mind, I think we can talk outside. My wife is not doing well, and I prefer to keep the house quiet. We can get coffee brought out to us on the patio, it will be private and comfortable."

Lovington agreed. What else could he say? The man's wife was dying; meanwhile, it was a gentle fall day and the sun was shining. Despite the warm temperature, Sheridan was wearing a tweed sport coat over an open-necked dress shirt. He walked slowly, as if he too were in failing health, his vitality sapped by the months of anguish, hopes raised only to plunge again with the results of a new scan. Lovington knew all about that. He'd walked that road, had been chastened by that torment.

They came to a paved patio secluded by shoulder-high bushes. An ornate iron table and chairs stood in the middle. On one side was a stone pedestal topped with a sundial. On the other was a statue of curving bronze that vaguely resembled a bird. Sheridan nodded for Lovington to sit. "Coffee?" He asked.

"Yes. A little cream, no sugar."

Sheridan pulled his phone out of a pocket and texted the coffee order to someone within the house. Then he turned to look at Lovington. "So, what are you going to do about that article?"

Chris Lovington had been dreading this moment. It was much worse than acknowledging his guilt in the anonymous darkness of the cathedral confessional. Here, he had to face a man he had admired, someone who had chosen him to carry on his vision for the state. He closed his eyes.

"I guess I trusted those guys because I wanted what they promised. It was also what you wanted, what I believed would be good for everyone."

Footsteps sounded on the gravel and Lovington waited while a young woman set their coffee cups on the table. She glanced at Sheridan.

"Anything else?"

He shook his head, "No, thank you, Yolanda. Can you look in on Mrs. Sheridan again, please."

When she had gone and they had taken their first sips of coffee, Sheridan laid his hands on the table and cleared his throat. "What happened years ago should not be driving what you do now."

Lovington's chest clenched. Shame flooded through him, hot and painful. So, Sheridan had done his homework. He knew all about Lovington's role in that old political campaign. He sighed. "Back then I was a different person," Lovington said. "It was like a game I could be good at. The more outrageous, the more successful I felt. I've lived with that shame for many years."

"You wrecked a man's career, and more." Sheridan's voice was low, his tone understanding but firm, oddly priestlike. Lovington hung his head. "I know," he said, barely above a whisper.

Sheridan looked away toward the Sangre de Cristo mountains, blue-gray in the morning light. Somewhere in the distance, a dog barked, a car horn honked. Then the quiet returned, broken only by the rustling of leaves. Sheridan picked up his cup again, took another sip, then said, "I think you should halt the solar project," he said.

Lovington's head jerked up. "What? How?"

Sheridan shrugged. "I'm sure you can find a way, some technicality, some permit they forgot to get, a missing signature. There are always ways. I just do not want the state to lose millions of dollars over this. There will be solar investment, but I think we both want it to happen the right way."

Manny's orange beetle was already parked at one side of the large gas station forecourt off Interstate 25 when Digger pulled in. She pulled up next to him and found him at a private booth inside the cafe area talking on his phone. She slid into the other side of the booth and waited while he finished the call. From the frown on his face, she knew he might be grumpy. He was.

"So, what's with meeting in all these weird places?" he asked.

"Come with me and I think you'll feel better in about five minutes." She led him over to a counter where a tiny woman in a white overall that didn't fit her, took orders for breakfast burritos. "Two with bacon, papas and green chile, please."

Manny rolled his eyes. "Gas station burritos, really?"

Moments later the tiny woman handed over two paper bags, and Digger paid. She led Manny back to the table and handed one to him.

"I defy you to tell me that's not the best breakfast burrito you've ever tasted. She peeled back the paper bag and bit into the warm tortilla, savoring the mouthful of crispy bacon pieces and hash brown potatoes with just the right amount of scrambled egg and green chile bite. Heaven.

Manny's eyes were closed as he munched. Then a smile spread

across his face. "Dammit, you're right, Digg. So, what have you got for me?"

She dug in her bag and pulled out the papers Marigold had given her. Manny nodded as she pointed out the contract details, dates, and amounts. Then she mentioned the family photo in Montoya's office.

"When she said her brother's name, I got curious. That's why I called my grandfather."

Digger took the time to fill Manny in about her grandparents' business, their interest in solar, and the strange case in Texas. "When Grandpa Jack told me about the Texas thing, it sounded familiar. That's when I started looking into it. I saw that name Randy Garcia and it rang a bell."

Manny looked puzzled. "How so?"

"Garcia is Julia Montoya's maiden name, and the guy in the family photo in her office—the one she said was her brother Raul—looked exactly like the guy named Randy Garcia in the old company prospectus that my grandfather found in his file cabinet and sent to me."

Manny stopped chewing, his mouth now half open.

"Thanks to my job and my grandfather's habit of saving everything having to do with business, we got lucky!"

Manny set the remains of his burrito on the table. They looked at each other. After what seemed like an eternity, Manny finished chewing, wiped his mouth with the back of his hand and said, "So, what do you think is going on?"

Digger stared down at her hands, noticing the wedding band as if she were looking at it from outside her body, marveling for a moment how new it was. Then she was back to the present, thinking how the more she asked questions about the solar project, the more she felt like she was venturing into a dark tunnel. "What I think, is that there's a link between what happened to an old project in Texas and the project Lovington announced."

"So, what's the link?"

"I think Julia Montoya's brother is linked with both projects, and maybe she is involved too. She clearly doesn't like Lovington, but I'm not quite sure yet why."

Digger was acutely aware of the silence in their booth, as well as the sound of pots and pans clashing, a toddler having a meltdown at the checkout counter, and the feel of her heart thumping in her chest. She hadn't meant to say all that to Manny until she began to put together thoughts that had been swirling in her head—part suspicions, part possibilities, and part guesses came together. Once she started talking about how all of her information came together, the words just came tumbling out.

Manny folded his arms and leaned across the table. His expression was serious, his voice low. "You said the case in Texas looked like it was politically motivated. Do you think Lovington's opponent could somehow be behind this?"

"Tom Sears, the Roswell guy?"

"Could be. He's got interests in a couple of those small drilling operations in the Permian Basin—that's a good reason to be against solar and wind."

Digger thought about it. What Manny said made a lot of sense. It was the most obvious answer. Instinct told her there was more, but she didn't know how to explain it. "I don't know," she said, finally. "Has Sears reacted to your story? I bet we're going to see a wave of negative ads from him."

Just then Manny's phone beeped an incoming text. He picked it up, read it and grinned.

"Bingo! You're right! Sears just put out a bunch of Tweets slamming Lovington and accusing him of fraud. I gotta go babe, the shit's hitting the fan and I've got a story to write."

CHAPTER 34

Izzy reached for the phone on the other side of her desk, knocked over the caramel macchiato latte she'd just set down, and cursed. She snatched the cup as a trickle of hot brown liquid dripped off the edge of the desk. The phone was still trilling.

"Hello!" She snapped.

"Hi, this is Matt, I'm the crew chief for Genro's Engineering, we're supposed to be doing work on the access road. There's a big chain on the gate and we can't get in. Any idea what's going on?"

Izzy watched the pool of coffee spread on the floor. She had no idea about the gate or why there would be a chain there. This solar project job was becoming a real pain, and they hadn't paid her invoice either.

"Sorry, can't help you there Matt. I'll call Tony and see if he knows."

She went out to the vending machine in the lobby and bought a Twix. Chocolate was the answer to a lot of life's constant irritations. Back in her office she punched in Tony Kramer's number and relayed the message. Kramer sounded as baffled as she had been. "I'll have to make some calls," he said, "Thanks for letting me know, Izzy. Can you call Matt and tell him we'll let them know when the crew can come back."

Kramer set down the phone and stared at the walls of his apartment kitchen. A cockroach was making its way along the side of a cabinet beside the refrigerator. He paced around the kitchen hoping the knot in his stomach would go away. He felt as if an ice bucket had been tipped over his head. His heart was pounding. What was going on? His hands were shaking. He sat down to steady himself, took a few deep breaths and called Chris Lovington's mobile. It went to voicemail. He tried the office number. When he asked for Lovington, he was put on hold for what seemed like forever. Finally, after a series of clicks, he heard Lovington's voice.

"Hello Tony."

"Chris! What gives? I got a call telling me the gate to the access road is locked."

Long pause. "Ah," Lovington said, "I asked my assistant to let your office know, but it seems the message didn't get through." Another pause. "An audit done a few days ago showed that Solar GRX hadn't applied for two of the permits required for the job. I'm afraid I can't allow work to go ahead until you have those permits."

"What the hell, Chris? Are you serious? What about the stuff I told you the other day? The investor, San Fermin? I thought you were in a hurry to get things moving before the election."

"I'm sorry Tony, but that newspaper report made me look like an idiot. It's probably derailed my campaign. So, until you can give me some real answers, you'll have to follow the regulations my agency has to adhere to. I'll have my assistant email you the necessary paperwork. Let me know when it's completed, and we'll be good." Lovington's voice was flat, distant, no compromise possible.

When the call ended, Kramer closed his eyes and clenched his fists. He knew he had to call Phoenix and tell them about the problem, but he felt as if he were sliding down a hill headed for a cliff. He shook his head to clear it, then dialed. Instead of Jeff's familiar voice it was Randy who answered. He relayed Lovington's message as briefly as he could.

"What the fuck is happening out there, Tony?" Randy's tone was far angrier than he'd ever heard it.

"It was the newspaper article. Lovington wants answers and I can't keep putting him off."

"Goddammit, Tony! Jeff told me you could handle that kind of thing. This was not supposed to happen."

Kramer clenched his teeth. He didn't like Randy's tone and he didn't like being yelled at.

"Then why don't you talk to him," he shot back. "You're the one that's always bragging about growing up in New Mexico."

He could hear Randy breathing loudly on the other end and he braced for an explosion. Instead, the man's words came through ice cold. "I thought you understood. I don't want to be publicly associated with this in any way. That is why we hired you. Are you clear? I expect you to deal with this, and fast." The line went dead.

Digger was putting together a presentation for the talk she was giving at the Coronado Historic Site near Bernalillo. She wasn't optimistic about the reception she'd get. Probably five old ladies with walkers and their families who were interested in building a family tree. Since the site was near Los Jardines, that meant she could get home early, but more and more she struggled to find the enthusiasm she'd had when she had started the job. Back then, she'd been so grateful to have a job to go to when The Courier closed its doors, one that gave her the chance to talk about her passion for the history and culture of New Mexico. Instead, she'd felt constrained, sidelined, and now increasingly uncomfortable with a boss, who was hiding something and dragging her into it.

A beep from her phone signaled an incoming text. The message from Maria said, "Can you call me ASAP." She picked up the phone and headed outside.

"Have you heard anything about the solar project?" Maria sounded anxious.

The question caught Digger by surprise. Maria continued before she had time to answer. "Alma just called me. She was driving back to San Fermin from Bernalillo, and she saw trucks parked by the access gate. The same place we were that day. She was curious, so she stopped to talk to the guys. They said the gate was locked, they couldn't get in and nobody was answering their questions."

"That's weird. I wonder if Izzy knows something."

Maria snorted. "Maybe, but you know I can't call her."

Digger wondered if the locked gate had something to do with the newspaper article. "I should probably call Manny," she said, "If he hasn't heard about this, he needs to know right away."

"Okay. I'd like to go talk to Alma too. The solar thing is a big deal for the pueblo, and I need their votes."

Digger looked at the nearly finished presentation on her computer screen. Her talk was scheduled for two o'clock. She should be free a little after three. "Okay. I've got to be in Bernalillo early this afternoon. Can you meet me there after school and we'll go to San Fermin together."

Digger finished her talk in under an hour but escaping from the small crowd of octogenarian family tree enthusiasts and their families took much longer than expected. Every time she thought she had wrapped up question time another arm would fly into the air with another question, so she had to quell her impatience and keep smiling. By the time she made it to their meeting spot at the IHOP restaurant, Maria was annoyed at having to wait. She signaled a "What gives?" gesture as Digger climbed into the Rav4.

"Sorry," Digger said. Leaning over to kiss her, she let her lips rest on Maria's cheek so she could savor the scent of her skin.

"Did I tell you I love you, yet today?"

Maria grabbed her close, bringing Digger's mouth to hers, kissing her deeply. When they broke apart, she laughed. "Don't you love being able to do that in public?!"

Digger grinned. "The Santa Ana hotel is right next door. Want to get a room?"

Maria gave her the mischievous look she found irresistible. "I wish. But I told Alma we'd be there in about half an hour."

The pueblo looked less deserted when they drove in than it had been the day Digger visited with Andy Whitaker and Izzy. A couple of boys were kicking a ball in a side street and some young women were standing in front of the health center, hanging onto toddlers. A thin pointy-eared dog eyed them suspiciously. Maria parked in front of Alma's gate. They threaded their way past a couple of downed bicycles, a red wagon, and a plastic trike in the yard in front of Alma's house where the meeting would be held. Alma was at the door ready to greet them, and waved them inside.

"Thank you for coming," she said. "I asked you here because people are worried. Governor Archuleta talked about this solar project, saying how much it would do for our people. But they see nothing happening. People are starting to doubt him. Now there's a rumor that it may go away. People are disappointed and upset."

"I'm not sure I can give them answers, but I want to listen," Maria said.

Six or seven people were gathered in the living room, deep in conversation. Some of them had been there when Alma held the fundraising event for Maria. Conversations hushed when they entered. Alma nodded at Maria and said, "This is my friend Maria Ortiz, she is running to represent us in Santa Fe."

Digger saw the anxiety on Alma's face and the faces of the men and women in the room. At that moment she realized it was more than just a series of puzzles that she was trying to make sense of. The solar project represented hope to this small community that desperately needed something to cling onto. She thought of Lovington's words when she talked to him at the campaign event, his sincerity. He believed in what he was doing, but more and more it looked like he'd put his trust in the wrong people. Why? And why did they promise so much? It was like a house of mirrors.

Maria turned to those in the room, her eyes bright and serious, her expression sincere. Digger saw it as she had seen it so many times. Maria inspired people. She invited their trust. One by one, they voiced their concerns; the old woman with the grandson struggling to find work, another whose daughter had gone missing, an old man who had lost his wife. What the solar project represented to them Digger couldn't fathom, but it was a symbol of how life could be better. "I have to be honest with you," Maria said, "I don't yet know what is happening, but I will do my utmost to find out and will do whatever I can. This is why I am running for office. The voice of San Fermin needs to be heard." The clapping seemed endless.

—

The sun was low in the sky as Maria drove them back to Bernalillo. The sunset lit up the Sandia mountains with a deep pink glow. Digger was silent, recalling the conversation she'd had with her grandfather. He'd said there was a lot of interest in the solar potential in New Mexico. If that were true, would another company be interested in building a solar array at that site?

"You're awfully quiet."

Digger looked around at Maria. "Sorry, I was thinking."

Maria reached out a hand and stroked her thigh. "You know what I was thinking? I think you and I ..."

Digger's phone pinged an incoming text. "It's Manny," she said, interrupting Maria. "He says it was Lovington that ordered the gate locked. Manny says Lovington did it because Solar GRX hadn't applied for the right permits to begin work."

"Seriously!" Maria's voice was heavy with sarcasm.

"Yeah. Sounds like BS to me. Maybe Lovington's getting a lot of flak because of Manny's story, and he wants to delay the project till after the election. Right now, that story gives Tom Sears plenty of ammo to attack him."

"Should I tell Alma?"

"Maybe...or see if he finds out more." Her phone pinged again. "Wait! That might be him."

It wasn't Manny. It was a Tweet from Danny Murphy: "She's doing it again. Maria Ortiz hates progress. She stopped the road to Los Sueños, and now she's trying to stop the solar project that will benefit San Fermin and Las Vistas."

"Oh shit!" Digger said.

CHAPTER 35

Tony Kramer glanced around, trying to read the room. Most of the other people seemed to know each other. That was no surprise since they were in a neighborhood recreation center. It wasn't so different from the center at the church in his former life. Same bland walls and tired plants, same cleaning fluid smell.

He had flown back to New Mexico that morning and picked up a newspaper at the airport. That's where he'd seen the notice that the Las Vistas Chamber of Commerce was holding a forum for candidates Danny Murphy and Maria Ortiz. He had been expecting a call from Murphy after the article came out, but he'd heard nothing yet. That was part of the reason he had come to the forum tonight. He wanted to see what kind of story Murphy was spinning on the campaign trail. He knew nothing about this Ortiz woman, but if she and Murphy were fighting it out for a state legislature seat, it was probably worth listening to what they said.

People were still arriving, milling around, gradually claiming seats. A tall woman with a helmet of auburn hair strode up to the podium at the front of the room. She picked up the microphone, there was a screech of feedback, then her voice. "Welcome everybody, I'm Denise Sowers, President of the Las Vistas Chamber of Commerce, thank you all for coming tonight. I'm afraid there's going to be a slight delay. One of our candidates, Danny Murphy, will be a few minutes late, so I ask for your patience. We will begin in about ten minutes."

A hubbub of conversations bubbled up around the room. Kramer had been about to take one of the seats in the back row when he noticed the slim young woman with spiky blond hair leaning against the entry door. She was vaguely familiar. It took him a minute to place her, then it came to him. She had been at the press conference when Lovington announced the solar project. Something about the way she was standing there, surveying the room, as if taking in every detail, made him wonder if she was a reporter. Manny, the guy who'd written that damning story had interviewed him once, but was he working with someone else?

Kramer made his way slowly toward the door. He was a few steps away when she saw him. He could tell she recognized him.

"Hello," he said, "I'm Tony Kramer."

"I know," she said. Her eyes were a piercing blue, chin firm, mouth in a tentative smile.

Embarrassed, he looked around to make sure no one else might overhear, then he said, "You were at the State Land Commissioner's press conference, weren't you? Are you a reporter?"

"I used to be. Not anymore."

"Oh. And you are?"

"Elizabeth Doyle. People call me Digger."

Kramer wondered if he should continue. Maybe she was cooperating with Manny. But what if she was? At this point, he didn't know if he could trust Lovington or the guys in Phoenix and he wanted to know how Murphy was tied in with them because he felt he had been played. He wasn't sure how to go on, but he wanted to find out more about this woman.

"Do you live in this area? Is that why you're interested in the candidates?"

Digger looked at him as though she was sizing him up. He was surprised how uncomfortable it made him feel. He was used to being the one who could control a conversation.

"Yes to the first question," she said, "And, not really to the second. One of the candidates is my wife."

"Oh," Kramer said, taken aback by Digger's frankness. In his former life, he'd been surrounded by people who were openly homophobic. He didn't think he was prejudiced but he'd never had a direct encounter. He cleared his throat. "And Danny Murphy, what about him?"

Digger shrugged. "He's someone I've been keeping an eye on for a while."

Kramer was intrigued. He guessed this Digger person knew a lot more about Murphy than he did. "If you were at the press conference, you know I live in Arizona. Still, if I were considering a vote for Mr. Murphy, what should I be aware of?"

Again, that unsettling look from her. "You should probably check the newspaper stories I wrote about a year ago. But if you've got time, I'll tell you, now," she said.

Kramer nodded. Digger continued. "Murphy was involved with a guy called Johnny Raposa, a big-shot developer around here. I found out the two of them had done property deals together in Scottsdale. Anyway, they persuaded the county to borrow several million to put in infrastructure for a fancy master-planned subdivision. But they had cut corners all around and the houses had a ton of problems. Only a few sold, and the whole thing went bust. The county sued to get the money back but somehow, they never got paid. Raposa is doing time. Murphy always claimed he had nothing to do with it. He runs the local golf club, and a lot of people think he's the best thing that's happened to Las Vistas."

Kramer felt a chill in his stomach. This was the guy who'd approached him to invest in the solar project. Jeff and Randy said they had worked with him in the past. He was wondering if Murphy had been involved with Jeff and Randy all along, and he was the one who was in the dark. If Digger knew details of Murphy's past, maybe she could help explain what was going on.

"If you're not a reporter anymore, why were you at that press conference? Were you working with Manny, the guy who wrote that article about the solar project?"

Digger appeared to consider before she answered. "Um. Yeah, he and I talked, threw some ideas around. But he did all the leg work."

"Hmm." Kramer wondered if he should let her know about Murphy's financial offer. At this point, he figured she or Manny were bound to find out anyway. "Did you know," he said, "That Danny Murphy contacted me, saying he was interested in investing?"

That caught her by surprise. "Wow!" She said, her eyes darting around.

Kramer hadn't expected his words to have such an impact. She was silent for almost a full minute, as if she were digesting the information. Finally, she looked back at him. "I can see how it might make sense. At the press conference, Chris Lovington said the state would put in a lot of money toward the solar project. Danny Murphy is planning to build some kind of upscale resort or hotel near the San Fermin pueblo. Maria and I went over there recently, and it looks like the access road to the solar array could serve both places. If the state was paying a lot of the costs, Danny Murphy could get a big bang for a small investment."

Kramer took in what she said, realizing it did make sense and wondering why he hadn't been more suspicious of Murphy's motives when he made the investment offer. Did he trust Digger? If she was married to Murphy's opponent in this political race, she had a vested interest in running him down. But still? She was looking at him as if she expected a response. Kramer decided to be honest. At this point, he figured didn't have much to lose. He was pretty sure this job wasn't going to last much longer. Meeting Digger's eyes, he said, "Just so you know, Murphy arranged for the investment money to be paid through a company in Phoenix. It's called SQS Developments, you might want to pass that on to your reporter friend."

Digger nodded slowly. "Thanks, I will."

She looked as if she were about to say something more, but just then the entry door opened and Danny Murphy walked in. He was wearing a dark blazer over a white turtleneck and charcoal grey slacks1. He stopped on the threshold, gazed around, spotted them, and walked over.

"Ah, Tony! I didn't expect to see you here. And Miss Doyle, nice to see again after. Still reporting?" He held out a hand. Digger hesitated, she didn't want to touch this man, didn't want to be near him, but she steeled herself and smiled.

"No, as you know, The Courier closed. I'm just here for Maria Ortiz."

"Oh, of course. Too bad. I thought you were one of my supporters," he said. "Sad about the newspaper. Is your friend Manny Begay here? That was quite the piece he wrote." Murphy made a show of surveying the room.

"No, I haven't seen Manny. There might be someone from one of those online news sources, but I don't follow them."

"Well, I better go alert Denise that I've arrived." Murphy then turned to Kramer, whom he'd been ignoring during the exchange with Digger. "Tony, stick around, I want a word with you when this is over."

CHAPTER 36

Digger slid into a seat at one side of the meeting room. As a reporter in Las Vistas, she always used to choose a spot that would allow her to check out the crowd. Tonight, there were a few faces in the audience that she remembered from the innumerable city council meetings she'd had to sit through. She knew from experience that some people found this kind of thing entertaining—and she had to admit—a political debate was like live theater. She expected plenty of drama tonight.

As soon as Murphy had left her and Kramer, she'd gone over to Maria and quickly relayed what Kramer had said about the investment. She'd hoped it would give her some ammunition against Murphy if he repeated his accusations that Maria had interfered with the solar project.

A hush fell over the room when Denise Sowers stepped up to the dais and announced the start of the forum. She began by introducing the candidates on either side of her.

"Daniel Murphy here is the Republican candidate. He's lived here in Las Vistas for two years. Some of you may know him as the manager of the golf course. He's been active in the Chamber and involved in several local developments. Maria Ortiz, the Democrat candidate has been a teacher in our local school system for seven years. She is a strong advocate for preserving local cultural institutions and businesses. Last year she led a campaign to save the chapel of Nuestra Señora de los Sueños, which has now been officially designated by the state as a historic site."

As Maria began her speech, Digger was aware of someone settling into the empty chair beside her. Glancing around she was surprised to see Dave Johnsen, the Las Vistas mayor. His eyes still focused on Maria, he leaned toward Digger and murmured. "She looks great tonight. By the way, congratulations, I heard you two got married."

"Thank you," she whispered. Johnsen had been a big supporter in getting the chapel's status formally recognized. She found it hard to believe they'd been married for nearly four months. All that time they had been caught up in the campaign, so little time together. Sometimes it felt as if they were being ground down, pressed, and squeezed like olives by the mill of daily life. Was she wrong to want more?

Maria did look good. Tonight, she'd let her dark curtain of hair hang down and it shone under the lights. At her neck she wore the thick gold chain Digger had given her as a birthday present, it made a bright crescent over her navy-blue silk blouse. She gazed around at the audience and smiled as she talked about her vision for the district, concern for the environment, and the urban, rural, and tribal residents. She cited her family heritage that stretched back two hundred years, the pride she felt, the concerns she had for the underprivileged and elderly, her desire to promote better job opportunities—all the usual points.

Digger wasn't sure how it would be received. The crowd tonight wasn't exactly her fan club. Some Las Vistas residents were angry when her campaign killed the road project. They wanted a quicker way to get to their supermarket and they weren't interested in some old Catholic chapel.

When it was Murphy's turn, he made a show of stretching out his arms and leaning over the table. "Been working on my swing. Any of you here play golf? Great game! And we've got a great club here! I'd like to give a shout-out to all the members. I think I recognized a few faces here in the audience."

"Mr. Murphy ...." Denise frowned disapprovingly.

"Oh. I am sorry, Madam Chamber President. Sometimes I get carried away." He beamed at the audience as though he were including them in a private joke. From then on it was as if a switch flipped in his brain and he went on the attack. "My opponent here, Ms. Ortiz, says she supports business. But last year, as I'm sure a lot of you remember, she led a movement to stop a road to the Los Sueños subdivision, and that has killed sales there and stymied the development of the commercial center. I tell you, people in Los Sueños now have to drive miles out of their way to get their groceries. And all for what? For a tiny church that no one was using, just because it was 'special' to her family."

Murphy's voice had been rising with each sentence. Now, he paused for breath, looking around to gauge the impact of his words before continuing the verbal onslaught.

"What else? She says she's concerned about the environment. Then why was she helping a journalist with an article slamming the company that wants to bring solar power to our district?"

"That is a complete mischaracterization!" Maria shot back. "I fully support solar power. We need to protect this land of ours. Building solar arrays can bring many benefits, but we need to make sure it is done in the right way. The article you refer to—which I had nothing to do with—pointed out that there are a lot of unanswered questions about the company that says it wants to build in our district."

"Ms. Ortiz ..." Murphy began, but Maria cut him off. "Maybe

you can answer some of those questions because I understand you are an investor in that project."

Murphy's face darkened and he shot a look out into the audience. Digger figured he must be looking for Tony Kramer. She wouldn't want to be Kramer when Murphy caught up with him after the meeting. Finally, he pursed his lips, then said, "I am a businessman. I saw an opportunity that could benefit people in this district."

Maria piled on. "And it would benefit you too, wouldn't it? I know you have big plans. Aren't you planning an exclusive development out near the solar site?"

There was some chatter in the audience, but Murphy simply shrugged, unfazed. "As I said, I saw an opportunity. Fostering businesses is one of the things I support."

Denise Sowers intervened to allow questions from the audience. The questions ranged from concerns about access to polling places on election day, to mundane items such as trash disposal. Murphy and Maria traded barbs for another half hour. Digger was proud of the way she remained unbowed throughout. Maria could be tough when she was backed against a wall. Eventually, the audience started to get restless, and a few people left. Denise Sowers thanked everyone and urged them all to vote "early and often," that old joke.

As soon as she was able to leave the podium, Maria came straight over to Digger and hugged her. "Thank God that's over. Let's go to Frankie's. I need a beer."

Immediately after the event, Danny Murphy went looking for Kramer. He caught up with him in the parking lot, just as Kramer was getting into his rental car.

"What's going on here, Tony? Somehow that Ortiz woman

knows that I invested in the solar deal. I can't imagine anyone else telling her."

Kramer turned to face Murphy but left the car door open. He didn't want this to be a long conversation. "Yeah, I mentioned it to that Doyle woman, apparently they're a couple so I guess she shared the information. You're the businessman, you said it would be a good thing for the district you're running for. What's the problem?"

Murphy moved in close, leaning against the car door frame in a threatening way so Kramer couldn't shut the door. "I'm wondering if you were the leak. Was it you talking to that reporter, that Manny guy?"

If Kramer had had doubts before, Murphy's words confirmed his fears. Murphy must have been in on the deal with Jeff and Randy long before he'd called Izzy and asked for the meeting at the golf club. Anger stirred in his chest.

"No!" He hissed. "I was the one spinning a line to the reporter, keeping everyone happy saying that we were arranging financing and everything would get moving real soon. Now, Randy says I'm supposed to sweet talk Lovington into letting us keep going. What is it you and Randy are up to?"

Murphy pointed a finger at Kramer's chest. "I don't think you're in a place to negotiate. I know about you and Janet and what happened with the church. You were hired to do a job for a few months and there's still a few weeks to go. So, my advice is, go talk nice to Chris Lovington and get him to forget about this permit shit, OK!"

CHAPTER 37

A blinking neon image of Betty Boop welcomed women to Frankie's. The bar was at the end of a sixties-era strip mall that had the negligently well-used look of a copy of People Magazine in a dentist's waiting room. Half a mile further south was the neighborhood locally known as "The War Zone." City leaders had optimistically renamed it "The International District," but that hadn't caught on.

Georgie, the heavyset Texan that Lexi employed to check IDs at the door, chuckled when she caught sight of Digger and Maria. "Well, you guys sure are a sight for sore eyes," she said in her gravelly drawl "Thought for a minute you'd forgotten us."

Digger realized they hadn't been to Frankies since the wedding reception—too busy with the campaign, moving and family stuff. All new to her lifestyle. Inside, she noticed Lexi was already getting into the Halloween spirit. Fake cobwebs hung from the pillars that supported the mezzanine floor, a cardboard black cat nuzzled around a portrait of Frida Kahlo and a broomstick-mounted witch sailed across the wall above the bar. Gena was playing a set of country music, a half dozen women were two-stepping on the dance floor and a couple more were gathered around the pool table.

They made for the bar where Lexi was filling beer glasses with one eye on the baseball game on the TV above the end of the counter. She did a double-take when she saw them.

"Hey! Look what the cat dragged in! How's domestic bliss suiting you?"

"Thanks, Lex. Good to see you too. Couple of Coronas, if you got 'em." Digger said. They took the nearest bar stools. Digger swiveled around, leaning one arm on the counter, her eyes on the dance floor. "Thought there'd be more people here tonight," she commented.

Lexi pushed the beer bottles across to them, followed Digger's gaze and frowned. "Yeah. Business isn't so great. I don't know what it is. People just aren't coming here like they used to. If it keeps up like this, I'm not sure I can keep the place open."

Digger swung around, shocked. "No. You serious?"

She'd been a regular at Frankie's ever since graduating from college. Frankie's was the place she could come and always feel comfortable, wrapping herself in the familiar atmosphere was like putting on a warm jacket.

"If they're not coming here, where are they going?" She asked.

Lexi shrugged. "Well, I could ask you the same question. That's the trouble. Women come here, meet somebody, then they get all cozy and stay home, or whatever."

Digger and Maria exchanged glances. Frankie's was the place they had met, and they too had gone on to nestle into their little burrow, no longer needing the ready companionship of like-minded women in the bar. Maybe Lexi was right—people changed, wanted different things, found their comforts elsewhere.

On the other side of the bar, in a corner behind the pool table, Izzy Chavez was sipping her way through her third Jack Daniels. After work, she'd swung by Panda Express and gotten some kind of Asian food for dinner. It had a name, but it didn't really make a difference. To her, it all tasted pretty much the same, just different colors. She sat around her apartment, eating from the container, half watching a cop show, and hoping Janet would respond to her text. Solar GRX still hadn't paid her invoices. When she'd finished eating, with still no word from Janet, she'd decided to go to the bar. Maybe she'd meet somebody. It had been quite a while since her fling with Cheryl.

Now, as she sat listening to Shania Twain, and watching couples two-stepping on the dance floor, it brought back a lot of painful memories. She imagined herself out there, leading Maria, feeling her twirl in her arms, effortlessly keeping the beat. They were so good together. She remembered the feel of Maria's skin, how their bodies fit together. She took another sip, closed her eyes, felt the hot burn of the whisky.

At the bar, Maria took a sip of her beer and glanced around. That's when she recognized the unwelcome form of her old girlfriend. She leaned over and whispered in Digger's ear. "Guess who's over there in the corner?"

She jerked her head toward the tables on the far wall. Digger peered through the low light, past the dancers. There was no mistaking the hairstyle, it was Izzy. Digger looked back at Maria whose eyes were hard, mouth tight, shoulders rigid. The next second, Maria jumped down off the bar stool and strode straight across the dance floor, knocking into a couple of women on her way. Digger rushed after her, ducking around the dancers, catching up to Maria just as she reached Izzy's table.

"You lying bitch!" Maria shrieked, "What the fuck did you think you were doing telling Cindy I was bringing drugs to school?"

Digger grabbed Maria's arm, afraid she was going to hit Izzy, who sat cowering behind the table. As she raised one arm to protect her face, her glass overturned, spilling her drink over the table.

"Maria, no!" Digger said, holding her back. One of the dancers yelled at them, "Hey! Your crazy-ass girlfriend nearly tripped us both. What the hell?"

The women at the pool table had stopped playing and were glaring at them. Digger held up her hands. "Sorry, sorry. It's Okay. These two women just had a bad situation. It's under control."

"It damn-well better be," said the dancer, a tall slim woman in a tank top who looked as though she probably practiced kickboxing in her spare time.

Digger looked from Maria to Izzy. "Maybe we should take this outside. You two seem to have a few things you need to discuss."

Izzy was on the floor, mumbling something unintelligible, her cheeks streaked with tears. Digger reached over and pulled her to her feet.

"Come on! Let's go," Digger said. Maria started to protest, gave an angry sigh, then took Digger's outstretched hand and went toward the exit door. Izzy followed.

Outside, the cool night air was filled with the sound of traffic on San Pedro and the pungent smell of frying from a nearby Wendy's. Above them a quarter moon hung partially obscured by clouds. Izzy stopped just outside the bar entrance and flopped back against the building wall. Digger realized Izzy was more than half drunk.

"I'm sorry," she slurred, "It was a dumb idea."

"Yeah, it was. You nearly got me fired. I could have ended up in jail or something," Maria spat back, still angry.

"I was jealous," Izzy said, her voice cracking.

"That was always your problem," Maria hissed. "I couldn't be with you because you wanted to own me, control everything I did."

Izzy hung her head. Looking at her, Digger thought of the time she had confronted Armando, the man who'd caused the crash that killed her parents. She'd always thought she wanted to make him pay for the pain he'd caused her. But when she did finally confront him, she understood that no amount of revenge would bring her parents back, and inflicting more pain won't heal that old hurt.

Now, she took Maria in her arms and hugged her tightly, feeling the sobs that shook her. They stood that way for what seemed a long time. At a sound from Izzy they eased apart.

"Guys, I'm so sorry. I need to make it up to you." Izzy mumbled.

Digger looked from Izzy to Maria, sighed and said, "Let's go over there and get coffee, okay?" She pointed at the Wendy's sign. Maria rolled her eyes, Izzy grunted unintelligibly, but they both gave in and followed Digger toward the restaurant.

When they were finally seated at a table with their coffee, Maria turned aside and stared sullenly out the window. Digger knew that look. They'd have a lot to talk about later. Right now, Digger wanted to take advantage of Izzy's contrite attitude and pump her for information. Up until the moment Maria spotted Izzy, she'd been preoccupied thinking about her conversation with Kramer and what he'd said about Danny Murphy. She hadn't had a chance to ask him why the project was stalled. As the PR person for Solar GRX, Izzy might know what was really going on. Then again, if it was bad news, as a PR person, anything she said could be spin. She decided it was worth a try. She waited while Izzy took a few sips of coffee. She looked like hell, but she was getting sober.

Making it sound casual, Digger said, "I talked to Tony Kramer tonight."

Izzy blinked but said nothing.

Digger went on, "He wouldn't tell me why Chris Lovington paused the solar project and I think there's something else going on besides the permit issue. You got any ideas?"

Izzy set down the coffee and pushed the hair out of her eyes, her face suddenly belligerent. "Why the hell should I tell you?"

"I think Maria is pretty upset with you, and for a good reason."

Digger rested her chin on her fist, eyelids half lowered as she regarded Izzy, waiting for a reply.

Izzy flushed and shrugged. "Look, those guys who hired me to do PR, made it sound like a big break. But they keep me out of the loop. All I know is that Kramer and his girlfriend Janet work for this guy Jeff in Phoenix who's got a construction company. It's Jeff's friend, Randy who's really calling the shots."

"So, tell me about Randy?" Digger prompted.

Izzy leaned on her elbows. "I don't know much. He seemed like he was more in the background. But the way he talked, I got the impression he truly hates Chris Lovington. It was as if there was something personal about it, like they have some history."

Digger and Maria left Izzy waiting for an Uber and headed home. Digger was at the wheel, and as they left the city behind them, she felt Maria's hand on her shoulder and heard her say, "I only want you in my life. Never forget that."

Digger reached up and squeezed her hand. For now, she didn't want to think about Izzy or any of the whole solar project mess. She wanted this moment to last as they drove on homeward, to where the night was dark, silent, and filled with stars.

Chapter 38

A strong north wind blew in overnight, stripping the golden leaves from the cottonwood trees. Aspens on the higher slopes of the Sandias were already bare. A light dusting of snow grizzled the dark outline of the crest. Digger worried whenever they left Abuela alone in the small adobe house on cold mornings. Lately, she'd been commenting about her hip hurting. Abuela wasn't one to complain, but she was in pain, and she made it known in subtle ways: a groan as she raised herself from a chair, and every now and then a wince. She would be eighty-one in November, a week after the elections. Maria had talked about having a birthday party for her, but she was much too busy to think about anything but getting through her workday and focusing on the campaign business.

When Digger left the house that morning, Maria had been on the phone to Dillon and barely paused to wave goodbye. The incident with Izzy had shaken them both. They'd talked about it late into the night. Maria wanted to pursue charges against Izzy for planting the drugs rumor. Digger thought it was doubtful any charges would stick, and going after Izzy publicly would only draw more attention to the rumor. Maria reluctantly agreed.

As she nosed her Subaru into the morning procession of cars commuting north on Interstate 25 toward Santa Fe, Izzy's words about Randy kept running through her mind. What was Randy's connection to Lovington? Izzy had referred to it as their "history." If Randy was Julia Montoya's brother, was it a shared history? Ever since Montoya had asked her to go to the press conference, she'd had the sense that her boss had an issue with Lovington. She'd assumed it had something to do with politics: either clashing egos, or some territorial quibble between their departments. But maybe it was even more personal than that.

As soon as she got to work, she texted Manny, asking if they could meet. Twenty minutes later he responded. "Crazy busy this morning but I can do lunchtime. Meet you in the Plaza."

"You can't get away earlier?"

"No. Sorry."

Digger stifled her impatience. She was supposed to be researching how the department could piggyback on a federal program that would pay college students to help stabilize centuries-old adobe walls at two Spanish mission sites. It was exactly the kind of project she had wanted to be involved in when she interviewed for the job. But her brain kept straying back to the solar puzzle.

Noon finally arrived and she slipped out of the office and headed to the plaza. Manny had texted he was on his way. She hurried along Don Gaspar, wondering where she'd find him. He just said one of the benches. Turning off East San Francisco into the Plaza she looked around anxiously hoping to spot him among the trees. And there he was, standing by the pergola where musicians played on summer weekend afternoons. He was wearing a red and black lumberjack shirt and a flat gray cap.

"Love the hat! You going for a new look?"

He grinned. "My girlfriend gave it to me. I kinda like it." He took it off, twirled it, and set it back on his head.

Digger slid him a sideways look. "Girlfriend, huh? Is Rusty the Rescue dog jealous of her?"

He mock-punched her shoulder. "Cut the crap, Digg. So, what was so urgent that you needed to meet me?"

Digger filled him in on what she'd heard from Kramer and Izzy. "It was the way she said 'history' that made me think whatever happened between Lovington and Randy was quite a long time ago. It could have meant anything, but it made me remember Abuela saying Julia Montoya's father ran for governor and when he didn't win it hit him hard. I've heard Julia mention her father's death a couple of times, and each time there was something really odd about the way she said it."

Manny rubbed his chin. "I don't know. Seems like a long shot."

Digger snorted. "I get that it sounds nuts, but we now know that Randy was involved in some kind of solar scam in Texas, and he's somehow connected to Solar GRX."

He still looked unconvinced.

Digger sighed impatiently. "Look, it's cold out here, let's go over to the library, it's just a block away. They'll have access to newspaper archives from all over the state."

Manny looked skeptical. He glanced at his phone. "Ok. I've got maybe an hour. Let's go."

The librarian at the counter shook her head when Digger asked if she could use her own laptop for the research. Most of the librarians Digger had encountered were only too willing to offer help. This one wasn't. Thin, fiftyish, and pale, she had the weary, barely polite attitude of a flight attendant on a low-budget airline.

"I'm sorry, but you'll have to use the library computers. Do you have a library card?"

Digger fished through her wallet and held out a card. The librarian glanced at it and frowned. "That's for the Albuquerque Bernalillo County system. This is Santa Fe."

Digger suppressed a groan. Manny leaned forward: Excuse me, "Ma'am," he said, "I've been in here before. The staff said they accept a card from any library system in New Mexico!"

She pursed her lips, nodded, led them to the computers, and

rattled through the instructions. "We're not busy right now, so I can let you use this one. But if a patron with a Santa Fe card comes in and needs to use it, they will have priority."

They sat close together, whispering to avoid upsetting the librarian any further. Digger started the search by tapping in Orlando Garcia's name and "governor." The top half-dozen hits were from twenty years before. They showed Garcia had been running as a Democrat. She recalled Abuela saying he'd lost the election, but the article indicated he'd dropped out a few months beforehand. The stories quoted him as saying that "he needed to spend more time with his family."

Digger looked at Manny and shook her head. "More time with the family! That's always code for something. Why would a guy who's polling well suddenly quit?"

Manny frowned. "Debts? Legal troubles? An affair? Keep looking."

They kept reading as Digger scrolled through the articles. Suddenly she stopped. "OMG. Look at this."

Manny hunched closer to the screen while Digger read the sentences aloud to him: "Garcia's Libertarian opponent ran an ad questioning his involvement with a charity that provided services to at-risk teen-age girls. Garcia denied there was anything inappropriate, saying he supported the organization to help those struggling with addiction."

Manny leaned back in his chair. "That sure looks like the attack that killed his campaign."

"Yeah, but his opponent didn't go on to win. I don't remember ever hearing that name and there's not much more detail about the allegations." Digger said. She was still scrolling, eyes glued to the screen. Seconds later she stopped again. "Here, look at this." It was a report of a fatal accident on I-25 south of Santa Fe at La Bajada Hill. She read, "State Police responded to a 911 call at around 11 p.m. from a motorist who said they saw a car traveling at a high rate of speed when it veered off the highway from the southbound lane...." she read out a few more details, then exclaimed, "Oh my God! The deceased was identified as Orlando Juan Garcia of Santa Fe."

Digger sat back, her eyes meeting Manny's. Seconds passed, thoughts whirling through her head: Abuela's concern about the Garcia family, Julia Montoya's strained expression when she mentioned her father's death. Manny drew in a long, slow breath. "We should talk to someone who was following this stuff way back then."

Digger's shoulders slumped. She knew Manny's instinct was right. "I wish Halloran was still here," she said, "He'd know who to talk to. He was always my go-to guy at The Courier."

Manny nodded. "Yep. But Halloran is gone, and I don't know of anyone at the Daily Post who's got that kind of institutional memory."

Digger thought about Rex. He was a photographer, not a reporter, but he'd been at The Courier for twenty-eight years—long enough to have been around when Orlando Garcia had gubernatorial aspirations. It was worth a try. When she ran the idea past Manny, he gave it his lop-sided smile. "At this point, I haven't got any better ideas. Call him and see if he'll meet with us!"

Digger used one of the private study rooms to phone Rex. When she came back, Manny already had his backpack slung over one shoulder.

"He wants us to meet him at his house tonight. Said he's got boxes of old clippings. He lives in Las Vistas. Can you do it, Manny?"

Manny consulted his phone, then gestured toward the door. "Okay. Can I meet you in Bernalillo at seven and follow you to his place?"

Digger nodded.

"Thanks. Gotta go." He turned to leave. Digger pointed at the back of the chair.

"Don't forget your hat. I don't think your girlfriend would be happy if you lost it."

CHAPTER 39

Rex lived on a short cul-de-sac in an older Las Vistas neighborhood with ranch-style homes, chain link fences, and front-yard basketball hoops. The streetlights showed that Rex's property had once been xeriscaped, but the pebbles had nearly disappeared, lost among the patches of scrubby grass.

"I guess Rex hasn't picked up any tips during his real estate job," Manny commented drily.

Digger chuckled. "Taking glamor shots of fancy homes isn't Rex. I think this is more his style, don't you?"

The old photographer greeted them with a big grin and a fist-bump for Manny. "Hey man, you look great. This is like a reunion!"

He led them into a living room dominated by an immense TV showing a World Series game. The air was heavy with stale cigarette smoke and something else. Digger identified it as soon as she spotted the large black and white cat curled on one of the recliners. Rex picked up a magazine from the coffee table and swatted at the chair.

"Mister, get down!"

Mister gave Rex an evil look, emitted a low growl, and jumped to the floor. Rex motioned for them to sit. "You guys want a beer?"

Rex had obviously had a few already while watching the game. A half-empty bottle stood on the table next to a full ash-tray and a bowl of Doritos. As soon as he went to get the drinks, Mister jumped back onto the recliner.

"Guess we know who's the boss around here," Manny said.

Rex returned, handed them their drinks, set his bottle on the table, turned down the TV, and frowned at the cat. "That damn animal! He's my daughter's but she can't have him in her student apartment. My wife loves him. She works nights and that's when he thinks he can get away with all kinds of shit."

Being a cat person, Digger had no problem squeezing in beside Mister. Once they'd settled themselves, Manny shot her a look. "You want to begin, or should I?"

Digger took the cue. "Like I said on the phone, Manny and I have been looking into the solar project. There's a lot about it that doesn't check out; like my boss, Julia Montoya, wanting me to keep an eye on it. It's got nothing to do with her department. I think she's got some kind of grudge against Lovington, and I imagine that her brother Randy Garcia may have been involved with the solar thing at some point—but I haven't been able to prove it yet."

Rex blew out a long breath and regarded her over his glasses. "So, why are you interested in Orlando Garcia?"

Manny set down his untouched beer on the table and leaned in. "Orlando Garcia is Julia and Randy's father. Digger thinks Julia's issue with Lovington might be tied to her father's political career, maybe even his death."

Rex's eyes widened, his eyes sliding from Manny to Digger and back. Slowly he put the cigarette he held to his lips and inhaled. He let the smoke curl out of the side of his mouth before he spoke. "Okay, guys. That was all a long time ago. I'll get the boxes."

He left and a few minutes later returned with a battered U-Haul box which he set on the floor by the table. Two more trips, two more boxes. He used his shirt tail to wipe a layer of accumulated dust off the surfaces. "I found these in the hotel room where Halloran had been holed up when he died. Notes from his old stories. They go back about thirty years. Help yourself."

Digger opened the nearest box. It held a pile of manila folders marked with dates. She picked one up. Inside was a thick bundle of newspaper clippings. Rex waved her away. "No. Wait a minute. You'll never find anything. I went through them before, and I figured out Halloran's system."

"Halloran had a system?" Manny laughed, "The guy's desk was like a bomb site."

Digger shrugged. They waited five minutes, ten minutes, or more while the voice of the baseball commentator droned in the background, the cat purred, and Manny crunched his way steadily through the bowl of Doritos. Digger had started to think the trip was a waste of time, when suddenly Rex, head deep in the last box, let out a muffled whoop. "Got it!"

He laid a folder on the table, licked his fingers, and leafed through the papers. "This is what I was looking for." He stopped, adjusted his glasses, and read through it. "Yeah, yeah! Here it is: "Orlando Garcia was an assistant attorney general. He made a name for himself with cases involving children and families." He flipped through a few more papers, added a few he thought were significant, then handed his carefully curated pile to Digger.

At the top of the pile was a photo taken by Rex. It showed Garcia behind a lectern, one hand waving as he smiled at an unseen audience. The headline said, "Garcia announces for Governor's race."

Rex sat back from the boxes and took a long pull on his beer. He wiped his mouth and frowned. "Back then, The Courier was considering endorsing Garcia. Halloran and I were following his campaign. He won his primary against some dairy farmer from Hagerman—a hick town near Roswell. Then, about four months before the election, this Libertarian guy named Bill DeSalles started gaining traction by stirring up some rumors about Garcia."

"What kind of rumors?" Digger asked though the gnawing in her gut told her she knew the answer. Rex looked from Digger to Manny and back again, like a third-grade teacher seeking the solution to a simple math problem. "So, you reporter hotshots tell me. What is the worst accusation you can throw at a candidate? I'll give you three guesses. Is it drugs? Stealing public money? Or…?"

Silence. Rex threw up his hands, exasperated. "Come on, you guys call yourselves journalists? You've been deep in election shit before this."

"Sex," Manny said.

"Bingo. You got it, Sunshine!" Rex grinned and dove back into the boxes.

Moments later he set down another file, unclipped one of the more familiar bundles, pulled out a large piece of poster paper, and laid it in front of them.

"I think this is what you're looking for."

The creased, much-folded poster showed a street scene at night. A man had his arm around a teen-aged girl. Beneath the photo a headline shouted, "Saturday night on Central Avenue, Orlando Garcia—Is this our next governor?"

Digger stared at the image, stomach twisting. Whoever took the photo was able to get up close and snap the picture without using a flash. The girl's eyes gazed blankly into the camera. Her hair was disheveled, mouth gaping, something moist was glistening on her chin. She looked about fifteen, dressed in a tank top and brief cutoffs that revealed multiple tattoos on her arms and thighs. The man beside her had an arm around her shoulder. His head was turned toward her, expression hard to read. But the face was unmistakable. It was Orlando Garcia.

"Where did this come from?" Manny gasped.

"That's the flier DeSalles used against Garcia. He somehow

got his hands on that photo and used it to make it look like Garcia was involved with teen-aged hookers."

"But was he?" Digger couldn't take her eyes off the girl's face. A bunch of questions crossed her mind: Was she drunk? Drugged? Was Garcia dragging her or was he helping her? Who took the photo, and why?

Rex kept his eyes on the picture too. As if reading Digger's thoughts, he said, "Garcia denied everything. Said he'd been donating time and money to an organization that helped adolescents with addiction. The leader of the organization even went on TV to defend him. But by then the picture was simply out there. The first time I saw it, I kept thinking, that could be my daughter out there. It made me sick."

Digger held onto the cat, her thoughts racing. The poster Rex showed them confirmed part of what she'd found out so far. Yet she knew there was more. "Is there anything in Halloran's papers about Garcia's death? A story we found said he died in a car accident at La Bajada Hill. Do you know if it was ruled a suicide?"

Rex laughed: short, sharp, and cynical. "A lot of people thought so, Halloran included. He was all ready to go after it. Then, guess what?" He looked over at them waiting to see if they were following his train of thought. They weren't. Not yet. Digger raised her eyebrows and shrugged. "I have no idea."

Rex responded with that cynical laugh of his again. "You remember how The Courier would pull a story when the Editor-in-Chief or someone else decided they didn't want a story to come out?"

Digger nodded. He didn't need to say more. She remembered the times when she was fired up about a controversial hearing, and suddenly she'd be given another assignment or just told "We don't think that's a good use of your time."

"But why do that in Garcia's case?" Manny wondered aloud. "It seems like such an obvious story to follow."

Rex emptied his beer. "A no-brainer, right? My guess is that the paper had been ready to endorse him, and they didn't want anything coming out that might put him in a bad light."

"And none of the other papers picked up the story?" Digger was incredulous.

Rex scratched his head, thinking. "Seems like there was something else that came up right then and everybody switched attention."

"What about that picture? Where did DeSalles get it?" Digger demanded.

Rex shrugged. "No idea."

Manny shot Digger a look of amazement. She could tell from his darkening eyes that he too was deeply frustrated. It seemed like every time they took a step forward, they came to another closed door. She knew he was probably thinking along the same lines. But how was Chris Lovington and the solar project connected to any of what they'd just learned tonight?

"We need to look at DeSalles," Manny said, pulling his laptop out of his backpack. Rex went to get another beer while Digger knelt beside Manny, bending over his computer screen. Ten minutes of searching through every hit that came up led them finally to a listing for an agricultural products business in Clovis, eastern New Mexico. It said DeSalles owned the company. Manny's fingers danced over the keyboard as he explored the company website. A tap on a link brought up a gallery of staff photos. There, listed as a salesman, was—surprise, surprise—a picture of a much younger Chris Lovington!

CHAPTER 40

Tony Kramer sat in the rental car with his head in his hands, wondering how he was going to get through the next couple of hours. He had to persuade Chris Lovington to allow work on the solar project to restart. If not—well, he didn't know what to do. It seemed like his life was unraveling. Last night, Janet had told him she was talking to her ex-husband again and she wanted to patch things up. Kramer's dream of moving to New Mexico, she said, just didn't work for her. He wasn't right for her. Everything he'd lived for in the last six months had been about Janet. Her words tore at his heart, but he still had to earn a living until he could find a new church to pastor.

Kramer got out of the car, found a bench to sit on, and stared at his shoes. Lovington had said he would be in Albuquerque that morning and asked Kramer to meet him in a parking lot beside a trail close to the Rio Grande. He wanted to walk and talk in the open air. The highly polished loafers Kramer was wearing were not right for trail walking. Nor was his office-casual clothing. He closed his eyes and wished he were somewhere else. His phone pinged a message. Lovington had arrived and would meet him by the Porta-Potty structure in the southwest corner of the parking lot.

When he looked around, he saw Lovington walking toward him, dressed in a fleece jacket, cargo pants, and eminently suitable hiking boots. Kramer felt like an idiot in his office clothes.

"Hi, Tony," Lovington greeted him. "Thanks for meeting me here. I know it's unusual, but I get tired of being cooped up in Santa Fe."

He led the way onto a paved trail with a channel of water on their left and a forest area to their right. Lovington had walked this path many times. He would have preferred diverging into the forest, but one glance at Kramer's shoes told him it wouldn't be a good idea. He knew why Kramer had asked for the meeting and he knew he held it in his power to let work go ahead on the solar project. He liked Kramer. The man was a pastor and they had recognized each other at a spiritual level. Despite all his doubts about Solar GRX, he wanted to trust Kramer. Or was it because what Kramer promised him fit in with what had led him to where he was?

Lovington felt at home here on the trail where the air was cool and brisk. Sunlight glinted on the water, warming one side of his body. The cottonwood trees were half bare, their yellow-brown leaves drifting around them. A group of brightly-clad cyclists pedaled past, chattering amongst each other. Lovington walked for a few minutes without speaking. Now he slowed, turning to Kramer. "You asked for this meeting because you want me to allow work to go ahead on the solar project, isn't that right?"

Kramer nodded, "Yes, we do want to keep going. We've made some good progress, including agreements with the pueblo and a major utility. It would be a shame to see all that work go to waste."

Lovington agreed. He wanted to approve this project. He wanted to ignore the nagging doubts. He turned to Kramer and smiled. "The idea of all those solar panels out there in the desert, it was like a dream come true for me."

As they walked along, away from the constraints of his office, Lovington felt his spirits lift. His mind strayed to fond memories of his early days. "I grew up in Clovis," he said, staring ahead, "It's a small town in eastern New Mexico, everything there is either about ranching or Cannon Air Force base. I never had much ambition and went off to Eastern New Mexico U. at Portales, came home, and thought I was doing well when I got a job with Bill DeSalles, the agricultural machinery dealer."

He paused for a few steps while his mind dwelt on recollections of working for DeSalles—the guy with big visions. How proud he'd been when DeSalles promoted him into sales and praised his skills. When DeSalles announced his intention to run for governor, Lovington jumped at the chance to volunteer in the campaign. Never mind that DeSalles had never held any political office, Lovington liked his boss's outlook.

Aloud he said, "Bill DeSalles was always talking about how New Mexico ought to be more independent from the federal government. Energy was his big thing. He told me he'd seen the wind turbines at the Llano Estacado site at Texico, just east of Clovis. There were only three of them, and they weren't very big, but he kept talking about them, saying power from the wind and the sun was the path of the future."

Lovington paused, thinking of DeSalles' booming voice, big chest, and thick sweep of sandy red hair. Everything about DeSalles exuded the confidence he, Chris Lovington, had long aspired to. He confessed to Kramer, "When Bill talked, it was like a call from God. He could have said jump and I'd have said 'how high.'"

He paused for a few steps, then sighed. "I should have listened to my dad. He warned me Bill wasn't who he made out to be."

"How so?" Kramer asked, forgetting about the pain in his feet from walking in his stiff office shoes.

Lovington later wondered why he'd started in on that story, because he knew it would lead him into that dark place he hated. But Kramer was a pastor, versed in listening and compassion. He felt he and Lovington had established trust. Once he started, the words just flowed.

He'd been so young, in his early twenties. He got a chance to go to Albuquerque. For a young guy from a place like Clovis it was like visiting the big city. He'd heard about the hookers on East Central and was curious. That night, he got a taxi to drop him off and he went looking for excitement. He hadn't been walking long when he saw a young girl with a much older guy. She was wearing a tank top and shorts that barely covered her crotch. Her face had the sloppy vacant look of someone who was totally wasted. He wasn't sure if the older guy was helping her or dragging her along.

Back then he loved photography and carried a pocket camera with him everywhere. When the couple got close, he snapped a few shots of them. He didn't think much of it at the time because the rest of the night was a bust.

At work on Monday, he was in the break room when he saw a copy of the Clovis paper with a front-page story about Orlando Garcia, the guy DeSalles was running against. He couldn't believe it. He recognized Garcia as the man he'd seen with the girl on Central. He was still staring at the paper when DeSalles came in and he'd joked with him, saying "Hey, guess who I saw in Albuquerque on Saturday night?"

Lovington remembered the way his boss had looked at the photo he'd taken, the grin that oozed across his face, the congratulatory thump of DeSalles' fist on his shoulder as he said, "This is pay-dirt, Chris. This is gonna be my ticket to the governor's mansion."

All these years later, he still asked himself why he showed

DeSalles the photo? Why did he listen to his sordid plan? And why was he so eager for DeSalles' approval that he went along with it? The plan DeSalles outlined was to use the picture for campaign fliers and ads insinuating that Garcia was consorting with, maybe even trafficking, teenage girls.

Lovington abruptly stopped walking, as if the memory was still toxic. Kramer, whose feet were increasingly painful, noticed a bench just ahead and suggested they sit for a while.

Lovington approached it and sat down, feeling as though he were still inhabiting a decades-old agonizing reality.

"What happened then?" Kramer prompted.

Lovington continued the story, his voice dreamlike. "It was radioactive for Garcia. He said he worked for a charity, and he was taking the girl to a shelter. But there was no way he could live down that picture. He shut down his campaign and about a month later he died in a car crash. The family accused DeSalles of driving him to suicide."

Kramer closed his eyes as he listened to Lovington's ugly revelations. He wanted to be the man he used to be, a pastor who cared for lost souls seeking salvation, not the salesman for some shady company's sunshine solution. Lovington's next words jolted him.

"Garcia's family tracked me down. They blamed me for ruining Garcia's bid for governor. I got threatening phone calls from his kids, Julia and Randy. It got so bad I had to take out a restraining order to protect myself from them."

Kramer's eyes snapped open. Did Lovington just say that family name? "Randy Garcia? That was Orlando's son?"

Lovington's head swiveled around, his eyes blinking as if awakened from a trance. "Yeah, his real name is Raul, but he's always been called Randy."

Kramer's stomach clenched. Suddenly it all made sense. The name itself was the synapse! It was the missing piece in his memory. He wavered. Should he tell Lovington what he knew? If he told him, was there still a chance he would allow the project to go ahead? Would that give him a chance to get his life on track again? Could he get Janet back? And if he didn't tell Lovington, would he be falling into the same trap as Lovington when he agreed to DeSalles' plan to distribute the photograph and destroy Garcia's dream of becoming governor?

Kramer stared ahead. The paved path looked out over a narrow channel of water and beyond it stood a Territorial style house with spacious lawns. In the distance, he could see the blue outline of the Sandia Mountains. The words of a Psalm drifted through his head, "I will lift up mine eyes unto the hills, from whence cometh my help." He closed his eyes to still the pounding in his head.

"Chris, you need to know," Kramer admitted, "Randy Garcia is the man behind Solar GRX."

Lovington exhaled a long slow breath, then another. Seconds passed. He stood, and said, "I might have known." Then, without looking at Kramer, he stood and began to walk back in the direction they'd come from. Kramer didn't move. Lovington was about twenty feet away when he turned around. "I know you came here to persuade me to allow the solar project to proceed. That project is really important to me. But I have fifteen million dollars and thousands of taxpayers to think about. If you can convince me that the investors are ready to go ahead, then I'll give the okay. If not, I can't. I'm sure you understand."

Kramer nodded, but he couldn't so much as move a muscle. He knew what he had to do next.

CHAPTER 41

All the way back to Santa Fe, Kramer kept wondering how he could convince Janet to change her mind and stay with him. She'd always said she wanted a new life, wanted to be free to be herself, be true to her spirit. Maybe they could find their way together here in New Mexico. The sight of the mountains inspired him with hope. Yet as soon as he got back to the La Quinta hotel room on Cerillos Road, reality hit. He was staying here in this bland chain hotel far from the city center because Janet didn't want to come with him on this trip. He sat on the bed, phone in hand, trying to pray. Finally, he tapped her number and waited, heart thumping.

"Hi, it's me."

"I know." Silence, then, "Tony, I can't do this anymore."

"But..."

"No. It's no use. I called Jeff this morning and quit. You know as well as I do this whole thing isn't going to pan out. You should get out now before these people burn you."

He heard genuine concern in her voice. "Janet, isn't there some other way? Couldn't we...?"

"I have to go now, Tony. Take care."

Then, just like that, she was gone, erasing him from her life. Tears stung his eyes and coursed down his cheeks. He curled over, head on knees, groaning. Minutes went by. Then, a tiny flicker of rage ignited, spreading until it filled his chest. Fists balled, he thumped on the bed as hard as he could. He took deep breaths. He needed to calm himself. He needed to refocus his thoughts, rehearse what he would say to Randy.

A woman he recognized as Jeff's assistant answered the phone. She told him Randy was unavailable. Kramer kept his tone light but firm. "Please have him call me as soon as possible. Tell him I have news about the solar project."

Ten minutes later his phone buzzed.

"Hey, Tony! I hear you've got something on this little project of ours."

"Yeah. I had a good meeting with Chris Lovington this morning."

"So, are we back in business?" Randy was all genial excitement.

"Well, he's prepared to give the go-ahead as soon as we provide proof that we have the investment backing."

He could almost feel the force of Randy's anger when he said, "Goddammit, Tony, he's just jerking us around!"

His tone fueled Kramer's resolve. At this point he had nothing to lose. "No," he said, slowly. "I think Chris has a very good point. He's a state official, he has fifteen million dollars of public money at stake, and he's running for governor."

He braced for another verbal assault, but this time Randy's tone was soft and cajoling. "I'm disappointed in you, Tony. Jeff spoke so highly of you."

Kramer had heard enough. "Maybe you can convince him yourself, Randy. As of right now, I'm resigning."

Randy switched back to hostile in an instant. "Listen to me Tony, you can't just quit. You've got obligations."

"Well, you haven't paid me for last month yet, and I've had Izzy complaining to me that she hasn't been paid either. I'm gone."

"You're going to regret this."

"Are you threatening me the way you threatened Chris all those years ago?"

Silence.

"Yeah, Chris told me everything," Kramer said.

Click.

Manny was arguing with his editor about the way he wanted to change the lead on his story. He was about to point out that although the wording his editor wanted might sound better, it didn't make sense technically and might even be factually incorrect, when—at that very moment—the theme music from "Mission Impossible" blared from his back pocket. Manny yanked out his phone and saw Kramer's name. "I've got to take this," he said.

The editor frowned. "Okay," he said, to Manny's retreating figure, "But get me a new lead and put something online as soon as you can."

Kramer sounded like a totally different person. Instead of the smoothly confident salesman-like tone, he spoke fast, his voice tense. He wanted to meet, saying it was urgent. He gave his hotel address and asked Manny if he could bring the "other reporter." Manny was momentarily confused. "What other reporter?" Kramer huffed with impatience. "That young woman, you know: the one that calls herself Digger. She needs to hear this too."

As soon as he got off the call with Kramer, Manny phoned Digger and told her about the meeting. Twenty minutes later, Manny turned off Cerillos Road when he spotted the familiar La Quinta sign and faux-Spanish architecture. The hotel complex occupied a chunk of real estate between a restaurant coyly named

"The Flying Tortilla" and a Kelly's liquor store. He pulled into the parking lot and looked around for Digger's car. He wasn't sure if she would be able to find an excuse to get away, but a moment later he saw the gray Subaru turn in.

She parked, got out, glanced at the hotel entrance, and winked at him. "Do you think we'll look like we need to rent a room for an hour?"

Manny waggled his eyebrows. "I'll remember this address for a future date. Come on, now. Kramer's room is at the back and he's kind of gone haywire, so I'm just saying don't be surprised."

Kramer opened the door and hustled them in. His normally perfect hair was mussed, his shirt half unbuttoned, his laptop was open on the desk, and papers lay scattered around it. He motioned for them to sit on the bed while he dropped onto the only chair. Manny sat awkwardly on one corner of the bed, Digger took the other corner and pulled a notebook out of her backpack.

Manny retrieved his own notebook and addressed Kramer quietly. "So, what gives, Tony?"

Kramer rubbed a hand over his face. His eyes were sunken, as though he were sleep-deprived. He studied them, took a gulp of water from the glass on the desk, and started talking. His stream-of-consciousness narrative went on and on. Manny and Digger scribbled notes as he outlined his work as a pastor, how he'd fallen for Janet, got fired from the church, and finally, had been approached by Jeff to sell the solar project. "I thought it was a great idea. I'd been doing some part-time work for Jeff, so that seemed the natural extension. Then he said he was going to be getting involved in something big in New Mexico. That's when he introduced me to this guy called Randy Garcia, saying we'd all be "business partners" for this important project."

Digger gave Manny a wary glance. "What was Randy's role?" she asked.

"That was the thing," Kramer continued, "It seemed like Randy was calling the shots, but he kept in the background. Never wanted his name on anything; insisted everything went through Jeff. He was the one who pointed me to Chris Lovington. I contacted Chris and we immediately connected. He talked about his passion to support renewable energy, and how he wanted to make it a key part of his election campaign."

Kramer said Jeff agreed to hire Janet to help with the project, explaining that Randy insisted it be under a different contract. Kramer said they told him she'd be paid through a different financial backer, but they never revealed who that was.

"Did you ever see Janet's contract?" Manny asked.

Kramer shook his head and exhaled. "No. Never."

Digger and Manny exchanged a glance, then looked back at Kramer who wiped his forehead and continued. "Anyway, I need to tell you the real reason that I had to meet with both of you today. This morning I met Chris Lovington and what he told me made me quit the project." He paused, looking at them both as though weighing his next words. "Judging from what he said, I've come to think Randy Garcia is just using the solar project to frame Chris because of what happened a long time ago."

Digger's brain immediately raced to the question that had been tormenting her since they talked to Rex. "Did Chris Lovington take that picture?"

Kramer's jaw fell. "You know about THAT picture?"?

"Yes, we've been doing a lot of homework on this, Tony," Manny said. "We know that Lovington worked for a guy named Bill DeSalles in Clovis, who campaigned as a Libertarian. We know that DeSalles not only ran ads but circulated fliers with a photo that showed Garcia in a compromising situation with an underage girl and that Garcia ended his own campaign and died in a car accident soon afterward."

Kramer's eyes darted from Manny to Digger. He licked his lips.

"You're right. That's what Chris told me this morning. He said Garcia's family learned DeSalles was the one responsible for the ads and blamed him for what happened. He said they threatened him, and he even filed a restraining order against them."

Digger's mind went back to the conversation she'd had with the mayor in Texas. "Does Chris Lovington think there's a link between Randy Garcia's threat back then and his involvement with the solar project now?"

Kramer frowned as if he'd considered that possibility too. He finally admitted, "All Chris said was 'I might have known.'"

They left Kramer sitting morosely at the end of his bed in the hotel room. He'd agreed they could use what he'd told them, but he didn't know if Lovington would agree to talk. The election was less than a month away and his opponents' ads slammed him for the solar project, saying it was a 'Flaming waste of taxpayer money.'

"Do you think we can get anything on this Garcia guy?" Digger said. Manny turned and grinned. "If there was a restraining order on him, I'll sure as hell find it."

CHAPTER 42

Digger had to jump aside as a tall man in a navy blazer and tan slacks marched across the lobby heading for the door. As he brushed past she noticed his handsome face was contorted with fury. But he was gone before Digger could throw the insult that rose to her lips. She swung around and noticed Marigold Ellis watching from the doorway of her office.

"Who the hell was that and who shat on his shoes?" Digger said.

"That," Ellis said, "was the secretary's brother."

Digger's jaw dropped. "Randy Garcia?"

Ellis nodded. "He used to come in here a lot, but I haven't seen him in a few months."

"He didn't look very happy," Digger noted.

Ellis folded her arms across her ample chest and frowned. "No. And in fact, I was going to come looking for you about that. I'll be leaving at five. Can you get away then so we could go have some coffee, I'd like to run something by you."

This was not like the secret donut-snacker Marigold Ellis with which Digger was familiar. Something had rattled her. Digger glanced at the clock on the far wall. It was already close to five. They'd spent longer than she realized talking with Kramer. She hoped Julia Montoya hadn't been looking for her. She checked her phone—no messages. Good. She turned back to Marigold. "I need to check a few things at my desk. You know the Inn of the Governors on Alameda? I'll meet you at the bar there about five-fifteen, okay?"

As soon as she got to her desk, Digger laid out her laptop and swiftly typed up the notes she had taken while Kramer talked. It sounded as though Randy Garcia's involvement with the solar project was a bizarre form of revenge against Chris Lovington. But why go to such lengths? If he wanted to wreck Lovington's political career, why not just plant rumors or craft an insinuating flier the way DeSalles did. Kramer seemed to have gone along with everything without asking many questions. And what about Janet Macy? Kramer had said hardly anything about her. Why was she hired under a different contract? And what did it have to do with Julia Montoya?

The chatter of voices made Digger realize her colleagues were packing up and leaving. She had a deadline for another presentation, but she figured that could wait. She'd just have to make up for lost time tomorrow. Meanwhile, she wanted to hear what Marigold had to say.

Marigold had ensconced herself in a cozy corner by the fireplace, at the Inn's Del Charro Saloon. She was not drinking coffee. The liquid in the thick-glassed tumbler on the table in front of her had the pale gold look of whisky. Digger slid into a seat opposite Marigold and watched as she took a sip of her drink, savored the taste, then gave a mischievous grin. "My father used to prefer a whisky called Famous Grouse. I like to indulge myself in his memory. Care to try one?"

Digger thought about the long drive home and decided now was not the time to enlarge her alcoholic repertoire. She ordered a Corona.

"So, what was it you needed to talk to me about?" Marigold's playful mood evaporated. She set down the glass and leaned forward, face deadly serious. "I've worked in state government for a long time, and I've been at this department for more than ten years. I've seen politicians come and go, but I don't like what I've seen happen lately."

"How so?"

Marigold glanced around the bar, then leaned even closer. "I had to take some copies into Julia this afternoon and when I got to her office the door was shut and I heard shouting inside. It was Julia and her brother Randy—you know, the one you saw storming out of the building. She sounded very upset, she kept saying, "I told you we could have done this another way." Then he shouted back, "You agreed to the plan. We did it for Papa." That's when she got really angry. It sounded like she said, "Okay, but why didn't you hire her?" and that's when he said to her, "You said you'd find a way to help us because we didn't have the money to pay her." Marigold eyed Digger over her thick glasses, gauging her reaction.

Digger met her gaze, thoughts racing. She had her own ideas, but she wanted to hear what Marigold might say. "Do you know anything about the plan they mentioned?"

Marigold picked up her glass and swallowed the rest of the contents, winced, then, eyes hard, she said. "I think you know. You were asking about the contract for that woman Jill Franks and the secretary had you following that solar project. I bet you think it's all connected."

Digger had to chuckle. She'd had Marigold Ellis figured all wrong. Sure, she had the air of an indulgent grandmother who had a sweet tooth and loved a little flattery, but she had sharp eyes—and she was no fool.

"Yep," said Digger, "I think Julia Montoya created a fake contract for Jill Franks, who was really Janet Macy, the woman with the solar project. From what you just told me, it sounds like Julia and her brother cooked up the deal together." She looked at Marigold, eyebrows raised. "What are you going to do about it?"

Marigold waved a hand toward the bar and ordered another Famous Grouse. Then she turned back to Digger, grinned, and said, "I have a friend in the attorney general's office. I thought I'd put a word in the right ear. Then I'm going to retire."

Kramer answered the knock on the hotel room door but before he could say anything the first blow knocked him back against the doorframe. Pain shot from his cheek through his skull. Murphy's eyes blazed with fury. He struck again with his fist. This time it hit him in the left shoulder. Brain scrambled, arms flailing, Kramer tried vainly to ward off another punch.

"Help!" He shouted.

"You idiot! You think you can just walk out on us like that!" Murphy snarled, "You get back on the phone now and tell Randy you made a mistake."

"Help me!" Kramer shouted again, hoping someone in the parking lot or one of the other rooms would come to his aid.

"Call Randy! Now!" Murphy said, stabbing a finger into his chest.

"Okay," Kramer gulped, "Let me get my phone. It's in the bathroom." He ducked quickly back inside the hotel room, but not before Murphy shoved his arm forward to hold the door open and stepped inside. Kramer hustled to the bathroom, pulled the phone out of his back pocket, and dialed 911. "Help, I'm being assaulted, La Quinta hotel, Cerillos Road, I'm on the ground floor on the south side. Please help me!"

Murphy was already halfway across the room, yelling again. "What the f...!" He began but a shout stopped him.

"Hey, what's going on in there? I'm gonna call the cops!" A

tall burly man in a black Steelers sweatshirt was standing in the doorway. Murphy swung round, hands falling to his side. he put on a smile. "Oh, nothing. My friend and I just had a little misunderstanding. Everything's fine."

"He's lying!" Kramer yelled and slipped past Murphy. The skin on his cheek burned where Murphy's fist had struck, and he could feel the tissue beginning to swell. He hoped the man could see it. He did.

"Looks like a little more than a misunderstanding, if you ask me, mister," He glared at Murphy.

"Nobody's asking you," Murphy snapped and made to push past him and out the door. The man barred his way.

"Not so fast." The three of them were standing on the threshold, Murphy eyeing the other two as if trying to decide whether he could talk his way out of the situation, when a squad car pulled into the parking lot.

It was almost dark by the time Digger turned off the freeway toward Los Jardines. A faint glow from the west cast the mountains in a deep blue. Lights in the expensive homes on the ridge line penetrated the shadow of the long valley that wound toward the village. A freeze was predicted for tonight, but the little house was probably already toasty warm from the fire that flickered in the wood burning stove. She arrived home to the unmistakable smell of green chile and found Abuela at work in the kitchen. "Oh Abuela, you spoil us!" she said, patting the old woman on the shoulder.

"You're my girls and I love you, so why shouldn't I spoil you! Maria said she's running late and will be here any minute. She had another meeting, of course." As if on cue, the familiar sound of her car engine said she'd arrived. The gate creaked and moments later Maria walked in. Digger took the shoulder bag from her, set it down in the nearest chair, and wrapped her in a full body hug. "It feels like I haven't seen you in so long!"

They had just finished their meal when Manny's call came. Digger eyed his number, tempted to let it go to voicemail. She wanted an evening with Maria—just the both of them, without thinking about the election or the solar project.

"If it's Manny, you should answer it," Maria said. Digger didn't want to, but she did.

"Guess what! Manny said in a rush. "Danny Murphy was arrested at the La Quinta for assaulting one of the guests."

"Kramer?"

"You got it."

CHAPTER 43

One Week Before Election Day

The story appeared a week before elections—front page, top of the fold, under the headline that read "Sunshine hopes clouded by investor worries at SLO solar site. He read it again:

> "Details remain unclear about the mysterious company behind a proposed solar array on state-owned land between San Fermin Pueblo and Las Vistas. State Land Commissioner Chris Lovington, who announced the project in June, pledged $15 million in state incentives, saying that the solar site would bring jobs and economic development to the area, while reducing dependence on fossil fuels.
>
> Under the contract, Solar GRX, the Arizona-based company behind the deal, is entitled to the incentive money as soon as it begins work on the project. But Solar GRX has yet to publicly reveal the names of any major investors. The company website shows no history of similar projects, and the office address is at a UPS store in Phoenix."

Then came his own quote, where he'd pointed out that he'd halted work on the project as doubts about the company mounted because he didn't want to risk state money. That's when the hard questions started. At first, Manny had asked around if publicity about the solar project would hurt his chances of being elected. Then the questions started rolling in. Did he think Solar GRX was genuine? Did he think the company's lack of transparency was deliberate? Might there be a political motivation behind it? Meanwhile, Lovington continued to deny it all, saying he had established a good relationship with the Solar GRX representatives, and he was confident the project would be good for New Mexico.

Part of that was true. Besides, he'd trusted Kramer. Why? He'd agonized over that plenty in the last few days. The more he thought about it, the more he had to admit it was because Kramer had previously been a pastor. Despite his salesman-like demeanor, he'd always thought he saw sincerity in Kramer's eyes, especially the last time they talked: when he'd shared his burden of guilt. When he'd learned about Randy Garcia.

Manny's article went on to say that he had tried to reach Garcia himself, but the man had not responded. Manny had even talked to Kramer, and he'd done his homework. He'd dug into all the old stories—though Bill DeSalles was no longer alive to interview—but he'd also talked to people in Clovis. He knew about the photograph, Randy's father, the threats, the restraining order. It was all there, all the sordid deeds he had tried so hard to keep hidden all these years.

While doing his research, he'd also found out Garcia was involved with a similar project in Texas that sabotaged an election. It was this last point that hit home. When Kramer had told him Randy was behind the solar project Lovington had wondered about his motive. Now he asked himself again, did Randy create this whole solar sham as an act of revenge because of his father? So that he, Chris Lovington, would lose the election and be publicly shamed for being stupid, naïve, and wasting millions in taxpayer money?

———◆———

Kramer looked at himself in the mirror. The swelling under his eye had subsided but the tissue around it was still a brownish purple. He read the article again and wondered what Chris Lovington was thinking now. He felt adrift. No Janet, no job, just the sickening thought that he'd allowed himself to be manipulated and walked into it with eyes wide open. He decided to call Jeff, the man who'd offered him a chance when the church threw him out over the affair with Janet. He held the phone in his hand, staring at Jeff's number on the screen. What would he say?

Did he want Jeff's help? No, he just wanted answers. He punched the number.

"Hey, Tony!" Jeff's tone was friendly, upbeat. Kramer wondered if Jeff had talked to Randy. Did he know what Murphy had done to him?

He cleared his throat. "Hi Jeff, I really need to talk with you about a few things."

"Sure, sure."

"You know I quit. I couldn't do it anymore."

A long sigh from Jeff. "Tony, don't you think you jumped the gun on this? We were really very close to starting work."

Kramer had already prepared to hear that accusation before he called. He liked Jeff, he did. They'd made such a good connection through the Fellowship at the church. But he wondered if the man really believed what he was saying. Now, there was no point in delaying. He had called because he needed to explain his position and ask the real question.

"Jeff, I told you I can't do that anymore. What I need to know is what was this all about?"

A long silence followed. Kramer stared at the bland walls of his hated apartment. He'd asked the big question. What would he do with the big answer? He didn't know. A long exhale, then Jeff said, "I guess I may as well tell you. After all, you trusted me. Remember how I was developing that subdivision with the solar panels? That place where high-dollar people could be off the grid if they wanted to? About then, I met Randy and he told me he'd worked in the industry and installed solar arrays on a big scale. Said there was a real future in it, good money to be made. He convinced me we could work together. He said he had all these connections in New Mexico he could put me in touch with. Said he wanted to stay in the background, for personal reasons. That should've been a red flag for me, but I just saw dollar signs. I thought maybe I could make a lot of money, too."

Jeff paused and sighed heavily. "You'd been helping me with some publicity and then you had that trouble with the church. By the way, I'm sorry about Janet. I heard she's back with her husband. Anyway, I knew you were in a bad way. That's why I offered you the job."

Kramer's ribs hurt. Nausea spread through his gut at Jeff's words. He thought of Lovington's story about the photograph and his part in ruining Orlando Garcia. But Jeff wasn't quite finished explaining.

"Once we'd settled on where the solar site would be, I got in touch with Danny Murphy. I'd known him way back when he and Johnny Raposa were developing in Scottsdale, and I'd heard he was planning a subdivision close to the solar site. Randy was happy to bring him in and we got together and talked about how it could be a win-win for all of us. But we needed investors to get the ball rolling. Murphy agreed to put up some money and that's exactly what we used to pay you."

Alarm bells rang for Kramer. "So why was Janet under a different contract through some New Mexico State agency?" he asked.

"Well, Murphy didn't have enough money for the startup, so Randy said he'd get help from his sister. He made it sound like she needed to be involved."

Kramer was running out of patience. Sure, Jeff had helped him out when he needed it, but he'd been duped and Murphy had attacked him, apparently on Randy's orders.

"Jeff, be honest with me. Were there ever really any investors? Or were you just going to take the state money?"

"Don't make it sound like that. We could have started work even without any investors and, according to the contract, so long as we "started" work on the project we were entitled to the startup money. It was all legal."

"Was Janet's contract legal?"

"Hmm," said Jeff, "That I don't know. "We didn't handle that. I guess Randy's sister did."

CHAPTER 44

The next morning, thick gray clouds pregnant with moisture loomed close over the Sandias. It hardly ever snowed this early, but the forecast predicted a frigid flow of air swooping down from Canada. Digger kept an eye on the weather as she followed the conga line of red taillights proceeding toward Santa Fe. If it did snow, the drive home could be tricky.

Right now, she didn't need any more stress. With the election just days away, Maria was jumpy and tense. Murphy's arrest was splashed all over TV and print news. Kramer was pressing charges, but Murphy's supporters weren't fazed. A group of them staged a protest outside the county courthouse. Manny's article provoked an even bigger media furor over the governor's race between Chris Lovington and Tom Sears. Hours after the story appeared the Twitter-sphere lit up with comments like "Sunshine Fantasy now a Nightmare" and "Solar Flop." Sears and his supporters painted Lovington's support for the solar project as an example of rampant corruption. Lovington's campaign hit back calling Sears a "Fossil Fuel Dinosaur" and accusing him of pandering to out-of-state corporations. He defended himself, saying he was a leader who would make New Mexico energy independent.

Digger read the comments and shook her head. No one seemed to see what she saw as the real issue. That the whole solar project was a giant scam planned and executed by a guy obsessed with getting perverse revenge against the man he believed had caused his father to commit suicide. She wondered what Julia Montoya's reaction would be.

———

Digger didn't have long to wait. If the air felt chilly when she got out of her car in Santa Fe, it was chillier still inside the Cultural Affairs Department. She sensed the atmosphere as soon as she walked into the building. Marigold Ellis was huddled by the door of her office with a couple of other women. They were speaking in hushed voices, glancing nervously down the corridor that led to Montoya's office. Digger approached and threw an inquiring glance at Marigold.

"What's going on?"

Marigold grabbed her arm, pulling her into the group. "There are some investigators here. They're going through the records we keep." She gave Digger a knowing look. Digger raised an eyebrow and nodded slowly. Marigold clearly hadn't wasted any time contacting her friend at the attorney general's office.

Digger continued toward her own area. She was almost there when she saw the door to Montoya's office open and two men come out. They wore dark suits and somber expressions. Neither smiled as they walked past her. Julia Montoya stood framed in the doorway, her face pale, hands tensed. Her eyes met Digger's. She beckoned Digger to come in and closed the door behind them.

Montoya walked over to the window and looked out at the gray sky. Even from where she stood, Digger could see a few light flakes of snow floating gently through the air. She waited.

Finally, Montoya turned around, her face an angry red. "I read the article," she said, "I don't think you were honest with me about how close you were with that reporter. That story had someone else's byline, but you gave him all the information, didn't you?"

Digger's heart raced and she took a large breath, trying to control her mounting anger. At this moment, she didn't care what Montoya thought. She wanted honesty, too. "Yes, I helped him with the research because that story needed to be made public. There were fifteen million dollars at stake."

Montoya's shoulders rose and fell. She fingered the silver pendant at her throat. Her dark eyes blazed. She grimaced, revealing a tiny smear of lipstick on one front tooth. "Well, we can stop pretending," Montoya said. "I'm glad you worked with him. That was why I asked you to keep an eye on the project. I knew a former reporter like you would suspect something and we wanted somebody to expose it. Why?" She paused; her face contorted into a sneer. "So, Chris Lovington would look like the murderous idiot he is." Her edgy laugh bordered on hysteria. She strode toward Digger, stopping just inches away. She was close enough that Digger could see a black eyeliner smudge under one eye. "What I didn't expect," she hissed, "was for you to knife me in the back. Yes, I know why the investigators showed up today!"

Digger didn't move. At this point, she had nothing to lose. "The Jill Franks contract?" she snapped. "So, what are you going to do? Fire me?"

Montoya drew herself up. "Oh, no. I'm the one who has to leave," she said bitterly as she stabbed a red-nailed finger into Digger's chest. "I want you to know my father was an honorable man. He was a good father. He was helping that girl, and that man—Chris Lovington—ruined his reputation and ruined the honor of my family!"

Digger felt as if she'd fallen into some kind of alternate reality. It was as if the always composed Julia Montoya, with her expensive jewelry, impeccable fashion sense, superb make up, and stylish hair, had suddenly shattered into a hundred pieces. Digger tried to find sympathy for her but all she could think of was that Montoya was perfectly aware of what she was doing.

"You knew that contract was illegal—and that there was a risk you'd be found out. If your brother pressured you into doing it, he should go down too," Digger said.

"Randy has already gone. You will never catch up with him." And with that, she turned away and walked out without bothering to shut the door behind her.

Digger sat at her desk, staring at the blank computer screen, unable to focus. After Montoya's abrupt departure she had instinctively texted Manny, letting him know about the investigators. The adrenaline that had ebbed away was replaced by disbelief as the full impact of Montoya's words hit home.

Montoya and her brother had made Digger part of their plan from the very beginning, and she had walked right in, believing all the while that she was doing the right thing. Yes, she had helped expose a multimillion-dollar scam. That had stopped Randy Garcia and the other guys behind Solar GRX, and probably Danny Murphy as well, from getting their hands on a share of the fifteen million. But, now she understood the whole scenario. Randy's real motive was to destroy Chris Lovington's political career in the same way Lovington had ruined the career of Randy's father. All the work she had done with Manny had probably accomplished that. She felt used, and it felt awful.

Halfway through the afternoon, a TV news alert came in on her phone. "Cultural Affairs Department Secretary Julia Montoya to step down." Moments later, Manny called. She let it ring. If she answered she knew she would have to tell him everything, and she just couldn't face all of that right now. Digger put her elbows on the desk and let her head drop in her hands.

Snow was still falling lightly as Digger left the courthouse and headed home. Trees and houses stood out starkly like a block print against the blue-white background of snow. Just beyond La Bajada Hill traffic slowed to a crawl and she could see the flashing lights of pileups in the distance. The unfamiliar weather had apparently claimed its first victims. Digger groaned.

It took her forty-five minutes longer than usual to make it back to Los Jardines. She'd once had doubts about moving in with Abuela, but she was glad of it now. The little adobe house, nestled within its hollyhock-lined walls was a refuge from the world. A fire was burning in the wood stove and the tiny living room was warm and snug. Best of all, Maria was already home, curled on the sofa with Lady Antonia on her lap. On spotting Digger, she dumped the cat aside and ran to her. "Thank God, you made it! I was worried about you on the freeway in this weather."

Digger sank into the hug. It was exactly what she needed here and now.

CHAPTER 45

It was election day. Digger woke in the dark, listening to the comforting sound of Maria's breathing. It would be time to get up soon. What would the day bring? She knew how much Maria wanted the chance to be a state legislator. If she won, would the dream be everything she hoped? The position would mean all kinds of new demands.

The legislature meets only thirty or sixty days, depending on the year, but there would be committee work. Constituents would be often contacting her, venting their grievances, and airing their demands. It could be dangerous too. Only last year, shots had been fired at the homes of two state legislators after they voted for a law to protect access to reproductive health care. Being "out" made her a target too.

Digger squeezed her eyes shut and told herself to stop worrying. Maria was a strong woman and if she didn't win today, she would always find a new cause. That was who she was and why she admired her.

Right now, Digger wondered more about her own immediate future. Montoya's abrupt resignation meant she wouldn't have to face her again.; however, it would be up to the new governor—depending on the result of today's election—to appoint a new

Cultural Affairs Secretary. She wondered if Lovington still had a chance. That sick feeling washed over her again as she thought of Montoya's revelation. She hadn't yet told Manny; she would wait to see how the votes played out today.

Tony Kramer looked at himself in the bathroom mirror. The bruising around his left eye had ebbed to the color of a mashed overripe banana. After the fight, Murphy's arrest, and the story about him that came out in the papers, he didn't know what to do or where to turn.

He'd tried praying. After all, he'd been a pastor, so he'd guided and comforted hundreds of people over the years. He tried reading the Bible that he kept in his nightstand drawer, but solace eluded him. He'd been a fraud. He'd deliberately ignored all the warning signs. If only he could be with Janet. Now Janet was gone. So, he sat in his bedroom and thought. Today, he knew, was election day and he thought about Chris Lovington.

In Santa Fe, the State Land Commissioner paced around his office. Sheridan had come to see him that morning. He arrived without warning, just a knock on the door and there he was, his tall frame filling the doorway, dark wool overcoat and check muffler tucked around his neck. At the sight of the outgoing governor, shame seeped through Lovington, as if his heart were leaking a corrosive fluid.

After brief greetings they'd sat awkwardly staring at each other. Sheridan's face was even paler than the last time they had met. His wife had died the previous month and he had hardly spoken to him since the funeral. Lovington wondered if he should express condolences again. But he knew Sheridan was here to talk about the election, so he waited.

Finally, the governor emitted a long sigh. "I'm disappointed in you Chris. I had hoped you could carry on my legacy."

"I know." There wasn't much else Lovington could say. There were no excuses. He'd risked too much, and it had all come crashing down. Did he still stand a chance with the voters? He'd soon know. In the meantime, he stared out the window and wondered what to do. If it were Friday, he could go to confession at the cathedral. But would it help? Maybe he could talk to Kramer. The man was a pastor or used to be. Right now, he needed spiritual guidance; and, after all, he and Kramer were lost in the same wilderness of their own making.

The polls closed at seven. Ten minutes later, Digger and Maria pulled up outside the small strip mall office rented by the county Democratic Party. If everything went smoothly, Digger thought, Maria could know the unofficial result within a couple of hours. Then they'd have to wait up to two weeks for the results to be certified to be official. On the other hand, a razor-thin majority might spark a demand for a recount, and that would be a nightmare.

She turned to Maria and squeezed her hand. "Are you ready for this?"

Maria nodded and opened the door. Inside, the heat was suffocating, and the air was thick with the smell of stale coffee. Campaign workers, volunteers, and a couple of candidates from other districts within the county crowded around computers and TV screens.

Everyone was talking on the phone or shouting across the room. Dillon spotted them and hurried over, exuding his familiar odor of unwashed clothing and rancid body. "Hey guys," he said, wrapping his arms around them. "Glad you all made it. I've set up direct links to the county clerk so we can follow the returns pretty much in real-time."

They followed him to a folding card table in the corner where his laptop sat among food wrappers, an empty Starbucks to-go cup, and a ragged brown watch cap. He sat down, took off his glasses, and wiped them on his shirt. Digger and Maria waited, but his attention was already back on the screen.

"Is there somewhere we could sit?" Maria asked.

Dillon looked around as if surprised. "Oh, uh, sure. There's some chairs in that storage closet over there. He pointed to the door behind them. Maria rolled her eyes.

They found a couple of folding metal chairs among brooms and cleaning supplies and set them beside Dillon. His laptop screen showed a list of precincts throughout the district. By punching a few keys, he was able to show a list for statewide races. He consulted his phone. "It's too early for any results yet. It'll be a while. You may as well get some coffee. Somebody's gone out to get pizza.

Over the next half hour, Digger felt like she was back in the newsroom at The Courier. She used to love election nights; the simmering excitement and tension, reporters' voices exploding into the overheated atmosphere like popcorn as they called out results. So-and-so is leading in this district, another trailing there, this one's too close to call. She looked at Maria, in her eyes a mix of anticipation and anxiety. The first few precincts in Las Vistas had reported results in Murphy's favor. She laid an arm on Maria's shoulder. "It's early days yet," she said.

Someone at the other end of the room yelled out "pizza!" Dillon jumped up. "Come on guys, or you won't get any."

Maria shook her head. "I can't eat right now." Digger wasn't hungry either. Dillon returned, his paper plate laden with pepperoni slices. The pizza smell mingling with the stale coffee and Dillon's body made Digger queasy.

They walked toward the front door. Halfway there a wall-mounted TV was showing a news program with election coverage: "And in the governor's race," the announcer was saying.

Digger stopped to listen. "Things are not looking good for Chris Lovington. With about twenty-five percent of precincts reporting, he's trailing his rival Tom Sears from Roswell by almost eight percentage points. Of course, this could all change in the next couple of hours, but it's not a great start. My colleague here has been doing the rounds at polling stations and talking to voters."

The picture cut to a young blond woman holding a microphone as she interviewed a heavyset middle-aged man wearing a baseball cap. "It was that solar thing," the man said, "He shoulda never listened to those people, that coulda hurt us taxpayers big time."

Digger's heart sank. She thought of all the work she'd done with Manny, all along believing she was doing the right thing. Then Montoya's sneer. It was all part of the plan to destroy Lovington.

Maria took Digger's arm and led her away. They went outside and stood for a while, saying nothing as cars whizzed by and the cold ate at them. Maria's voice brought her back to the present. "It's not your fault," she said quietly, "Chris Lovington made his own choices. You did the right thing."

"I know. I just hate being used."

"Come on, we better go back inside." Maria kissed her gently and they went back into the maelstrom.

"Where the hell have you guys been?" Dillon shouted, "We're at nearly ninety percent of precincts reporting and you are pulling ahead, girl." He grabbed Maria's arm and dragged her over to the desk.

Digger followed. Peering at the laptop screen she noticed that the remaining precincts were all in Las Vistas—Murphy's stronghold. It could still go either way.

"And the governor's race?" she asked.

Dillon snorted. "AP's already called it. Lovington went down in flames."

Digger looked at Maria. Her lips mouthed the words "Not your fault!"

Fifteen minutes later it seemed like it was all over. Dillon let out a whoop and flung his arms around Maria. "You did it girl! It's helluva close but you did it!"

Maria hugged him back, then whirled round to grab Digger, tears of joy streaming down her face. Volunteers crowded around, hugging, laughing, and congratulating them.

They finally made it out and were almost at the car, Maria was on her phone to Abuela when they heard Dillon shout. "Hey guys, wait!" He ran toward them. "Bad news!" He panted. Murphy called just now. Said he's going to demand a recount."

Maria's jaw dropped. "No! He can't do that, can he?"

Dillon hung his head. "Yeah, he can. The margin's just under one percent."

CHAPTER 46

One Month Later

The night was already brilliant with stars and the air so cold it bit the skin. Digger was standing by the blue gate waiting for guests to arrive. She thought of the night nearly two years ago when Abuela had invited her to join the family in making tamales on Christmas Eve. She had been an outsider then, afraid of commitment, yet longing for a family. Tonight, they were celebrating Abuela's eighty-first birthday, albeit a little late. Confusion following the election had consumed them all for three agonizing weeks. In the end, the recount Danny Murphy demanded didn't change any votes and at last they could also celebrate Maria's victory.

There was more to be grateful for. When she'd called her grandparents to give them Maria's good news, Grandpa Jack had given her the names of five companies he'd worked with who, he said, were interested in developing solar resources in New Mexico.

"Now she's a real politician, Maria should call them up. Tell them about that location. A lot of the preliminary groundwork's already done," he said.

Digger laughed. "If I know Maria, she'll be on the phone tomorrow. How's the heart?"

"I'm busier than a one-armed monkey with two bananas."

Now, as she looked down the street, she could see Maria's parents' car turn the corner. Ever since the Labor Day barbecue they'd had weekly visits from Consuela and Humberto. Maria's relationship with her mother was still fragile, but at least they could stand side-by-side over a pot of posole without an explosion.

They parked and approached the gate, laden with packages. Consuela wore a coat with a faux fur collar so big that when she leaned in, to air-kiss Digger, the fibers of the collar tickled her nose. Digger led them through the small walled yard which was lit for the occasion by the glow of a dozen tiny solar lamps. When she opened the door, Maria was standing by the entrance, dressed in a white silky blouse that showed off her olive skin. At her throat was the Celtic design silver necklace Digger had given her as a wedding present. Consuela reached out and embraced her daughter.

"Felicidades, mija." She looked around. "Where is your abuela?"

"She's still in her room getting ready, she left Ana and Cristina in charge of the kitchen."

Maria's sisters were busy sampling from pots on the stove. Humberto joined their husbands standing in front of the fire. Moments later Lexi and Susan arrived. Soon the little house was buzzing with conversation. Digger almost didn't hear the old cowbell that hung beside the front door. When she opened it, she found Manny with a young woman beside him. Digger figured it must be the new girlfriend.

"This is Lina," he said, introducing her.

"Ah, the giver of the hat?" Digger pointed to the flat cap Manny was wearing. Lina grinned shyly. She brought them into the kitchen and while Lina was talking to Maria and the others, she took Manny's arm and whispered in his ear. "She looks familiar, but I can't place her. Where did you two meet?"

"That rainy day in the cafe at Museum Hill, remember?"

Digger laughed. "You're a sly one. Hey, if you've got a minute can we talk?"

Manny shrugged. "Sure."

"Let's go out to Maria's studio, where it will be quiet." She caught Maria's eye, signaled that she had to go talk to Manny, and they slipped out.

The studio felt glacial after the warmth of the house. Digger plugged in a fan heater and rubbed her arms. She wondered where to begin.

"There's something I've been meaning to tell you."

Manny frowned. "Let's have it."

Digger leaned against the wooden wall beside a portrait that Maria had painted of her grandmother, as a birthday present. She regarded Manny, sighed, and finally said, "Julia Montoya was playing us all the time."

"What?" His breath puffed in the cold air like a cartoon speech balloon.

Digger recounted the scene in Montoya's office. Manny folded his arms across his chest as he listened. When she had finished, he drew in a long, slow breath, then exhaled loudly.

"Shit! We knew Julia and her brother wanted to get back at Lovington for his part in wrecking their father's life and they came up with the solar scam to do it. Now you're telling me they used both you and me as a way to make the plan work. That is so sick." His eyes shot all around the studio, then swung back to Digger. Do you think that's why she hired you?"

"No!" Digger shook her head. "She contacted me last year, before The Courier shut down. Lovington announced his plan to run for the governor's job early this year. That's probably what gave Randy the idea. He'd already been involved with the guys who'd pulled something similar in Texas, so he saw his chance."

"Yeah, the timing fits. Randy and Julia wanted revenge. Jeff and Murphy were just in it for the money."

They looked at each other. The sound of voices and music

drifted in from the house. Finally, a slow smile spread across Manny's face. "Well, I bet you'll be glad to know that Montoya is in deep trouble. The investigators uncovered all the evidence about the thousands she'd swiped through that phony contract."

"It's just too bad they can't get Randy too."

"I'll keep an eye out for him," Manny grinned. Then, as an afterthought, he said, "There's something else I heard today. Sounds like Lovington and Kramer have teamed up and they're starting some kind of church, calling it the "Home of Faith and Light."

Digger just shook her head.

Manny cocked his head toward the door. "Come on, my girlfriend will be getting jealous."

Even as he spoke, the door opened, and Maria rushed in. "Come on! We're going to do presents. We need to get the painting."

Digger helped her wrap the picture in a large drop cloth and carry it through to the house. The others were gathered around. The dining table was piled with presents, but the birthday honoree was missing.

"Abuela's still not ready?" Maria said, concerned anticipation in her voice.

Ana shrugged. "I just knocked. She said she'd be out in a minute."

Just then, Abuela emerged from her bedroom and stood beaming at them. The old woman had broken with custom and put on a dress. It was the first time, except for the wedding, that Digger had seen her wearing anything but baggy corduroy pants and a denim shirt. The floral pattern of the material was reminiscent of the 1970s. Her footwear, however, was the same as ever: brown cowboy boots with scuffed toes.

Digger eyed her up and down. "Love the dress, Abuela, but you should have let me polish the boots for you."

Abuela waved a hand, as if she were swatting at a fly. "I just thought I should dress up a little," she said primly.

Later, when the guests were all gone and Digger and Maria had finally finished cleaning up the remains of the enchilada dinner, they found Abuela asleep in the armchair by the wood-burning stove.

"Should we wake her?" Digger said.

"Maybe not." Maria raised an eyebrow and slid her eyes toward the bedroom. But the sound of their voices roused the old woman. Her eyelids fluttered open and she looked around, taking a moment to become fully present.

"Oh, the guests! They're all gone?! Are you going to go too? Now that you've won your election, you don't have to stay here anymore. If you want, you can move back to Albuquerque."

Digger looked into Maria's eyes and knew the answer. She knelt and laid her head on the old woman's lap. "Abuela," she said, "You gave us a home. This is where we want to be.

The next morning dawned bright and clear. Digger rose and went to the window to see the light play over the mountains. She heard Maria's barefoot steps and felt the warmth of Maria's body press against her.

"I love waking up with you," Maria said.

"And we have a lot of mornings to look forward to," Digger murmured.

She was thinking about Maria's political future and what Manny told her just before he and Lina left. He'd said there was a job opening up at the newspaper.

THE END

Dear Reader,

I hope you have enjoyed Digger and Maria's story in *The Sunshine Solution*. Please take a minute to write a review on Amazon and Goodreads.

Be sure to follow me on Facebook and my website RosalieRayburn.com and you'll find out what happens to Digger and Maria in my next novel, *Windswept*.

Printed in the USA
CPSIA information can be obtained
at www.ICGtesting.com
JSHW021105191123
52268JS00003B/119